Spores, Don't Even Breathe

DOUGLAS PARKER

Version: 1.0

First published in 2016 by Belmont Creative.

National Library of New Zealand Cataloguing-in-Publication Data

Parker, Douglas 1963
Spores, don't even breathe
by Douglas Parker

ISBN 9780473356668 (Softcover), 978-0-473-34221-0 (ePub), 978-0-473-3422-7 (MOBI)
ISBN: 047335666X

1. Parker, Douglas, 1963 – Fiction. 2 ….

Cover illustration by Catherine Caldwell, Belmont Creative.

Author photo by Val Buckland.

Kindle layout by DIY Publishing Ltd, www.diypublishing.co.nz.

www.sporesdontevenbreathe.com

PROLOGUE

The Humvee swung wildly as it took the corner, smashing side on into the cars parked on the far side of the street. The sound of breaking glass and crumpling metal was drowned out by the roar of the diesel engine as the driver accelerated hard and sped away from the scene.

The soldiers inside weren't bothered by the crash. They'd been in Fallujah long enough to know their best defense in these back streets was to keep moving, and fast. They checked their equipment one more time and shouted to each other over a soundtrack of indecipherable thrash-metal music.

"You know where these fuckin' Hajis are man? I'm sure we've been down this street twice already."

"Don't ask me. All these chicken-shit houses look the same."

The shouting stopped as the Humvee skidded to a halt in a pall of choking yellow dust. Within seconds the local people had cleared the street and the truck stood alone as the dust slowly settled.

"Go! Go! Go! Go!" The back doors flew open as the soldiers leapt from inside, running at full pace towards a wooden door set into the low stone wall of the nearest house.

They kicked furiously at the door until it splintered from its hinges then raised their guns and rushed in through the doorway. Within seconds they had searched every room of the house and the shouting began again.

"Shit! Get the fuck over here. You gotta see this."

"Are you clear back there soldier?"

"All clear! You gotta get the camera back here sir. It's fucked up."

The soldier stood in the center of a small room next to a video camera on a tripod. It pointed toward a banner on the far wall, covered with Arabic writing. Beneath the banner were a pile of rifles and a box of grenades.

On the floor lay four young Arab men and a woman, their clothing soaked in congealed blood. A second soldier appeared with a camera.

"Fuckin' crap what's that smell?"

"Dead Hajis man. These fuckers have been rotting for days. Make sure you get some nice close-ups."

The first soldier knelt beside one of the bodies and carefully lifted up the clothing with the barrel of his gun, checking for booby-traps. When he was sure there were none he relaxed and pointed at one of the bodies.

"They're clean. Get a shot of this, no bullet-holes."

The camera zoomed in on a young man's body, recording his bare chest crusted with black-red blood, but no apparent wounds. The blood had gushed from his nose and mouth which were now clogged shut. Beyond the body were dark stains that covered half the floor and soaked into the plaster of the walls.

The kneeling soldier looked at the camera.

"What the fuck happened?"

He was answered by a third solider standing in the doorway.

"Fuckin' puked themselves to death man. Ain't none of them's been shot. There's more in the back room."

The cameraman carefully went through every room in the house but the other soldiers just stood and stared, uncertain what to do on finding their enemies already defeated.

The mission was ended by Sergeant's voice echoing through the house.

"OK let's get out of here. They're fuckin' dead enough already."

Within thirty seconds the soldiers had gone and the house was quiet again except for the sound of flies and the distant rumble of the retreating Humvee.

1

"Need a hand there Dale?" A woman's voice carried across the room in a carefully practiced tone. Loud enough to be heard, but quiet enough to be calm, there was no mistaking its authority and it stopped the argument immediately.

Officer Dale Reynolds sighed in exasperation. "No Chief we're fine. Got a language problem is all. Just trying get this guy calmed down a little so I can understand him."

"Well you won't do it by shouting at him."

"Ten-Four Chief."

Police Chief Marion Quirke allowed herself a wry smile. Her sixty-one years gave her much more experience, and much more patience than her officer. Hell, he'd been a kid when she moved to Fulton over thirty years ago.

They had been thirty very happy years too. Marion was entirely content in her little town. She had given up on her ideal weight a long time ago and allowed a few extra pounds to accumulate, allowed her hair to fade to its natural grey and only wore make-up on the most serious of her official duties.

Marion waited for Dale to relax then returned to her paperwork. She would sort him out soon, but right now she had to answer this damned letter from the Department of Homeland Security.

She read the title again: 'Counter-Terrorism Suspect Individual Identification Procedures - Mandatory Training.' It was the third reminder. "Chief Quirke, You are hereby required to present yourself at the specified DHS training center for participation in the above-mentioned training."

She had to go this time, even though it was all a waste. In Fulton 'Suspect Individuals' stood out like hogs in a henhouse. She didn't need a training course to spot them.

Marion knew the locals well and made a point of knowing the criminals among them better. If a car was stolen, or a house was burglarized, she knew exactly who to visit and who to arrest.

She looked over at Dale and his guest, a Chinese man who'd been found wandering around on Sherman's farm. Was he a suspect individual? She had no doubt the DHS would think so, until he could prove otherwise. But most likely he was just a lost tourist.

Marion checked the dates again and shook her head at the timing. The course would finish only a week before the Presidential election. It wouldn't cause problems in Fulton but she was sure it would make the DHS folks even jumpier than usual.

She sighed and started ticking boxes on the form. Yes, she would be attending at the Washington D.C. training center. Yes, she had read the attached non-disclosure agreement. No, she did not require any kind of special assistance.

The letter was followed by forms FPD1730-4B (request for expenses), FPD2984-1C (absence on official business) and FPD2860-14A (budget variance authority). Finally she stuffed the whole irritating pile into a large brown envelope and dumped it in a tray for the administrator to deal with.

At least she would be able to see her cousin Joe in D.C. That would be a nice break and it was something to look forward to. She started to make the call but put the phone down when there was a sudden increase in volume from Dale.

It only took her a moment to cross the room to where the two men were sitting. "Alright Dale you just calm down now and tell me what's going on."

"You know the story Chief. Found him wandering around on Sherman's farm. Spent the last half hour trying to tell him that he just can't do that, but it's not sinking in. Seems like he's deliberately—"

"That'll do for now Dale, don't go getting all worked up again. You go have yourself a coffee or something."

"Yes Chief."

Marion waited until he'd gone then pulled up a chair and sat so she was facing the Chinese man. He was late middle aged, carefully groomed and wearing a light gray business suit that looked almost new. An expensive leather briefcase was on the floor beside him. His glasses and cell phone were on Dale's desk.

He was still red in the face from arguing with Dale and Marion waited for his breathing to slow a little before she spoke. "Now sir, what is your name?"

The man straightened his back, looked directly at Marion and answered in a clear voice. "I am Du Rui Kuang. You must call me Mr. Du. It is how you show respect."

"Okay Mr. Du. Do you have your passport?"

He reached into his jacket and pulled out the document, but held it close as he began to speak again. "In China I am given great respect. Never shouted at. I am a Senior Party Official. Entrepreneur. Chief of Jouchou Industrial Machinery and Jouchou High Quality Textile Company. *Owner* of Jouchou Cement Works. Director of the Jouchou Peoples Special Medical Laboratory. As Director I am in United States on official visit. I visit National Institute Health. I am *diplomat* when I am here." With that he handed the passport to Marion, holding it carefully so she could see the gold embossed letters on the cover. 'Peoples Republic of China. DIPLOMATIC PASSPORT.'

Fuck! He really was a diplomat. Marion paused as the thoughts 'Department of Homeland Security', 'International Incident' and 'Suspect Individual' all bounced off each other in her head. She might be only a small town cop, but Marion Quirke knew trouble when it knocked on the door.

"Alright Mr. Du. I apologize for the misunderstanding. We don't get many foreigners around here, and fewer diplomats." She handed the passport back, feeling irritated at the look of satisfaction on Mr. Du's face.

"Mr. Du, I need to know what you were doing on Sherman's farm. It's private property and you need to get the owner's permission to go there."

"I am diplomat when I am here."

"Yes, I know that, and you are being accorded all due respect." She paused to let that sink in.

"Mr. Du, you need to understand that this is a small town. If folks think you're causing trouble then they'll cause trouble for you. If you tell them what you want though and ask them nice, well they'll go out of their way to help you."

"So why am I arrested?"

"You're not under arrest Mr. Du, and I'm doing my best to keep it that way. I just need to know what you were doing out on the farm. If there's a good reason, then I'll explain it all to Ted Sherman and I'm sure that will be the end of it."

"Then no arrest?"

"Not if you have a good reason."

Mr. Du took a deep breath and allowed himself to settle back into his chair. "My visit to America not just work. Also for family. My great-grandfather come here to dig gold. Leave wife and children in China. Men with ships say America has much gold, plenty for everyone. Great-grandfather work hard for years. Find no gold. Gold gone long before the ships leave China.

"Great-grandfather need money to get back to China. He work digging roads. They bring him here. Chinese all live together. People spit on them. Winter come. Great-grandfather die."

Mr. Du was no longer a Senior Party Official, an entrepreneur or a diplomat. He was an old man sad at the memory of his Great-grandfather, unwelcome, suffering and dying in a foreign land.

Marion asked quietly, "Is he buried near here?"

Mr. Du reached into his coat and carefully pulled out a plastic bag which he laid flat on the desk. Inside was a single sheet of paper, yellowed and frayed with age. It displayed a simple map, hand drawn with thick lines of charcoal and smeared almost to nothing over the years. Mr. Du put his finger on a spot where two lines crossed. "Here."

It didn't look like anywhere around Fulton. Marion leaned back on the old wooden chair and let herself relax. An international incident seemed unlikely now, and of course Mr. Du turned out to have legitimate business in the town.

"Are you staying here for a few days Mr. Du?"

"No not here. Masons Tourist Cabins, two days then gone."

Marion smiled. "Well, that's just up the road. You're at Masons for the next two days?" He nodded agreement.

Marion picked up the phone and dialed. "Hello Bernadette? It's Chief Quirke here. You tell old Tom he's in a lot of trouble and he better get to the phone right away." She waited for a few seconds then began to shout into the phone when the old man answered. "Tom! What are you up to? Haven't heard from you in weeks. Uh-huh, okay, okay.

"So are you free tomorrow? I've got someone here with a historical enquiry. He'll be a challenge for you Tom and I know you like a challenge."

Marion's smile was broad as she put down the phone. She had smoothed the ruffled feathers and soon Du would be off her back. She could get back to her regular work, at least until that damn training.

"Okay, Mr. Du. Can you get back to Fulton tomorrow morning?"

Again he nodded agreement.

"Did you see the old church as you drove into town?"

Another nod.

Marion was writing now and she handed him a piece of paper. "You meet Tom Sutton tomorrow, up at the old church. He's head of the local historical society. He's got the records and he can show you around, maybe he'll find your great-grandfather for you."

Mr. Du took the paper and stood up. "Thank you."

Marion watched him leave then returned to her desk and tidied away a few papers. Dale came back into the room just as she stood up again. "Fuck Dale. Did you know he was a diplomat?"

"What? No, he never mentioned it."

"Well he was. You nearly got us both buried in a mountain of shit with that one. What are you going to do different next time?"

"Well Chief, I uh—"

"You'll stay calm and you'll pay attention and you won't make a mess that your Chief has to clean up. Now I'm finished for the day. You try not to cause too much trouble on the night shift, OK?"

"Right Chief"

Dale would lock the station and head over to Sam's bar soon after she left. No doubt he'd spend a couple of hours there having dinner and making a fool of himself over young Tiffany. Everyone in town knew where he was though, and if there was any trouble it would probably start at Sam's anyway.

2

Shona Price grew up in Washington D.C. Tall and strikingly beautiful she was young, gifted and black, just like the song. Always ahead of the other kids at school, she found the work just plain easy.

But she was young, *poor* and black also. She knew what hard times were like and she knew what prejudice was.

Young Shona was always told it was a good thing, to be gifted. But being gifted made her different and being different meant she never really felt accepted, even at school amongst her peers.

Her answer to the problem was over-achievement and she threw herself into the world of books and learning. It was a place where she could shine, a place where success was measured by standardized tests that didn't care who she was or what she looked like, just whether she knew the right answers.

If the other kids called her names, well, she *knew* that she was smarter than them. If they didn't shut up then she knew that she was taller than them too. It wasn't long before even the bullies had learned to leave her well alone.

Shona's overachievement continued into adulthood. She was the youngest ever black woman to graduate from the University of Maryland. She qualified as a doctor then earned a PhD in microbiology.

After university she joined the National Institutes of Health in Washington D.C. She loved research and felt more comfortable in the academic environment than she had anywhere else.

The Institutes provided a fast-track to success. By age thirty-four Shona had been promoted into management, was serving on the National Academy's Committee on Women in Academic Science and Engineering and advising several congressional panels.

Thirty-four is young for a mid-life crisis, but that's when Shona had hers. A year of counseling led to the conclusion that despite all her success she was, emotionally, still back in the playground; fighting like hell to prove that she was worthy. So at age thirty-five she changed direction and moved to the country, looking for a slower pace and time to think.

She'd been the doctor in Fulton for two years now. There were of course some folk who didn't like that she was a black woman, but they kept their distance and got their doctoring somewhere else. Fewer patients gave Shona more time to herself and for the first time in her life she wasn't weighed down by the pressure to succeed.

Yes, Shona was happy enough in Fulton, but today she was also very worried. First it was Bernadette Sutton, then Sarah Cummings. Now Steve Foster and young Tommy Sherman were ill.

Four sick people in Fulton were nothing unusual but it was their progression that concerned Shona. It started off like a common flu. The patients were tired and aching, then after a few days they developed a cough. Bernadette was in her eighties, she'd come to the see Shona straight away, but the others hadn't worried until the rumors started.

When Bernadette came back for a check-up she'd been ill for a week. Shona gave her a thorough exam and ran a few tests, but what disturbed her was the distant rumbling, gurgling sound in her stethoscope. Fluid on the lungs is not a good sign in anyone, and especially not in the elderly.

Doubtless the old woman hadn't stayed in bed as recommended. She was one of those people who insisted on staying active, convinced it was better to keep moving than be still.

Shona had patiently explained at the first visit that this would only make the infection worse, but it clearly hadn't worked. She was about to launch into her standard old-folks "Now you look after yourself better speech" when Bernadette changed everything by taking out her handkerchief.

Scented with lavender it had delicate embroidery around the edges and a fancy monogrammed 'B' in one corner. Shona had no difficulty imagining Bernadette sitting by the fire in the evening, embroidering that 'B' with the casual skill of a lifetime.

Bernadette coughed in to the handkerchief then drew it away from her mouth. Tiny spots of blood were now scattered across the formerly pristine white fabric. A cold shock spread through Shona's body at the sight. She hadn't seen these symptoms since treating immigrants in New York on her internship.

If Bernadette did have tuberculosis then others in the town would probably have it also. With a high proportion of elderly people the last thing Fulton needed was a TB outbreak.

Shona took a moment to calm herself. "Now Bernadette, looks like you haven't been taking care of yourself too well." The standard speech was coming in handy after all. "I want you to go back home and wrap up warm. Okay?"

Bernadette nodded agreement.

"I'm going to take a sample from your mouth, send it off for tests. Just to be safe. Also, you let me know if anyone around you gets sick, it's very important. Sooner we can treat folks, the better."

It didn't take long for Bernadette to spread the news. First it was Steve Foster, then Sarah Cummings who came bursting into Shona's office. Half an hour later Tommy Sherman appeared at the insistence of his mother.

Shona told them all the same thing. It was probably nothing to worry about, just a virulent flu, but when someone started coughing up blood then caution was the best approach. She took samples from all of them and sent them away again, all agreeing that yes, they would take better care of themselves better.

By lunchtime Shona was much more worried. She'd done some basic tests and all four patients showed blood in their saliva. She now had four sick patients who had progressed in a week from flu like symptoms to…

what? Again she thought *this is probably nothing*, but she still felt a need to prove herself to the town, so she took two steps.

First, the samples were carefully labeled and sent to the medical laboratory for testing, then Marion Quirke was called. Shona didn't have to call the cops, but in a town as small as Fulton it was a matter of courtesy, especially with Bernadette spreading rumors far and wide. So at two-thirty on a Friday afternoon Marion Quirke entered the doctor's offices.

"Marion. Thanks so much for coming. We have a problem you need to know about."

"Well, the problems all end up on my desk eventually. What have you got for me?"

"I've had four patients in today all with blood in their saliva. It could turn out to be nothing but there's a chance it's tuberculosis."

"Okay, so it could be serious. What can I do to help?"

"Nothing for now, but if it is TB then we'll need to test a lot more people, anyone who's been in close contact. In a town this size, that's everyone.

"Also, Bernadette Sutton was the first one to get sick. I had to ask her about contacts and now she's telling everyone there's some terrible disease sweeping the town. She doesn't know it might be TB, so Lord only knows what she's making up. The test results should be back in a week. Until then you know as much as I do."

The Chief paused before replying. "So there's nothing practical to do before the tests arrive?"

"No."

"Well your timing couldn't be worse Shona. I'm leaving town in the morning and I'm going to be away for the next two weeks. You'll have to rely on Dale to keep folks calm. I'll tell him to keep an eye on the troublemakers. You let him know too when the tests come back and make sure he calls me. Oh and thanks for keeping me informed."

The two women shook hands then Marion hurried away. Shona called after her "Good luck in D.C.!" but Marion was already out the door.

Shona had expected to feel better. She'd done all the right things but the worry hadn't gone away. Had she overreacted? But what if it *was* TB?

She tried to put it out of her mind. The tests would be back in a week. Then everyone would know for sure.

Saturday started out much as Friday had in Fulton. Much, in fact as every day did. The old wooden houses sat content behind the white picket fences. The wind rustled gently through the leaves of long-established trees. On Main Street the stores were opening and the townsfolk starting to appear. It all looked just like the photo on the front of Fulton's tourist brochure, so pretty and oh, so peaceful.

Shona's Saturday morning was particularly peaceful. She worked from ten until two on Saturdays and so an extra hour's sleep was followed by a relaxed breakfast then a leisurely stroll through the town to her office.

"Damn!" Shona dropped the toast onto her plate, turned down the radio and picked up the phone. It was Tom Sutton. Shona heard the panic in his breathing even before he spoke. "You've got to come up to the house Doctor, its Bernadette."

"Okay Tom. Take a breath to calm down then tell me what's happened." Shona kept her voice as steady as possible.

"She's having a heart attack!"

"Tom. Can you tell me exactly what's happening to her?"

"She's got chest pains bad; she's shaking like a leaf, and bleeding." Tom was shouting now.

Chest pains, so that's why he thought it was a heart attack. The shaking was odd though and the bleeding was a major concern. Was she bleeding from her throat like yesterday?

Shona had been silent for a moment while she analyzed the situation, but that was too much for Tom and he shouted down the line. "Please Doctor. I don't know what to—"

"Tom!" Shona spoke sharply to make sure she was heard. "I'm coming over right now. You keep an eye on Bernadette. If she has trouble breathing you give her mouth-to-mouth. You got that?"

"Okay, okay. Please—"

Shona didn't wait for the reply. She had already put the phone down, thrown the toast into the sink and was heading for the car, dialing for an ambulance as she went. So much for a quiet Saturday morning. *Damn again!*

Five minutes later she arrived at the Sutton place. It was a big two sto-rey farm house, surrounded by carefully tended gardens and immaculate in a fresh coat of white paint.

Shona grabbed her doctors' bag and emergency kit from the back seat of the car and ran toward the front door. It was not locked and she let herself in. There were voices upstairs so she called out "Tom!" and went up immediately.

Bernadette was lying in the bed with Tom sitting beside her, holding her hand. Shona started to speak but only managed to say "I…" The old man turned and stared at her blankly, tears streaming down his face. As he turned, Shona got her first clear view of Bernadette and then it was Shona's turn to stare blankly.

The old woman was shaking violently and muttering incoherently to herself. Then she began to shout "Get out! You just get out of here or else!" although she didn't seem to notice Tom or Shona. She also didn't seem to notice the thick pink frothy blood that sprayed from her lips with every word.

3

Du Rui Kuang worked nearly a hundred hours in his first week back in China. It was tough, and he could have delegated more, but that would have given his underlings too much authority. It was far better to work hard and stay in control.

There would be time soon enough for him to relax and enjoy the success of his traveling, and there was much success to enjoy. All of his businesses had new sales contracts and his medical laboratory was to exchange research data with American government labs.

In contrast, his visits to the foreign places of his ancestors were disappointing. It was two weeks since he'd met the old man Tom. They'd spent a full day driving around looking at fields and forests and old campsites by the rivers but there was little to see.

The Chinese settlements had always been makeshift and they quickly reverted to forest or farmland when the workers moved on. Graves were marked with simple wooden posts which rotted away after only a few years. Du and Tom went to several places where his great-grandfather might have been but they found nothing.

In the evening Du had met the local historical society. They all wanted to help and threw themselves into the task with admirable determination. They looked at Du's ancient map and asked him many questions. With each answer they would search their own maps and their lists of names then return with further questions. In the end however, the records just weren't good enough.

Australia had been more pleasing although he had only been there for three days, stopping over on his return from the US. Du had living relatives in the small town of Miltonah which sat amid the vast desert of the Northern Territories.

Du's great-great uncle had trekked that desert looking for gold. When he reached Miltonah he fell in love with a local woman, married her and settled down. They ran the hotel where Du's uncle ensured success by offering gambling and prostitution along with the accommodation and alcohol.

Du was welcomed by the family who now owned land all around Miltonah. On one plot they kept a well maintained graveyard and Du was deeply gratified to see the graves of his great-great uncle, the uncles' wife and many of their descendants.

The rest of his time was spent with the children, telling them all about his life in China. A place they only knew from books and the lurid kung-fu movies rented out by the local store.

Yes, Australia had been a great success until the phone had woken Du that morning.

"Du, it is your cousin Jiao."

"Jiao Heng?"

"Yes Du. I must ask you if you are well?"

Du sat up in the bed and swung his feet to the floor. He shook his head to clear the drowsiness of his sleep and checked the clock.

"I think I am well Jiao, but it is four in the morning here and I am not fully awake. You should check the time before you call me from Australia. Now what is going on that you would call me like this?"

"It is the children Du. They have fallen ill since your visit."

"What? I was just there and your children were fine. Are you saying—?"

"Please Du! We are not blaming you. Your visit was a blessing and the children loved you, but they are sick now and we do not know why. The doctors have given them drugs but the little ones are still getting worse. They are coughing now and there is blood and the doctors are confused."

Du stood and left the bedroom. He didn't want his wife being troubled by the news. "I am very sorry for this Jiao, but what do you want from me?"

"When you were here you talked about your laboratory. You said you had a doctor there, a scientist so good that the lab was offered far more work than he could do."

"That is Dr. Fen and yes, he is very good, but he can't be released from his duties here to fly to Australia." If Fen was a lesser man then Du might well have sent him, but without him the whole research program would grind to a halt.

"But he could talk? On the phone."

"Well yes, but Jiao there will not be much he can do for you that way. He is a good doctor but without seeing your children—"

"Please will you ask him Du? He can speak to the doctors here and they have seen the children. I just hoped he might know what this thing is."

Du thought for a moment. This was not a good omen, to have sickness associated with his visit, and if anything happened to Jiao's children he would feel responsible. "I will talk to Dr. Fen but you must remember he is a busy man. It may take him a few days to find some time for you Jiao."

"Thank you Du, but please tell him to hurry, this thing is moving fast."

"I will tell him, Jiao."

Du returned to the bedroom and woke his wife. He would not sleep now and there was a busy day ahead. First he would inspect the cement works. Photos of the machinery were needed for an American company that was tendering for an upgrade. Then he must prepare for the afternoon when his laboratory would be visited by officials from the Jouchou Central Party Offices.

He would make a great impression on the visiting officials. It would bring good fortune to the laboratory and soon everyone of importance in Jouchou would know of his success. Du put all troubling thoughts out of his mind as he began his day.

4

A stain of deep red soaked Bernadette's nightgown and formed a spattered semicircle around her on the bed. But it wasn't the blood that froze Shona. Doctors and kids growing up in poor neighborhoods see plenty of blood. What did it was the look of horror on Tom's face.

"Please!" He cried. "What's happening to her? I can't bear it."

Tom and Bernadette had been married for over sixty years, long before Shona was even born. She could only imagine his pain.

"Please!"

Tom's second cry shook Shona from her paralysis. She wasn't going to help anyone just standing there. The emotion was pushed away as she forced herself to focus on the job that had to be done.

Shona walked to the bed and stood beside the old man, speaking as calmly as she could while she reached into her bag for the stethoscope, gloves and a face mask.

"Tom, how long has she been like this?"

He could barely talk through his tears. "She was complaining about the pain. Then she was shaking and coughing and bleeding. Then I called you, and..." he broke off, sobbing.

"Come on Tom. I need you right now. Tell me what happened after you called."

"She was talking to me, complaining like I said, then she was just… gone. Couldn't hear me, couldn't see me. Yelling nonsense and jumping all around like that."

Thank God there was an ambulance on the way. "Okay Tom. I need you to give me some room now." The old man nodded and slowly stood up from the bed while Shona put on the gloves and mask to check Bernadette.

No fever, that was a big surprise. In fact she was cold to the touch. Her heartbeat was erratic and her breathing labored. The gurgling from the lungs was much worse than at her last examination but that was not a surprise, given the quantity of blood being produced.

Then there was the shaking. Shona was sure it had gotten worse in the few minutes since she arrived. The spasms seemed to be taking over Bernadette's entire body.

It was vital to stabilize the old woman as soon as possible. Shona administered a muscle relaxant for the spasms, and an antiarrhythmic for the heart, but she didn't really know if they would help. She monitored Bernadette's pulse and watched her breathing carefully, praying they would hold out until the ambulance arrived.

Bernadette calmed down when the muscle relaxants took hold. The shaking eased and she only muttered now, still seemingly unaware of her surroundings. Shona tested her pupils with a flashlight. One reacted to the light, the other didn't, yet her eyes were tracking together. What on earth caused that? Must be some kind of neurological damage.

Tom hovered beside the bed. "Is she better now? Can I hold her hand?" His voice was thin and dry and he didn't take his gaze from his wife for even a second.

"Yes Tom, she's stable now."

So Tom sat next to his wife again, holding her hand and talking to her gently, saying he loved her and everything would be all right. Shona stood next to them, waiting for the ambulance and willing her patient to stay alive. Trying desperately to think what this illness could be.

It just didn't make sense. Bernadette had symptoms of several diseases, but not enough of any one for a clear diagnosis.

Shona was used to being the smart one. She was the one who solved the problem when no one else could. It was agonizing to sit like this in the old couple's house and watch their torment, unable to help beyond treating the worst of Bernadette's symptoms.

She heard the siren as the ambulance arrived but stayed with Bernadette, still trying to solve the riddle. Tom was fixated on his wife and didn't move either. It was only when a paramedic called out from downstairs that Shona remembered tuberculosis.

How could she have forgotten? Perhaps because this didn't look like TB anymore, but she couldn't take the chance. Shona leapt from beside the bed and out into the hallway, still wearing the gloves and mask. The stethoscope swung wildly from her neck and it connected with the door-frame then clattered to the floor.

"Stop!" She yelled down the stairs but the paramedics had already stopped at the commotion. "I don't know what this is, but it could be TB, it's almost certainly infectious."

The paramedics retreated to their ambulance and kitted up in masks and gloves. They returned to the house with a gurney, lifting Bernadette onto it from the bed and securing her with straps.

Shona followed as her patient was carried out of the room. She told Tom to stay where he was, she would come back for him. Yet when they reached the bottom of the stairs he was right there with them, refusing to be separated from his wife.

The end came as they carried Bernadette down the small flight of stairs beyond the front door and out into the light. She called out suddenly, a primal cry of agony that came from deep within her.

The spray of blood from her mouth caught Shona and the paramedic closest to her. He almost dropped the gurney in surprise but somehow got it safely to the flat ground below the steps.

Bernadette was screaming now, her body arched and straining against the straps of the gurney, and between the screams the raw rasping sound of her breathing. They didn't need a stethoscope to hear it now.

Tom ran towards his wife, shouting above the screams. "It's alright honey. I'm with you, I'm with you." Shona barely had time to grab him and hold him back. He struggled desperately to escape her, but the only hope for Bernadette now was with the paramedics. They lifted her again and rushed her to the ambulance with its array of life-saving machinery.

Bernadette died within sixty seconds of leaving the house. Her body gave one final, mighty spasm as her heart stopped and she fell silent.

Tom stopped struggling at the same moment, standing motionless for a few seconds before slowly slipping down through Shona's arms and onto the ground.

The paramedics worked on her for five more minutes, trying to restart her heart. All that time Tom sat on the ground, staring silently through his tears towards the ambulance that held the body of his wife. Shona sat next to him, one arm around his shoulders. There was no use for her now except to be a comforting presence.

Eventually the senior paramedic came over. "We have to go now." Shona stood and together they got Tom to his feet, guiding him to the ambulance to be next to his wife. The paramedic spoke again. "He'll need to be held for observation. You should be tested too."

Shona nodded. "I know, but I have urgent calls to make. Other people have been in contact with her. I'll come to the hospital later. Look after Tom for me."

The ambulance drove away and Shona was alone now with the horror of the last half hour. It would have been so easy just to curl up into a little ball right there on the driveway and cry, but instead she took out her phone and put it up to her mouth. It was only then she realized she was still wearing the blood-soaked mask.

The first call went to the police station so Dale would know what had happened. Next she called her receptionist Marcy to cancel the day's appointments and asked her to contact Sarah Cummings, Steve Foster and Tommy Sherman's mother. They must all go to the hospital right away. Then she called the lab and urged them to hurry with the tests.

Shona's stethoscope was still inside, lying in the hallway where it had fallen. The house was utterly silent as Shona picked up the instrument and she took a long look into the bedroom. The crumpled sheets lay half off the mattress, a pile of bloody blankets next to them on the floor. *Poor old Tom. He has to come back to this.* She resolved to come back first, and clean it up before he saw the mess. It would have to wait though, there was far too much to do today.

5

It was midafternoon before Marion arrived at Joe's house in D.C. He was out on the driveway washing his truck and he gave a cheerful wave as she pulled up at the curb and got out.

"Marion! It's good to see you. I didn't think you'd be here until dinner time."

"Well you know us country folk Joe. We get up with the chickens."

"Yeah I guess you do." Joe stood and looked at Marion for a moment then shrugged his shoulders. "Hey, I'd give you a hug, but, you know." His old t-shirt was soaked with water. His arms were still dripping with foam from cleaning the truck.

Marion laughed as she replied. "That's okay Joe; you can save it for later. Tell you what though; I could use a hand with these bags."

"Sure." Joe wiped his hands on his shirt and waited for Marion to hand him a suitcase before they walked across to the house.

Marion nodded her head toward the truck as they walked past it. "Looks like you got a new one of those. I thought times were tough?"

Joe beamed with pride. "Had to upgrade now the twins are older, wasn't room for them in the other one. This one seats five in the cab; it's got a bigger tray and three-ninety horsepower. Don't know how I managed without it."

Marion smiled to herself as they walked into the house. Joe had always loved his toys.

When they reached the hallway he dropped the suitcase. "You want a beer?"

"Sure Joe, so long as I'm not keeping you from your work."

"Hey, my long lost cousin is here, I gotta be sociable!"

Marion followed him into the kitchen. "Where's Kathleen and the twins? Hope she's not staying away on my account, I can go stay in a hotel you know."

Joe reached into the fridge and retrieved a couple of bottles, flipped the lids off and handed one to Marion. "No way. Kathleen doesn't mind you staying here. She took the boys to soccer is all."

"Well so long as you're sure. I get the feeling sometimes she doesn't like me."

"Oh hey no. She's just cautious 'cos I told her all the stories from the old days. You know like when you broke that guy's wrist up in Alaska. Guess I might have exaggerated too." He winked as he took a swig from his beer.

"Gee, thanks for that Joe. No wonder she thinks I'm a bad influence!"

"She's their mother, can't blame her for being protective. But the twins are older now and she's a lot more relaxed. So don't worry about it, okay?"

"Okay. So tell me—" Marion's question was interrupted by a chime from her pocket. She took out her phone and looked at the screen. "Better take this Joe, it's Dale." Joe took another swig from his beer as Marion answered the call.

"Hello Dale."

"I thought you ought to know, Chief. Bernadette Sutton died this morning."

"Damn! I spoke to Shona about her yesterday. It didn't sound that bad."

"Well, turns out it was. Shona called me from the Sutton house. They were loading Bernadette into the ambulance when she just up and died on them. Look Chief, I wouldn't have bothered you but it sounded bad up there. Shona was real shook up. Never heard a doctor that upset about someone dying. She said there's a chance it's tuberculosis so I'm thinking we might be putting people into quarantine."

"Dale Reynolds!" Marion paused, pleased to be met with silence, it meant he was listening. "You calm yourself down now; you're a cop, not an old woman. Start spreading rumors like that and you'll have a town full of crazy folk to deal with.

"Now you answer some questions for me Dale. Number one, do you know that it *is* TB?"

"No Chief, but Shona said—"

"I don't care what Shona said. There's tests being done at a proper laboratory and we'll know exactly what we're dealing with in a week. Question two. Shona told me three other people were sick like Bernadette. How are they?"

"We're still finding out. Shona's got them coming in to the hospital. Tommy Sherman went fishing for the day, we'll get him tonight. Oh, and Tom Sutton is sick too. He's already in the hospital for observation."

At least Dale was concentrating on the facts now. He wouldn't want to be told-off again. "Well then Dale, it sounds like Shona has it all under control, which leaves me with Question three. Do you think you can keep the town from falling apart until I get back?" She said this with just a little mischief in her voice.

"Yes chief. I read you loud and clear. No rumors, no panic, no anarchy. I'll keep the folks in line and you can come home to a nice quiet little town, just the way you like it."

"That is indeed the way I like it Dale. Now here's what you do next. First you go ask the pastor to announce Bernadette's death at church tomorrow. Tell him I said to add a little something about the wickedness of spreading rumors and how it's not Christian to get people all riled up.

"Then you talk to Shona. Make sure she tells everyone that comes through her door that there's no need to worry and test results will be back real soon. You got that?"

"Yes chief."

"Okay then. You keep things quiet and don't let anyone pour gas on that fire."

"Ten-four Chief."

Joe waited for Marion to put the phone back in her pocket. "Trouble in the old town?"

"Probably not. We'll know soon enough."

"So you'll be staying then."

"I have to stay Joe. Can't get out of this damned training even with a good excuse. I've put it off twice already."

Joe seemed pleased at that and he smiled. "So what have you got planned?"

"Like I said Joe, training for two weeks. But I don't get up to D.C. that often so I'll do some exploring too. I've got a few places I'd like to visit."

Joe finished his beer before he replied. "I thought maybe at the weekend we could take the boys out hunting. They need to get into the forest more often, just to sharpen their skills. We won't shoot anything."

"Hell Joe, I don't mind if you shoot something. We've been hunting together plenty of times before."

"Yeah I know you don't mind, but Kathleen does. The boys are nearly fourteen and she still thinks they're too young. Anyway we'll take them out there and get them some experience."

Marion put her empty beer bottle on the counter. "Thanks for asking Joe but I didn't drive all the way to D.C. just to turn around and go back to Virginia for the weekend. Tell you what though, why don't you all come out to Fulton sometime after the training. Kathleen can't say no to a family trip and once you get there well, what else is there to do?"

Joe seemed pleased with that and he nodded his head and smiled. "Okay then, let's get those bags upstairs."

Marion walked up the stairs to the guest room looking forward to a rest before dinner. She thought about Fulton as she unpacked her bags. By the time she returned Shona would have the test results and whatever it was making folks sick, it would be under control. There was nothing for her to worry about, nothing at all.

6

Four days had passed since Bernadette died, but Shona Price was still feeling shaken. It was so sudden. So bloody and so wrenching to see old Tom lose her like that. Worst of all was her sense of failure. She had been right there but Bernadette had died anyway.

The old man's body was holding out surprisingly well, despite his lungs having the same worrying rumble as Bernadette. His spirit though seemed to be broken. Since his wife's death he had withdrawn from the world, refusing to stay at the hospital and choosing instead to sit at the kitchen table in his house, staring silently into the distance.

Folks from the historical society were staying with him, cooking, cleaning and mostly just trying to cheer him up. Shona visited each day and though the disease was not progressing she was certain that Tom was dying. She had read about cases like this, where a person felt they had nothing to live for and just gave up, allowing their life to ebb away.

Stop it! Shona scolded herself for letting her emotions take control. She could *not* afford to do this. The town needed her and she must keep a clear head. She took a moment to look at the papers on her desk and the walls of her office, dragging herself back into the present.

There had been no more deaths but there were still had a bunch of sick people in the town and an illness that just didn't add up. With the morning appointments over Shona had two hours before the afternoon session began. Those two hours would be used for sorting the mess out.

Faced with this mysterious illness Shona had slipped back into the role of trained researcher. She collected what data she could and tried to organize it, looking for patterns that might help her to understand.

There were eight people in Fulton who were probably infected. Without a clear diagnosis though, it was not certain. Even if it had been the question remained; infected with what?

Tuberculosis was still most likely and after Bernadette died Shona had started the other patients on Isoniazid. It was a standard treatment and she hoped it was responsible for slowing the progression.

Full tuberculosis treatment wouldn't start until TB was confirmed. A combination of drugs was required and they had to be used for at least six months. If treatment ended early the most resistant germs would survive and reproduce. Subsequent infections would be that much harder to cure. Even the Isoniazid was a risk.

"So doctor" she muttered to herself, "let's review the evidence."

All of the patients were members of the historical society or living in close proximity to members. The patients were also in contact with the wider community but so far there were no infections beyond the smaller group. That was good news at least.

Shona identified at least thirty people in the 'close contact' group, but only eight were infected. That was more good news. Transmission and susceptibility were high, but not overly so.

Unfortunately that was the end of the good news. There had been time since the weekend for Shona to perform more tests but she had found nothing conclusive. X-rays of the patients with the worst breathing difficulty showed discoloration in the lungs. That was a tick in the TB column. Skin samples however tested negative.

Five of the patients complained of strong body odor prior to the lung infection and three had small red lesions. All reported occasional pins-and-needles sensations. Perhaps the lung infection lowered their immunity, resulting in skin infections? Maybe it was a single infection that attacked both the skin and the lungs?

Leprosy would explain the body odor and lesions. Shona recalled her microbiology classes. Both tuberculosis and leprosy are caused by mycobacteria. The patients couldn't have TB and leprosy. *Or could they?* Shona dismissed that as implausible.

But could it be some other mycobacterium? There were many others but they only infected humans with compromised immune systems and in the US that usually meant AIDS. The thought of eight members of the historical society having AIDS was also implausible.

Shona didn't have the resources in Fulton to do more specific tests. She would have to take additional samples and send them away. Even a good, powerful microscope would help and Shona longed for her old university lab.

For now though that was the sum of her knowledge, and it wasn't good enough. Feeling frustrated, Shona decided to call about the samples she had sent the previous Friday, but the phone rang before she could pick it up. It was Marcy calling from the outer office.

"Shona, I've got a reporter here from the local paper. Do you have a minute?"

Oh God. Just what I need! It would be that idiot girl Tiffany. Still, it was better to talk to the paper than to say nothing; she might even get some real information out there.

"I just need a few minutes Marcy." It was definitely time to call about the tests.

The lab answered with recorded music but eventually a man's voice cut through it. "Supervisor."

"Hello, this is Shona Price from Fulton. I'm trying to get the results on a set of TB samples I sent in."

The supervisor gave her a practiced and disinterested reply. "Your samples have been prioritized and are with the infectious diseases team. Notification will only be given by mail to authorized parties to avoid miscommunication and consequent litigation issues. Thank you for your enquiry and—"

"Wait!" Shona wasn't about to let him hang up. "I know the procedure, but we've already had one death and folks here are starting to panic.

Can't you give me some indication?" Shona didn't know of anyone actually panicking yet, but if she didn't give them answers soon then they would be. For good measure she added "I've got the media on my back too, if I don't give them something they'll be calling you next."

There was a long silence before the supervisor answered. "I can let you talk to David, he's doing your tests. Strictly off the record though. If anyone asks this laboratory we will deny everything, especially to the media."

Gotcha! Shona managed to speak politely through her smile. "Thank you. I would very much appreciate that." The music returned and Shona waited as she imagined the supervisor warning David not to say too much.

"Hello Shona?" David sounded young and far more relaxed than his supervisor.

"That's me."

"You have excellent timing. I've just finished your tests and I'm putting them on the database for checking. Not great news though, they're inconclusive. We got some activity but not enough to meet the criteria for a diagnosis. This is absolutely off the record okay, but I'd say there's only a five percent chance it's TB. I think you've got something else out there."

He was right about it not being great news. Shona was no further forward now than she had been with her hunches. "Are you sure about that David?" Perhaps he'd forgotten to tell her something, the one seemingly irrelevant thing that would solve the mystery.

"No Shona. I'm not sure. That's what inconclusive means. The formal report will state an insufficient margin of confidence to make a determination. There's really nothing more I can say."

Shona hoped the disappointment didn't come through in her voice. David and the supervisor had broken the rules to help her and she was grateful. "Thank you David. I do appreciate your help."

She thought for a moment how to present all this to the reporter then picked up the phone. "Okay Marcy, you can send her in now."

Tiffany Masterson did not look anything like Shona's image of a newspaper reporter. Dressed in a tight t-shirt and tighter skirt, Tiffany showed off a full three-inch band of teenage midriff. Just like all the carefully groomed girls who danced and jostled for attention in the music videos on her iPad.

Tiffany spent nearly every evening at Sam's bar, hanging out with her friends but creating enough of a display to be sure every man in the bar was watching. Then she would share her drunken opinions with anyone in range who could be bothered to listen.

"Oh God! I'm not like, *staying* here. I'm just doing the reporter thing because my Dad *made* me. First chance I get, I'm outta here. I'll go somewhere cool and exciting and I'll never, never come back."

In fact, everyone in the town knew she would stay exactly where she was until she turned twenty-one. That was when she inherited her share of the family money and that was precisely when she would be 'outta here.' Still, the job did have its perks. She got lots of attention and it was her *job* to be nosy and to gossip.

Tiffany sat herself on the edge of Shona's desk and said "Hi!" in her chirpiest voice, smiling broadly and flicking back her long blonde hair. Shona found it all very irritating. Tiffany didn't need to bother with her usual act; it might work on all the men in town but it wasn't going to work in here. Maybe she didn't know how to turn it off?

Shona waved at the empty chairs in front of her desk and said, "Please Tiffany, take a seat".

"Uh, sure, whatever." The girl shrugged her shoulders then hopped off the desk and sat down.

The interview itself was brief and pointless. Tiffany really wasn't interested because, as she said, "diseases are like, so icky."

Shona answered the few questions in a flat, distracted voice. "Yes, Bernadette died unexpectedly but she was very old. Yes, more people are sick. No, they aren't dying. Yes, something is being done; the patients are on preventive drugs. No, it isn't tuberculosis. No, there is nothing to worry about, the situation is under control."

When Tiffany was finished Shona asked to be shown a draft of any article before it was printed. This would help ensure accurate reporting.

Tiffany stood to leave and squeaked "Don't worry about accuracy Doctor, I *can* write you know."

Shona took a deep breath and did her best not to worry about what the paper would print.

With the girl gone there was one task left before Shona could take a break. She turned to her computer and typed 'Martyn Fortescue microbiology' into Google. *Not bad*. The search returned with 'Results 1 - 10 of about 1,800 for Martyn Fortescue microbiology.' The motto of the academic world is 'publish or perish' and Martyn had obviously not perished.

Shona knew Martyn from her post-graduate days when he was an exchange student from England. Martyn had finished his degree then moved to Atlanta and a job at the Centers for Disease Control and Prevention. Shona hoped he was still there and that he would remember her. She needed a friend in her corner right now.

It did not take long for Google to confirm that yes; Martyn was still at the CDC, although it could not confirm if he remembered Shona. She found his public email address and clicked it, but how best to catch his attention? She thought about Martyn for a while then entered: 'Need your help. Have found an exotic new disease.' That should work. Any new disease would need a lot of research and that of course would lead to many papers published in prestigious scientific journals.

Shona went on to describe the symptoms and what was happening in the town. Did Martyn have any ideas and could he please forward the details to the most appropriate person at CDC? That done it was time for some lunch. Shona left the office and walked out into the street, trying to forget her problems and relax, just for a few minutes at least.

7

Alison Grove arrived outside her office in Atlanta. She was proud to be a research analyst at the CDC, working for the National Centers for Preparedness, Detection, and Control of Infectious Diseases. Precise to a fault, it bothered Alison that in five years she had never heard anyone else at the office pronounce that name in full.

She stepped off her bicycle and checked that the time on her watch matched the time on the bike computer. They both agreed that it was seven forty-eight. This was the time Alison arrived every morning, although until recently she had always arrived at seven fifty-three.

The extra five minutes were required for Alison to lean her bike against the little coffee cart in the courtyard and smile at Matt. It took Matt ninety-three seconds to make a single shot decaf espresso and Alison would smile silently at him for every one of those seconds. Then, espresso in hand, she would walk her bike to the rack and wonder what exactly was the right thing to say to captivate Matt.

It was seven fifty-seven when Alison arrived at her desk, still carrying the espresso, which she set down on a folded paper towel to the right of her keyboard.

The first fifteen minutes of this Friday morning had been allocated to deal with a rogue email. It had troubled her since it arrived because it did not follow the correct procedures. Alison did not like that and consequently she did not like Martyn Fortescue either.

She scanned the email for the third time since she'd received it. Martyn had a friend who was a doctor. She was having trouble diagnosing a pulmonary disease. The details were attached – could Alison help?

The proper course of action would be to send the message back with a terse reminder to use the official channels. Unfortunately that allowed for the tiny possibility of Alison letting something important escape her.

The symptoms described were not consistent with a regular pulmonary disorder. The coughing and blood were common, but the body odor and skin lesions were unusual, and the manner of the old woman's death was extraordinary. A standard dose of Isoniazid seemed to help, but it was difficult to be certain with such a small sample of cases.

Alison ran a few queries against the main databases; first the official ones, then her personal one, the one that was properly organized. After that she checked the reliable on-line journals but there was nothing conclusive. All the reported symptoms had been seen before, but never grouped together like this.

Strange little infections popped up all the time. They appeared like this one then disappeared just as quickly, never to be seen again and rarely doing much harm. The public seemed to think that all diseases were known and understood but there were billions of undiscovered micro-organisms and any of them could give rise to a new illness.

Alison logged the details in the official database: date, location and symptoms but gave it the lowest priority. She fully expected this entry would sit unnoticed amongst the thousands of similar entries, never to be referenced again.

A standard response was emailed to Martyn Fortescue and Shona Price. The reported illness was not recognized. If there were any further developments they should respond through official channels. A list of possible disease agents was attached along with a few suggestions for further diagnostic work.

The clock on Alison's desk showed that only fourteen minutes and five seconds had been consumed. With a deep sense of satisfaction she selected today's page on her calendar and marked the job as complete.

8

Events in Jouchou had been accelerating for the past week and as the time approached midnight Du Rui Kuang was about lose any sense that he had the situation under control.

The first call had come mid-morning while Du was playing golf. It was the nurse at his cement works and she was clearly overwhelmed.

Single-handedly responsible for all medical matters at the works, the nurse was not qualified in any way. Qualified nurses were too expensive. Until now this hadn't mattered as her role was only to apply bandages to cuts and hand out painkillers. The important thing was to get injured workers back to work as quickly as possible.

On Friday morning a worker had reported to the nurse with severe breathing problems and gone home unable to work. The symptoms were nothing unusual; workers got sick from the cement dust all the time. It *was* unusual that the worker had gone home. His pay would be docked for the time he was away.

By Saturday morning five more workers had similar symptoms and were also unable to work. The family of the first worker had called to say he was hallucinating and could the nurse do anything to help?

This was all of great concern to Du. Absent workers meant lost production. Lost production meant missed deadlines, and missed deadlines meant financial penalties to the works.

Du ordered the nurse to have all sick workers report to his medical laboratory immediately. Then he called his production manager to ensure replacement staff had been found. Next he called Dr. Fen, the senior researcher at the laboratory. Fen was sternly instructed to stop whatever he was doing and cure the workers immediately.

With that done, Du relaxed. The important decisions had been made quickly and the situation was under control. He assured his golfing partners there would be no further interruptions and returned to the game.

Six hours later Du's phone rang again. This time it was Dr Fen and he spoke in a rush. "Du, it is a grave situation here. One of your workers has died. Four more are hallucinating. There are now twelve workers with early symptoms. This is not a normal lung problem. Something else is going on."

Du grunted acknowledgement but allowed the agitated doctor to keep talking.

"If they keep coming at this rate I will soon be overwhelmed. This is a research laboratory and we are not equipped to cope with an emergency. I should be sending them over to the People's Hospital."

"No! Do not do that." There would be enough rumors in the town without letting the public see sick workers over at the hospital.

"Listen Fen, I don't care how many there are. You keep my workers there at the laboratory. I will come over later to sort this out." Du hung up before Fen could argue. Sometimes his subordinates behaved like scared children. Du had always supposed that was why he was in charge. He would not allow the panicky doctor to ruin his day.

At home, Du ordered his wife to prepare him an early dinner as he changed into a business suit. It was seven in the evening before he arrived at the medical laboratory. With luck there had been time for Fen to have calmed down, diagnosed the illness and begun proper treatment. There would be nothing to do except for telling him to carry on.

The laboratory had two large accommodation rooms, each with twenty hospital-style beds. These were normally used by volunteers during experiments but now the beds held sick workers. Du saw his faith in doctor

Fen had been misplaced the moment he stepped through the door of the Day Patients Room.

It was chaos. All the beds were in use now and the space between them was crowded with frantic relatives. Two nurses were moving from bed to bed, desperately trying to relieve the suffering of the sick men and, at the same time, calm the crowd.

The laboratory had only two security guards on duty; both young and inexperienced. They stood frozen, just inside the doors of the room with their eyes wide. They were utterly outnumbered and had given up trying to keep order a long time ago.

Some of the relatives were speaking to the sick men, trying to soothe them. The rest were wailing to themselves or shouting at Dr Fen and the nurses to do *something, anything.* Fen stood in the center of the room, crushed by the crowd and unable to move. He was shouting to be heard above the din. "Please, I cannot help if you surround me like this. Tend to your sick and let me get on with my job!"

Beneath all the shouting was another noise. A strange unnatural sound, it somehow caught Du's attention more than all the other turmoil in the room. It was a deep and rumbling sound, a terrible boiling cough that came not from the throat but from the very core of each of the sick men.

Du forced his way through the crowd and grabbed Fen by the arm, dragging him out of the room and into the lobby. "How could you let this happen? You are a disgrace! You will never get these men back to work if you do not impose some order on this chaos!"

Fen countered with anger of his own. "I told you on the phone. This is a research facility not a hospital! We have just one doctor, a few unqualified nurses and a couple of scared boys posing as security guards. How are we supposed to treat all these men at once? How are we supposed to keep the relatives out? More sick men are coming here Du, this is only going to get worse. If you want to impose order then you'll have to call in the police."

Du was not about to call the police, no matter how angry his doctor was. The police would have to be paid to keep quiet and that would be expensive.

Du did not reply to Fen. He had taken out his phone the moment Fen had uttered the word "Police." He spoke rapidly for half a minute then snapped the phone shut and returned his attention to the doctor. "Workers are coming from Jouchou Industrial Machinery plant to assist the guards. They are big men and these people will have to do what they say."

Fen looked horrified but said nothing.

"Is this it then?"

Fen lowered his head. "No Du, there is more. You must come." This was said quietly and with such a deep sense of helplessness that Du forgot his anger and followed Fen without another word.

The Night Patients room was used for experiments where patients had to stay for long term monitoring. There were only five occupied beds in this room, one nurse and a dozen or so relatives. No one even looked up as Du and Fen entered the room.

Du stood transfixed, still holding the door open but aware of nothing except what he saw. It could not possibly be happening. He was proud to be a leader. Proud to be a strong man with a strong will, resolute and unbending. The sight of the Night Patients room crumpled that will in an instant.

9

The DHS training course was worse than Marion had expected. It was held in a bland government building filled with identical offices on identical floors. Indistinguishable people scurried between the identical offices and took the elevators between the identical floors. All of them doing... what? Marion didn't know and no one was about to tell her.

Presentation Room 7A was as bland as the building that contained it and the course presenter seemed to have been carefully chosen to match. How could any human being have that much life drained from them and still function? By Wednesday Marion had it figured out. When he wasn't training others, he worked in one of the offices in this building.

The course material was disappointing. It was practical stuff, but anyone with commonsense could have worked it out for themselves. There were hints now and again of meatier material between the lines. Secrets gleaned from spy satellites and covert interrogations. Information smuggled around the world in diplomatic bags, or carefully encrypted and bounced off yet more satellites. By the time it reached Presentation Room 7A though, it had all been thoroughly sanitized. What was the point of dragging hard-working cops away from their jobs and then withholding any really useful information?

Marion was glad when the first week of tedium was over. She arrived at Joe and Kathleen's that Friday night well after dinner while they were watching TV. They glanced at her and said "Hi" but were too absorbed in the drama of 'The Hero Project' to say more.

Marion detested The Hero Project. In each episode a group of 'ordinary people' were given a week's training in how to be a firefighter, cop, paramedic or whatever. These supposed heroes were then turned loose on an unsuspecting public, all the while competing for cash prizes and desperately trying not to be 'eliminated.'

Marion's hosts were settled in their favorite chairs, the ones with the best views of the TV. There was a comfortable couch but it too had a good view of the TV and was close to the surround-sound speakers. That left the old chair in the corner, the one that had almost no view at all. Tonight that chair suited Marion fine and she fell into it with relief.

It was only five minutes later when Marion's phone rang. She stood quickly and left the room before answering. The 'Congress of Heroes' was in session, votes were being cast and blame was being laid. Joe and Kathleen would not appreciate being disturbed, besides which meetings of the Congress could be very loud

When Marion got to the kitchen she pressed the 'talk' button. "Hello Dale. What's the news?"

Dale's response was calm, which was a welcome sign. "Might be good, might be bad – I'm not sure. Shona came over today. She's got preliminary lab results. They're saying it's not TB and I think she agrees with them. Seems to me—"

"Just give me the facts Dale. We know it's not tuberculosis, do we know what it *is*?"

"No, we don't. The lab said it was inconclusive. Shona says it looks like a lot of things, kinda like leprosy, kinda like TB, kinda like something else. She said if they all had AIDS it would make more sense but they can't all have AIDS. Then again, maybe those history folk do more than just shuffle papers up at that old church."

"Christ Dale! You keep thoughts like *that* to yourself. Now, is there anything else I might actually want to know?"

"No Chief, that's it for today. Oh, the Mayor's office keeps calling. They're worried about the town's reputation. I just keep telling 'em everything's under control."

"Good boy Dale. Don't give those damned politicians any excuse to get involved or they'll screw things up completely." She had given Dale this lecture a hundred times before.

"Sure thing Chief. You have a good weekend."

Marion assured him she would, and ended the call.

Back in the living room the Congress had made its decision. Tyler was eliminated for rescuing the cat and leaving the old man in the burning building. "But I like cats!" he wailed beneath the closing credits. "That cat was glad to see me but the old guy was crabby. Shame on the Congress I say. They've been out to get me from the very start."

Kathleen clicked off the remote as Joe went to get a beer. There was half an hour for conversation before his football game started. She waited for Marion to sit back in the old chair before she spoke. "You look worried. Was that bad news from the town?"

"Not bad, not good. Just news. The tests have come back and it's not TB. Beyond that nobody knows. Dale's done a good job at keeping things calm and by now everyone's getting used to the situation. It's amazing how scared folks get when something like this comes along; but you know, most of the time it'll turn out to be nothing."

"I don't know how you can be so casual about other people's lives. Even if this isn't tuberculosis it's something bad enough that an old lady died. Aren't you worried about that?" "No Kathleen. I refuse to worry until it deserves to be worried about. If it turns out to be a real problem, then I'll deal with it head-on. For now though the town doctor is doing all the right things and so is Dale. We're not ignoring the problem you know."

"I suppose not. I just couldn't be as calm about as you are. I have my boys and I worry."

Joe came back into the room holding a beer. "Worry about what honey?"

"Oh, about everything Joe, you know me. I was just admiring Marion for being so relaxed when no one can figure out this disease in her town. I'd be a mess."

Joe settled in his chair. "Well you're right honey; it could be anything up there. They could have the bird flu or the swine flu, or maybe even something new, like ah... the groundhog flu. You get many sick groundhogs out there Marion?" Joe cast a mischievous smile at Marion and she shook her head in disbelief.

"No Joe, no sick groundhogs, and it's going to take something a lot worse than that to rattle my cage."

10

Mike Fanning rang the bell at the Olde Worlde bed and breakfast at about the same time Marion was going to bed in D.C. After a moment he was greeted by a cheerful voice from behind the polished wooden door. "Hello, hello." The ancient door creaked open to reveal a woman who was elderly but every bit as cheerful as her voice had been. "You must be Mike, the journalist from D.C."

Mike nodded and smiled. "That's me."

He walked into the ornately decorated hallway of the house as the woman fussed around him. "Well Mike, welcome to Fulton. I'm Selma. My husband will get your bags. You sign the register, and thanks for calling to say you'd be late; otherwise we'd both be in bed by now."

Mike had called to confirm his booking, not to say he would be late. It was only nine in the evening now and that didn't seem late to a journalist. He kept smiling. "You're welcome Selma. Say, you don't know anywhere I could get something to eat do you."

"That would be Sam's. They won't have much food left at this time of night but you can be sure they'll have plenty to drink."

Mike ignored the tone of disapproval in her voice. "Ah Selma, you know just what a journalist wants to hear. How do I find Sam's?"

Selma laughed at that. "This is Fulton Mister Fanning. Sam's is on the main street along with everything else."

As Mike drove towards Sam's he hoped the weekend's work wouldn't intrude too much on the relaxing and fishing he had planned.

Mike Fanning had been a reporter at the Washington Record for longer than most people could remember. He joined the paper as a junior reporter in 1972; just months after the Watergate break in.

It was a heady time to be a journalist. Each day the papers revealed still deeper levels of corruption and it was not long before the powerful men of Washington D.C. began to fall at the onslaught. The reporters Woodward and Bernstein became celebrities to the public but to Mike and his colleagues they were more than that, they were heroes. Suddenly it seemed there was no limit to what a determined young man with a pencil and a notebook might achieve.

It took a few years but inevitably the glamour faded from the job. After all, a scandal the size of Watergate just doesn't come around too often. Mike worked diligently at unearthing corruption but the public had become jaded. They just assumed all politicians were on the take and there was no surprise or even interest in further revelations.

Readers and advertisers drifted away from the papers and towards TV. Budgets were cut and the Record stopped spending money on serious investigations. Reporting for Mike became a mundane activity.

Then in the eighties the new media barons arose, consolidating once independent papers into their vast empires. They didn't care much about journalism, and didn't care at all about fairness or accuracy. Profit was the only motivation and a newspaper was no different to a factory or a fast food store.

Mike's role changed and to his dismay he was often reduced to simply paraphrasing the press releases of politicians or corporations. There was no time to ask questions or do real research.

He struggled to do what he considered proper journalism, but rarely succeeded and the strain took its toll. He gained weight, developed ulcers and became permanently irritable. He was almost glad when his wife left him and took the children with her. It wasn't their fault after all and they shouldn't have to watch his slow deterioration.

His will was finally broken by an interview with an economist; a man who saw the world entirely in terms of incentives. He patiently explained to Mike how the papers main incentive was to sell advertising, that's where the profit came from.

To sell advertising they needed to attract readers and that was the sole purpose of Mike's stories. The best story of course was the one that drew the most readers for the least cost so anything requiring a lot of Mike's time would be ruled out.

Of course, it was necessary to maintain a veneer of journalistic integrity. The readers still should believe they were being informed, but only a veneer that was required.

For Mike himself the incentives were clear. He should produce as many stories as possible in as little time as possible. This strategy reduced the costs he imposed on his employer and maximized the revenue he generated. The papers incentive was then to reward Mike in preference to any of their other journalists.

The economist's words haunted Mike for days. They were so heartless and yet they rang so true. They robbed Mike of any lingering hope that he might be doing something worthy with his life. With no energy to fight what now seemed beyond his control, Mike capitulated and adopted the economist's strategy to the letter.

Now he wrote only the type of stories the paper wanted and he wrote a lot of them. He refused to worry about the impact of those stories or whether they were good journalism. He just came in every day, did what was asked of him and went home again.

The excess weight was long gone, the ulcers had cleared up and his face was frequently relaxed into a smile. His family had not returned and he did not expect them to, but he had made his peace with that a long time ago.

In fact the only thing that continued to disturb him was a tiny nagging voice telling him he'd sold out. This voice didn't reach his consciousness often but it was there nonetheless. He wondered sometimes if that was the reason he spent so much time alone, but he was close to retirement now and there seemed little point wallowing in the past.

Despite Mike's self-doubt the economist's strategy had worked and he was considered a valuable asset by the Record. The paper sold a lot of advertising and, recognizing his contribution to that end, gave him a small amount of leeway in his use of the paper's resources.

Take this little trip to the country for instance. Mike had needed a break, just a few days away from his routine would do. He'd scanned the news archives and the first article to catch his eye was by Tiffany Masterson of the Fulton Echo. It was perfect for his needs. Almost certainly nothing, it could easily be made to *look* like something. Enough of something at least to have the paper pay for a trip to the countryside.

Mike's pitch to the editor was brief and, he hoped, not too obvious. Folks from a small town historical society were getting a mysterious illness and one of them had died. Maybe they'd dug up some infected bones? Maybe it was bird flu from the local chickens? Maybe it was the start of something big? You couldn't be too careful these days. It had to be worth a look.

Mike was sure the editor wouldn't believe a word of it, but he was also sure the trip would be approved. A weekend in the country was small price to pay for keeping such a productive journalist happy, so long as the expenses could be justified to the accountants.

"What'll it be?" It was Sam himself who asked.

"Uh, Heineken thanks, and do you have any food?"

"Sorry buddy, kitchen's closed. They usually leave some sandwiches in the fridge though."

"That'll be fine,"

Sam made conversation as he poured the beer. "You just passing through or stopping to pay us a visit?"

"Staying for a couple of days. I'm a reporter with the Washington Record." Mike produced his card with practiced ease. "Saw a story on the wire and thought I should check it out."

Sam lifted an eyebrow. "You must have the wrong town mister. Nothing much happens in Fulton."

"Well I wouldn't be so sure. You've had a few sick people out here recently. The story made it onto my desk."

"Oh that. You're wasting your time buddy. It's just young Tiffany trying to make a name for herself."

Mike wasn't surprised that Sam would try to kill the story. A bar wouldn't sell much beer if everyone stayed home for fear of being infected. He pushed ahead. "That would be Tiffany Masterson right? Where could I find her?"

Sam flicked his gaze towards the back of the room. "That's her down there. You'll have to buy her a drink though, or she won't even notice you."

Mike saw a gaggle of young women sitting around a table littered with empty glasses. They were all dressed provocatively and laughing too loud. He waited until he'd finished his sandwiches then ordered another beer, which he took with him as he walked towards the commotion.

"Tiffany!" Mike had to shout several times before he was noticed. One of the young women looked up at him as he held out his card.

"Hang on." Her attention went back to her phone as her thumb frantically tapped out a message on the keypad. Mike waited and looked down at Tiffany and her friends, suddenly feeling very old and pale and aware of just how saggy his face had become.

He shouted again, now eager to get this over with. "I'm Mike Fanning from the Washington Record. Saw one of your articles. Wondered if you could fill in some background for me, maybe tomorrow?"

"Oh. You're not trying to pick me up then?" This was met with an eruption of laughter from Tiffany's friends.

"Professional interest only."

Tiffany picked up an empty glass from the table in front of her and waved it at Mike. "I'll need another one of these."

"Sure, in a minute."

One of the friends chimed in. "Washington Record Tiff. You're going to be a famous reporter!" With that the group threw their hands in the air and dissolved into a mass of whooping, giggling, silly little girls. Mike could not tell if they were genuinely excited or if it was sarcasm. He knew one thing though, they were definitely very drunk.

When the group calmed down Tiffany spoke. "Okay Mike, you give me a call tomorrow." Simultaneously she sent the single word "Tiff" to the mobile number on his card then handed it back.

Mike walked back to the bar and ordered "another one of whatever it is she's drinking." Sam took a bottle down from shelf behind him. "That'll be five bucks, anything else?"

"Yeah, how do I get in touch with the local doctor?"

11

The nurse in the Night Patients room looked over at Du, her eyes pleading with him to make this better. The thick foamy blood that caked the front of her uniform had dried into a brown crust. The blood on her face was smeared thin where she had wiped it with her sleeve and wet where her tears had washed it partly away.

Du did not move and the nurse returned to tending the sick, doing what little she could to help them.

Each of the men in this room was strapped to his bed with whatever had come to hand. When bandages had not been strong enough sheets from the spare beds where knotted together, thrown across the men then tied beneath the bed frames.

The restraints were barely adequate as the men's bodies jumped and twisted, their backs arching and muscles straining from relentless waves of spasms. Some of the relatives were trying to hold the men down, putting their full weight on them to keep them from hurting themselves.

The noise in this room was unlike anything Du had heard before. The beds rattled and banged beneath the convulsing men. At times the bare metal legs lifted clear off the floor then crashed back down with a din that echoed from the white tiled walls.

The men themselves were all shouting. Incoherent nonsense that came gurgling through the blood that frothed and sprayed from their mouths.

The blood was thrown first to one side then the other as their tormented bodies danced. It covered the men's faces, their clothes, their relatives, the walls and the floor. It had been flung to every corner of the room so there was hardly a surface left that wasn't flecked with its horrid red decoration.

Du was only vaguely aware of Fen's hand on his arm, leading him back out to the lobby.

When the doors had closed and the noise was trapped behind them Fen handed a phone to his boss. Du took it and held it up to his face but then stood motionless again, the blue light of its display illuminating his cheek.

Fen prompted gently. "We must call the authorities sir. We do not have the facilities for this. We are overwhelmed."

Du did not want any of it to be true, but Fen was right. It was clear that the men in the Night Patients Room would die. It was clear that those in the Day Patients Room would soon follow them.

When he spoke his voice was as quiet as Fen's had been. "Get these men to the hospital. Call the police. Call the army if you have to. You are the doctor. I leave these men in your hands."

Du Rui Kuang, Senior Party Official had never felt such a knot of fear in his belly. He drove back to his home and woke his wife and daughter. They must leave immediately. They would be safe with their relatives in Fujian province.

His wife argued until she heard the scream of sirens passing the house. Then she picked up her child and hurried off to pack.

The call to Miltonah was answered by a man with a strong Australian accent.

"Hello, who is this calling?"

On a normal night Du, would have barked at the man and demanded to speak to his cousin. This was not a normal night and Du said quietly, "I am Du Rui Kuang."

The stranger was not satisfied. "No Mr. Kuang, I need to know why you are calling this number."

Westerners often got Chinese names backwards, but for the first time in his life, Du didn't bother to correct the mistake. Again, his voice was quiet, "I am calling from China. Where is my Cousin?"

The voice became softer in a practiced way. "I am Sergeant Thompson of the Miltonah Police. I'm sorry to have to inform you Mr. Kuang that your cousin and his family have all been evacuated by air to the nearest hospital. One of the children is gravely ill and they have all been put under observation. I am presently securing their property."

Du no longer needed to fear for his family in Australia. The worst possible thing had already happened to them. Why had he not done more when he heard that the child was sick?

"Mr. Kuang? Would you like the number of the hospital?"

Du wrote down the number. "Goodbye Sergeant."

"Goodbye Mr. Kuang. Please know we're doing everything we can to help."

Du helped his wife and daughter into the car and watched them drive away to safety. Then he went to bed, but there was no sleep. Each time his eyes closed he saw his family; screaming, bloody and dying as the helpless doctors looked on.

He tried to make sense of events. It was possible that one of his research organisms had escaped the lab. It was even possible the organism had reached the cement works independent of his movements. But it was *not* remotely possible it had reached Australia without him carrying it there. There was no way out, he *must* be the cause.

Du knew little of what his researchers actually did, and until now he had been happy to keep it that way. The most lucrative work of all was done for the army. Even as Director of the laboratory Du was not authorized to know the details of that research.

The army work was carried out in a separate section of the building. Only Fen and the two most senior researchers ever worked on it. What were they doing in there? For the first time Du resented his army contracts.

Yet if he was the cause, how did the cement workers get infected? Du had visited the factory but only to meet with his supervisors. If Du carried the sickness and it was that virulent, why were they ill but not his wife and daughter?

He must have been infected before leaving China for the U.S., so why were there no infections until he reached Australia? A chill ran through him as he realized perhaps there were infections in the U.S. He could only imagine the consequences of a senior party official, with diplomatic status, releasing a disease that should not even have existed.

Du wrestled with his questions but answers were not to be found. When dawn finally arrived he gave up the struggle and got out of bed. He did not have the stomach to eat so he showered and changed into his most impressive business suit.

There was nothing more to do except return to the laboratory and the terrible failure that waited there.

12

"Damn!" Shona dropped the toast onto her plate, turned down the radio and picked up the phone. It was almost exactly the same time as old Tom had called last week.

"Shona here."

"Doctor Price?" The voice that replied was perfectly calm. Thank goodness for that.

Shona paused to swallow some coffee. "Yes."

"Good morning doctor. My name is Mike Fanning. I'm a reporter with the Washington Record. I was wondering if I could interview you today about the mystery illness going around your town?"

How the hell did the Washington Record know about that? If she spoke to another reporter the Mayor's office would go ballistic. She'd already had a lecture about Tiffany's article, even though she'd explained to them she hadn't said a tenth of what was printed.

If she refused to speak though, he could print what he liked and Shona could write that story herself. "Town doctor Shona Price refused to be interviewed but local gossips were happy to fill in the details." That wouldn't help the town's reputation either.

Her train of thought was interrupted by the reporter. "Tell you what Shona. Seeing as I've already ruined your morning how about I buy you breakfast?"

Shona thought for a moment about the next lecture from the Mayor's office then decided they could go to hell. She was the only one in town qualified to talk about the illness and she was an independent business-woman besides.

"Okay Mr. Fanning. I'll meet you at the bakery, nine-thirty." Then, just to cover her back she added, "Oh one condition though. I'll need a copy of your notes from our interview. It's policy." That wasn't true but it sounded better than *I want some ammunition so I can tell the Mayor's office to go fuck themselves.*

"Sure, no problem, I'll see you there." The reporter sounded amused by Shona's request and she hoped she hadn't made things worse. You never could tell how the media would choose to spin a story.

Shona arrived at the bakery exactly on time. Her morning practice started at ten and she didn't want to give the journalist any longer than was necessary. He waited until they had their food then started with general questions. What had been the sequence of events so far? What were the symptoms? Who seemed to be the most susceptible?

Shona was relaxed and enjoying her breakfast by the time he asked his first real question. "So tell me about the old lady that died. I hear it was kinda nasty?"

Shona stopped enjoying her breakfast. Yes, it was 'kinda nasty' but there was no way she would let those details be published. She tried to smile. "Look Mike, I'm going to have to invoke doctor-patient confidentiality on that one."

"She's dead Shona, what harm can it do?"

"Well her family could sue me into bankruptcy for starters. Then there's the professional misconduct hearings, the never working as a doctor again."

She must have made her point because the reporter changed tack. "Well what about causes then? You don't know exactly what this is, but do you know what's causing it?"

Shona replied with a patronizing tone. "That's the same question twice. If I knew what was causing it then I'd know what it was."

"Okay, but I'm talking about where it came from. You know, is it something local that's got away on you or is it something that's come in from outside? There've been suggestions of bio-terrorism."

"What?" Shona's voice was loud in the little bakery and the other patrons turned to stare. She had been spreading cream cheese on her bagel and was so startled by the question that now a smear of it went half way across her left hand. She was angry at letting Mike get the better of her, but did her best to hide it.

"I haven't heard anything about terrorism, rumors or otherwise. You've probably been talking to Tiffany. Most of her so-called journalism comes directly from her imagination."

"Yes, but you can't rule it out, can you?"

Shona gave up hiding her anger. "I can't rule *anything* out Mike because I don't know what the hell it is. For the *record* it is *not* terrorism and you should be ashamed of yourself for even bringing that up. What we have here is a small number of sick people and one elderly lady who died. There's a million micro-organisms out there that we know nothing about. Not having a firm identification at this point is not unusual, it's not alarming and it certainly *is not* evidence of terrorism."

"Okay Doctor, I get it."

"Good, now if you don't mind I'd like to finish my breakfast in peace."

"Sure."

Surprisingly there were no more questions and the reporter sat silently until she was done. Then he thanked her for her time and stood to leave.

Shona pointed at his note-book. "I need a copy of that, remember?"

"Sure, you want to do that now?" Mike flipped the book open so she could see the pages. Damn! It was short-hand and useless to anyone except Mike. She should have known he was an old-school reporter when he didn't pull out a lap-top.

He was smiling now. "Sorry about that but I have to use short-hand. It's policy."

Touché you smart-ass.

He walked to the door of the bakery then called back. "I'll send you a transcript on Monday."

"I'll be waiting for it. Good day Mr. Fanning." She deliberately avoided thanking him for breakfast.

13

The weekend passed slowly for Shona. She tried to relax but her thoughts kept returning to Bernadette and the other sick folk. What on earth was wrong with them? If only she could have figured it out before that damned journalist turned up.

She found it hard to concentrate too at her Monday consultation. The problems of her regular patients just didn't seem important now and she was almost glad to be interrupted by an urgent call from Mary Sherman.

"Doctor Price, it's my Tommy. He was just tired yesterday but now he's coughing up blood. You have to come see him." Mary's voice was strained in a way that said far more than her words.

Shona didn't want another mistake like Bernadette and she was already standing up as she replied. "Mary you get him over to the hospital right now. I'll meet you there." She apologized again to her patient, packed her doctor's bag and was driving to the hospital within three minutes.

Tommy was in the emergency department when she arrived. The hospital doctor had already begun treatment so Shona told him the little she knew and what had happened to Bernadette.

Mary sat on the edge of Tommy's bed, stroking his head and singing a gentle lullaby but the boy didn't seem to notice. His body heaved with the effort of breathing and each time he coughed more blood soaked into the tissue held gently to his lips by his mother.

When Shona spoke it was as much to reassure herself as it was for Mary. "He'll be okay. He's young and fit and strong. Bernadette was very old. The staff here will watch him twenty-four hours."

The singing stopped, but Mary did not turn away from her son. "I sure pray you're right doctor. I sure pray you know what to do for him."

"We're doing everything we can Mary, but I need to know what happened. Did anything happen to Tommy to make this worse?"

Mary whispered her reply, so the boy wouldn't hear, but the fear in her voice was unmistakable. "He was doing fine. Tired, you know, but okay. I kept him at home all Saturday and he seemed to be getting stronger. Sunday after church he went down to the river with his friends. Said he felt good and even went swimming. He ate okay on Sunday night, went to bed and drifted off to sleep like always. Then this morning...."

Shona had never thought to forbid swimming. From the little she'd seen this disease appeared first on the skin then somehow moved into the lungs. Could swimming have transferred infected water droplets? The idea might help some of the others, but it was no use now to Tommy or Mary, so Shona kept it to herself.

She stayed with them until the hospital paperwork was completed and she was sure that Tommy was stable. By then it was nearly two-o'clock and she spoke quietly to Mary. "I have to go now. They'll look after Tommy here, but you call me if there's any change."

Mary nodded acknowledgement but still did not take her eyes off the boy.

Back at her office Shona found the small waiting room crammed with patients. She explained there had been an emergency, although in a town as small as Fulton they would already know where she had been and why.

She walked toward her office, calling out, "Okay Marcy, send the first one in."

Marcy hesitated, holding out a small piece of paper. "You might want to look at this first. It could be important."

An email had arrived from someone named Alison Grove at the CDC. "Okay Marcy, I'll be five minutes."

The email was a disappointment. It told her nothing useful, except that Martyn had forwarded her message and Alison had received it. Shona picked up the phone and called the contact number listed at the end.

Alison had many questions, but Shona did not have any answers except for the news about Tommy Sherman. The call was turning out to be as disappointing as the email.

Shona was about to hang up when Alison asked: "Oh, one last thing. Have you had any visitors from Australia recently?"

"Australia?" Shona repeated to make sure she had heard right. An image of a kangaroo in the desert passed through her head. "No. Well, not that I know of, but I can ask around. Why Australia?"

"We've had a request for help from Australia. A family there has gotten sick and the symptoms are *identical* to the ones you reported for the elderly woman who died."

Shona found it hard to believe there was any connection between Australia and Fulton. "I don't remember anyone from Australia. This town's lucky to get any tourists at all. I had a German backpacker in here with a septic cut, but that was last week after people got sick."

"Okay. Well thanks for your help."

Shona gave herself a moment before the next patient was shown in. Fulton had been such a sleepy little town since she'd arrived all those years ago. But now, what the hell was going on?

14

Monday's training seemed particularly dull to Marion after a weekend exploring the capital city. By the end of the day she was feeling drained and went directly back to the house. She would relax tonight and go to bed early. Maybe do some reading, maybe just sleep.

Her plans were changed by Kathleen who called out the moment Marion entered the house. "Marion, have you heard? Come and see this!"

Marion assumed that one of the contestants from the 'Hero Project' had done something particularly outrageous, but the TV screen was showing a map of China. The subtitle read "Mysterious Disease Outbreak."

Kathleen and Joe were both planted in their usual chairs but Marion stayed standing, more interested in a hot bath than in China. She waited with her arms folded, ready to leave the room the instant the item was over.

The anchor spoke rapidly in the excited-but-serious voice that newscasters everywhere use. "...Chinese authorities have denied they are overwhelmed and insist it is simply a cluster of industrial disease cases. They say the sick workers are being treated at Jouchou hospital and everything is under control. Rumors are spreading in Jouchou however that the outbreak started at the nearby Jouchou Peoples Special Medical Laboratory. This has also been denied by the authorities."

Marion was sure she'd heard the name Jouchou before. Hadn't that Chinese diplomat mentioned it? The one who cause a fuss up at Sherman's farm a couple of weeks ago? Marion spoke involuntarily. "Goddam!"

Joe looked up and mumbled "Huh?" but the conversation went no further as Marion was now staring intently at the screen.

The graphic behind the newscaster zoomed in to show a close-up map with a red 'X' to mark the location of Jouchou. The 'X' was skewered by the needle of a hypodermic syringe with the word 'OUTBREAK' written down its length.

The newscaster changed to a more somber tone. "The following video footage was posted on the internet over the weekend and purports to show the scenes in Jouchou. We must warn you that some viewers may find these scenes disturbing."

The map/hypodermic graphic remained on screen as the newscaster was replaced by grainy low-quality images and a new subtitle: 'Amateur Video.' Voices shouting in Chinese could be heard beneath a stilted English translation.

"This is Jouchou Peoples Special Medical Laboratory. Staff work all night on sick workers but no good." The commentary stopped as the camera panned around a room filled with hospital beds and shouting, crying people.

The camera was carried over to one of the beds where a nurse stood. Even with the dim light of the room and the poor color of the video it was obvious both the nurse and the bed were covered in blood. The man in the bed jumped and twitched uncontrollably as the nurse tried to hold him down, but could barely even hold onto him.

Marion had heard Shona's description of how Bernadette had died. Could this be the same thing? She wanted to call Shona immediately but could not take her eyes off the screen.

The camera panned back around the room and the commentary started again. "These men came from—" A new voice cut through the cacophony in the room and clearly came from someone used to being obeyed. The camera swung rapidly towards the doors where it captured a brief shot of armed soldiers standing in the doorway before it dipped towards the floor as the video dissolved into broken lines and static.

The newscaster returned. "Shocking images there from China, just shocking. We'll be back right after this break for some expert commentary on that video."

The image changed instantly to an over-groomed couple and their unfeasibly cute child. For twenty-five seconds they were confused about which juice box had the most vitamin-C. Thankfully a cartoon giraffe was able to resolve the issue just as their allotted thirty seconds expired.

The news-spell was broken now and Kathleen turned to Marion. "Isn't that *horrible*? Aren't you worried? Do you think that might be what you have in Fulton?"

This time Marion was worried. "Yes Kathleen, that is horrible and I am worried. I better make a call."

There was no answer from Shona so she tried Dale. As she listened to the dial tone she thought more about Du Rui Kuang and exactly what kind of research they did at the Jouchou Peoples Special Medical Laboratory.

Dale was unusually brief when Marion spoke to him. "Yes, I saw the news, but nothing new to report here."

Marion relaxed a little at that. "You remind Shona about that Chinese diplomat we had in town. I'm sure he worked at the laboratory they mentioned on the news."

"Uh, sure chief, anything else?"

"Make sure Shona's on top of this, and find out from her what the CDC are doing. If there's any link to China then they need to know. You get onto this right away. Got it?"

There was a long silence before Dale replied. "Sure I got it. Uh, Chief."

"Yes?"

"How's it going at Homeland Security?"

"Well it's not the most exciting thing I've ever done but it's going fine. Is there some reason it shouldn't be?"

"Uh, no Chief, just makin' sure."

"Okay, well you take care then."

Marion wondered why her officer was being vague, but there were more important things to worry about for now. She returned to the living room but the news had moved on to other issues.

She knew about events in Australia. Dale had relayed that news from Shona before the DHS got to him. She asked Joe, "Did they talk about Fulton at all? And what about Australia?" Joe looked confused, "Australia?"

"Yes you know, crocodiles and men with big knives."

"No, they only talked about China, and why would they mention Fulton anyway? You think there is some connection?"

"I hope not Joe, but we had a Chinese guy in Fulton a couple of weeks back. Nearly got himself arrested for trespassing. I'm sure he was from Jouchou, he even mentioned that laboratory."

"Christ Marion! You don't think he was spreading this thing on purpose?" Kathleen gave Joe a disapproving look at his use of profanity but only Marion saw it.

"He was a diplomat Joe, not a terrorist and he was trying to find his great-grandfather's grave."

"But there is a connection, you said so yourself, and think about the timing. It's only a couple of weeks until the presidential election. He could've been running around out on those farms spraying diseases all over the place. Those people don't care about themselves. Hell, they'd get sick on purpose and just walk around infecting anyone they could."

"Sure Joe, some people would do that. But don't you think a terrorist would choose a bigger target than Fulton?"

"Maybe, but then maybe it was a test run and the main attack is still to come."

"So what's he doing back in China?"

Joe paused. "Hmm… must be more of 'em I guess. You gotta admit, it's possible."

"Okay Joe, I admit it's possible and I certainly can't prove you wrong. But *you* have to admit it could just as easily be an accident. Maybe this guy got the groundhog flu out on Sherman's farm, brought it into Fulton then took it home to China."

"Stalemate then?"

"Stalemate, and I hope to God we're both wrong. Now I'm tired and I'm going to get some rest. You two enjoy the rest of your evening."

Marion went to bed but the images from China had stuck in her head. Fuck it! Without that damned video the story wouldn't even have made it to air. She would have been fast asleep by now, not lying awake wondering what *was* going on in her town and if there really was a connection to Jouchou?

A lot of folk would have sided with Joe and assumed the worst. The fact was however that at the moment all she had was an unidentified disease and no evidence, not a *single shred* of evidence, that there was anything more to it than that.

15

"Alison." The voice came from Dean, her boss. He waited for Alison to stop typing and look up. "I need you to come down to my office, it's important."

Alison went back to her typing. "Okay Dean, I'll need about five minutes to finish up here."

"No Alison, now" and with that he was gone.

Alison stopped typing and looked at the spot where Dean had been. It was unusual for him to interrupt her work and she let out a disapproving sigh before saving her document and heading to his office.

A man she didn't know was sitting behind Dean's desk talking on a cell-phone. He wore a dark blue casual shirt and black pants. Dean was sitting in front of the desk in one of the visitor's chairs. A second man, also unknown to Alison, sat next to him in the other one. The second man was dressed in a black suit and white shirt. A wire appeared from beneath his shirt-collar and curled its way up to an over-sized earpiece.

Just like in the movies Alison thought.

All three men looked up at Alison as she entered the room. Dean smiled but the two strangers just stared as the one behind the desk finished his phone conversation.

There was nowhere for Alison to sit and she became increasingly self-conscious. She put her hands in her pockets, then took them out again and folded her arms. She stepped back so she could be further away from the men, leaning awkwardly against a filing cabinet.

Alison did not like meeting new people. She especially didn't like being stared at by them, and extra-especially didn't like it if they were men. She was worried too by the power structure in the room. Why had Dean been cast out from his desk and replaced by a stranger?

The phone call ended but it was Dean who spoke first. "Alison, this is Special Agent Luke Johnson from Homeland Security. He wants to talk to you about the alert you raised on Friday; the pulmonary infections in Virginia."

Alison said only "Okay," but her mind began to race. What could DHS want to know about a pulmonary infection? She was sure she had followed protocol to the letter and began to review Friday morning's events in her mind. What had she done wrong?

Agent Johnson took over from Dean. "Ms. Grove, we have reviewed the infection alert you raised and we have a few questions. Given the current situation, you understand we must be very careful."

Alison had no idea what current situation he was referring to, maybe Australia? The entry she had made on Friday was not even an alert. It was simply a record of events. She didn't bother to correct him though; she was still busy trying to figure out her mistake.

The Agent began his questions. "What is your relationship with a Journalist by the name of Mike Fanning?" Alison's mind stopped racing for a moment. The question seemed irrelevant and she had no place for it in her mental filing system.

"Uh, who?"

"Mike Fanning, do you know him or not?"

She was certain she'd never heard the name before. She searched her memory for a while but came up blank. Eventually she answered, still hesitant "I don't know anyone named Mike Fanning."

"Do you read the Washington Record?"

Again, the question made no sense. Alison scorned all the mainstream media. She couldn't understand why people relied on a source of information that was so clearly compromised by commercial and political influences.

These people didn't seem to have done their background checking very well at all. Alison asked a question of her own. "Why do you need to know that? Are you sure you're interviewing the right person?"

"Just answer the questions Ms. Grove."

"Well I get my news from the web mostly, from the better blogs. Does Mike Fanning work for the Washington Record?"

"Please Ms. Grove, just answer the questions directly. Then we'll be finished a lot faster. Are you aware that Dr. Shona Price has qualifications in microbiology?"

The idea of these men being finished faster was very appealing, so Alison said only "No."

"What information do you have about the disease outbreak in Jouchou?"

Fuck! Just when I've started to cooperate they ask a question like that! Where the hell is Jouchou?

"Uh, I have no information about Jouchou."

Agent Johnson looked surprised; it was the first emotion he had shown. He turned to Dean. "Surely you keep your staff informed about relevant current events?"

"Yes we do sir. You'll find the appropriate personnel in this office are fully informed. Alison however works with a very high level of detail. We don't interrupt her important work with speculation. To date there is no confirmation from China."

Agent Johnson sighed. "Well, Ms. Grove. Your boss seems to have a high opinion of you." His tone made it clear that he did not share that high opinion. "There has been an infectious outbreak in Jouchou, China. The symptoms are similar to the pulmonary disorder in Fulton and we were wondering if you could give us any information beyond what you put in your alert."

Alison thought carefully before she replied. "I have spoken to Doctor Shona Price. Until today she has had only one serious case, an elderly woman who died. This morning she learned of a ten-year-old boy whose symptoms have become serious overnight, but not critical. He is in hospital and stable.

"I also received an official request for information from the Australian Department of Health and Ageing. They have a case similar to Fulton and are asking for——"

"Australia? Are you sure? Why isn't this information on the official database?"

"Yes, I am sure. I received an email this morning. The information was added to the official database immediately." Then, because she couldn't stop herself she added "I guess you've not been very competent with your spying on me."

Dean grimaced but agent Johnson ignored the comment. The other agent took out a phone and tapped out a text message.

Johnson repeated his earlier question, "So you have no information about Jouchou?"

"No."

"Are you *sure*?" He stared directly in to Alison's eyes.

"Yes!" *What the hell is his fixation with Jouchou?*

When Alison finished Agent Johnson did not speak or move. She felt increasingly uncomfortable in the silence but had told the man everything she knew, so she simply looked back at him.

It was Johnson who gave in and spoke first. The little victory was not lost on Alison. "Ms. Grove, have you discussed this with anyone apart from Dr. Price?"

"Just you."

"How did Dr. Price come to contact you?"

"Through a former colleague, Martyn Fortescue; he works at CDC, he knew where to forward her information."

"So you *have* discussed it with him?"

"No. He just sent me the email."

"Okay."

With that the questions were over. Agent Johnson had taken no notes but Alison assumed he was recording the conversation anyway. He leaned back in his chair but did not relax; it was just a change of position.

"Your continued cooperation in this matter would be most appreciated Ms. Grove. You will continue to collect and analyze whatever information you can obtain regarding both the Australian and U.S. situations. Don't bother about China, leave that to us. I must instruct you formally that this is a matter of National Security and as such, you are not to communicate any information whatsoever with anyone except authorized representatives of Homeland Security. You especially should not communicate to anyone that Homeland Security is involved. If you breach these conditions you may be arrested and detained." Johnson paused for effect. "Do you understand?"

"Yes."

Agent Johnson stood to leave. "That will be all for now Ms. Grove."

"Wait! How do I contact you?"

"You don't. Just keep your database up to date. We will contact you if we need to." With that, Agent Johnson of the DHS and his silent companion were gone.

Alison turned to her boss. "Why didn't you give me some warning?"

"I didn't get any warning. They just turned up and said they had to speak to you."

"Well they won't get very good answers if they don't give me time to prepare!"

Dean gave her a serious look. "Please just cooperate with them. We are all on the same side after all."

Alison agreed that yes, she would cooperate and returned to her desk. Before sitting down she did a physical check. Maybe they had planted a microphone or put some spy chip in her computer. Everything seemed perfect however, exactly as it should be.

It occurred to Alison they could get everything they wanted by tapping the office network anyway. God! They were probably monitoring her web-cam. She smiled at it and waved then turned it around to point at the wall of her cubicle.

The men of the DHS were also busy in Fulton that afternoon. They visited Shona Price, Tiffany Masterson, Dale Reynolds, Tom Sutton, the hospital doctors and the proprietors of the Olde Worlde. All were asked what had they heard, who had they heard it from, what had they said, who had they said it to?

All were left with the same instructions. This is a matter of National Security. Continue to listen but do not communicate with anyone. Do not mention Homeland Security. You will be arrested and detained if you do not follow these instructions. None of them were given any instructions on how to contact the DHS. If it was necessary the DHS, in its own good time, would contact them.

16

Michael Stonehouse did not like surprises. It was a point he made abundantly clear to those around him and, because he was one of the most powerful men in Washington D.C, they usually obliged. Yet here he was on Tuesday morning with an appointment on his schedule that he had not authorized. An appointment marked Urgent and Confidential.

Few people beyond D.C. had heard of Michael Stonehouse but within the town he was so well known that he was universally referred to as just 'MS.' He had never been elected to public office because he'd never seen any need to stand. That kind of power came with too many checks and balances.

Instead, MS built his power carefully through personal connections and business arrangements. His corporations now contributed more money to political fundraising than any other group and they were also awarded the largest value of Government contracts and special dispensations.

There would be hell to pay if this morning's appointment was not of the highest importance. MS pressed a button on his intercom and barked "Send him in!"

MS gave his visitor a moment to settle then asked "Well?"

"We have a problem at the Advanced Biologicals lab, a possible breach of containment."

The man paused but MS did not react.

"We had a Chinese guy visit the lab a while back, about three weeks ago. He's a business man but high up in the party too, so he had diplomatic credentials. The State Department asked us to show him around and we need those guys on our side, so we took him through the academic labs. All public domain stuff and most of it real simple. Then we answered a few of his questions, gave him lunch and sent him on his way."

MS began to sort through the papers on his desk as the director spoke, eventually selecting one to read. It was a request for funding from one of his political allies. He waved at the man to continue as he scanned the document.

"We do that kind of visit all the time and nothing unusual happened with this guy. But now there's a disease outbreak in China. I fished out this guy's card and there it is – Jouchou Peoples Special Medical Laboratory, the same place they've got rooms filling up with dead bodies."

"Hmm..." MS did not look up as he spoke. "Why do you think there is a breach? You haven't presented any evidence for one."

"I don't have any evidence for one, but if it has occurred then it's serious."

"Because?"

"Because if there's a breach then it's Project Longarm."

The papers dropped to the desk as MS transferred his full attention to his guest. "You're not sure of a breach but you *are* sure it's Longarm?"

"As sure as I can be without going to China. Since you got clearance for the lab I've been in the loop for intel reports on this kind of thing. I've seen the detailed symptomology. It's exactly what we saw in the field trials for Longarm. That's why I had to see you in private. If this gets..."

"I don't need you to fucking tell me what happens if this gets out again!" MS stood and began to pace the floor behind his desk, but he kept his gaze firmly on the director.

"That damned thing is black ops and you're supposed to have it stuffed back in its bottle with the lid shut tight! Do you have any idea how many favors I called in around D.C. to keep that ball of shit away from the fan the first time? Do you have any idea what it cost me individually; never mind the losses to my corporation!"

The man opened his mouth to speak but it had been a rhetorical question and MS did not slow down. "Of course you don't! Shit! I should have you stuffed into a wire cage with a bunch of those damned monkeys you like to experiment on so much down there."

The room fell silent as MS continued to pace but with noticeably slower steps. "Still, you have an excellent track record and it was me who appointed you as director of that lab. So I guess you stay out of the cage for now."

When his breathing returned to normal MS sat back down. "Okay. How's our deniability on all this?"

"Within our community it's good. There's almost no paperwork and after the pressure you applied last time most folks in D.C. will do their best to keep this tucked away. But there's two possible weaknesses."

A yellow legal pad sat on the desk in front of MS and he began making notes, but he did not interrupt the director.

"First problem is the Chinese. If they figure this out they've got no incentive to keep it quiet and they might even see it as a deliberate attack."

MS continued writing as he spoke. "You leave the Chinese to me and concentrate on your own back yard. Now what's the second weakness?"

The director cleared his throat. "It's my Head of Security. He disappeared about two weeks ago."

"Fuck! You didn't tell me?"

"It didn't seem to need that level of escalation. I was concerned of course, but even now I don't *know* if there's any link to Longarm. What you need to be aware of is that I reported it to DHS."

"Our friends at DHS, or just the regular guys?"

"The regular guys. I have to for something like this; it's in all of the government contracts. So they're sniffing around but they won't get anywhere near Longarm, it's way above their clearance."

MS leaned back in his chair. "Okay. Is there anything else I need to know?"

"No."

"Right then, this is how you stay out of that monkey cage. First you go back to your lab and contact *our* DHS people, the ones who know about

Longarm. You get them looking for your Head of Security and you tell them Longarm might be compromised and they need to make damned sure they've got their deniability in order.

"Second, you do whatever you can to find out if this thing in China is Longarm or not, but *don't* make waves. And you'll report to me in person every day, nothing in writing and nothing traceable. I'll have someone set it up."

With that the director was dismissed and MS set to work. He pressed the intercom again. "Get in here; we need to clear some space in my schedule."

17

Mike Fanning had finished his Fulton story on Saturday afternoon at the Old Worlde. After the disappointing interview with Shona he'd driven over to the hospital, betting that the paramedics from the previous Saturday would be on shift again. He found them sitting outside in the sun, waiting next to their ambulance.

They knew they weren't supposed to talk to journalists but Mike could be charming when it suited him. He soon had a firsthand description of the scene at the Sutton household. Strictly off the record, of course.

By lunchtime Mike already had enough material to justify his weekend away. He didn't bother with Tiffany and returned directly to the Olde Worlde. Choosing a comfortable chair in the guest living room he set up the lap-top he had deliberately not taken to his interview with Shona.

The story was written in a suitably exaggerated style. Facts were stated in the minimum possible space while speculation and rumor were emphasized. Nothing written was untrue and yet the reader was encouraged toward dramatic conclusions for which there was, in fact, no evidence.

To summarize: A report from the Fulton Echo could be confirmed. A mystery illness had killed one person and infected others. Confidential sources confirmed the death was unusual with blood soaking the victim's bed and sprayed onto medical personnel. Authorities (this sounded better than 'town doctor') confirmed they could not identify the cause of the illness and despite official denials, bio-terrorism could not be ruled out.

Thanks to the magical technology of his satellite network gizmo, Mike's story was at the Record in D.C. only seconds after he typed the final period. Happy with his work, Mike had put his lap-top away and moved on to the beer and fishing that would occupy him for the rest of the weekend.

Monday had been spent working from home so it was just after seven on Tuesday morning when Mike returned to his desk at the Record. To outsiders it was a cluttered mess, indistinguishable from every other journalist's desk. To Mike it was *his* clutter, as warm and familiar as his favorite sweater or his old leather couch. This morning the clutter was almost completely hidden beneath a sheet of faded newsprint. Scrawled across it in black felt pen were the words 'SEE ME NOW.'

Mike walked into the editor's office with a grin on his face. "What's the problem Bob?"

The editor answered without looking away from his computer screen. "The problem Mike is all the fishing and working from home. It must be wearing you down."

"Nope, I'm coping just fine, must be my executive killer instinct."

"Hmm…. Well with that kind of instinct you'll know all about the news from China, right? Lots of people dying in China, Mike. That's nothing new of course, but today they're dying like that woman you wrote about from Virginia. So you drop everything else and follow up on this thing."

"Jesus Bob there's nothing to follow up on. I had to use a hell of a lot of window dressing on that story, just to make it even remotely interesting. The doctor had no idea what was going on and if I hadn't got a description of the old woman's death from the paramedics I'd have had nothing."

"Well congratulations Mike because you *did* make it remotely interesting. Now there're people dying on the evening news in glorious Technicolor and I've got to print something or I'll look like I'm asleep at the wheel. Your story is the closest thing I've got to an exclusive on this so you need to get off your backside and do some real journalism."

"Maybe you should send a real journalist then Bob." It was a stupid thing to say and Mike immediately regretted it as all the old memories began to surface. "Uh, what I meant was—"

"I know what you meant Mike but you brought it up, not me. Sure I know you like to be all cynical and sure I know you decided a long time ago not to care. But the truth is you *are* an investigative reporter and a damned good one when you set your mind to it. Maybe the kids around here don't know it but I'm as old as you are and I've seen you do it. So there's no more argument. You found this story and you're sticking with it."

Mike was reluctant to disturb the life he'd created for himself at the Record, but he wasn't about to quit and look for work elsewhere. He told himself there couldn't possibly be any connection between his story and anything that was happening in China. He'd do a little digging, come up with nothing and that would be the end of it.

"Okay Bob, you win. Got any leads?"

"Sorry chum, you'll have to watch TV like the rest of us."

Mike started with the news agencies but they all claimed the video had just turned up on the internet; they had no idea who the source was. The Chinese authorities refused to comment beyond declaring the video to be 'spreading unnecessary panic when the situation is under control.'

An attempt to re-interview Shona Price was equally unproductive. It didn't matter how many times Mike apologized for their last meeting; she just would not say anything and would not give a reason. The Fulton police were equally uncooperative and even the girl, Tiffany, was surprisingly quiet.

Mike needed a new approach. He guessed that Shona might have contacted the CDC and a search for the word Fulton turned up a public alert from the previous day. Frustratingly, it mentioned Fulton and Australia, but there was nothing about China.

Several calls to the CDC in Atlanta produced only an official response that an alert had been issued and it would be updated when further information came to hand. Mike had not dealt with the CDC before but they seemed uncooperative for a body devoted to public health.

The trip to the editor's office was brief.

"I'm going to need a budget for this one Bob. Someone's trying to put a lid on it and that's pissing me off."

"You mean you're actually going to investigate?"

"Only if you can come up with the dough Bobby boy, otherwise my hands are tied."

"Well it's good to see you back in the saddle. Bring me the forms and I'll sign them off."

Mike drove to Fulton wondering if there really was a story there, something worth getting his teeth into. The prospect gave him a sense of purpose he hadn't felt in years.

He arrived to find Shona Price walking down the street, heading away from her office. He up pulled up beside her and called out. "Doctor Price!"

The doctor stopped walking and leaned forward, peering into the car. "I've got nothing to say to you Mr. Fanning. I made that very clear on the phone." She stood up straight, looked away and continued walking.

Mike assumed she'd seen his story in that day's Record and didn't like what he'd written. It wouldn't be surprising given how he'd chosen to present her information. It wasn't going to stop him though, Journalists needed to grow a thick hide or they simply didn't last in the job. He parked his car and ran to catch up with Shona.

"Listen. I'm sorry about the story. I know you didn't like my angle, but I've got a hungry editor to feed."

"I didn't read your story and I don't care about your angle." Shona looked directly ahead as she spoke, walking faster now. The words drifted back to Mike who wasn't used to moving this quickly at all.

"You didn't read it?"

Shona kept walking fast and still wouldn't look at him. "I don't read the Record, Mike. I get my news from reputable sources."

Mike made a supreme effort, passing Shona then turning back towards her and blocking her path. The ten-foot sprint was almost too much and he forced out his words through labored breathing. "If you haven't read my story then *what* is your problem?"

Shona stopped and glared at him. "Like I said on Saturday, Mike. What we have in this town is a few sick people and one old lady that died. There's no good comes from people like you making up stories and printing them like they're true. All your talk about terrorism, getting folks around here in trouble with the government."

The government? Mike kept his voice quiet, hoping the doctor would calm down. "Shona, what do you mean, in trouble with the government?"

She didn't calm down. "You know and I know that I can't talk about it." She stepped around Mike and started walking again.

Mike didn't know, but he wanted to. What was the government doing in Fulton and what kind of trouble were they causing for Shona? He puffed along beside her, adopting an awkward trot to try and keep up with her angry pace.

"Who told you not to talk Shona? Was it the CDC, the cops?" He kept asking questions as they hurried side by side through the little town but it was no use. She said nothing, refusing to stop or even look in his direction.

When they reached the lawn in front of Shona's house she stopped and turned toward him. "This is my house. You step on my land and you're trespassing. I do not want to speak to you. I do not want you on my property. Is that clear?"

Mike knew when he was beaten. "Yes" he puffed "it's clear."

Shona went into her house and locked the door with what seemed a deliberately loud turn of the latch. Mike stood for a while longer to catch his breath then headed off towards Sam's bar.

Tiffany Masterson was exactly where he expected her to be. Sitting at the bar, waiting for her friends to arrive for the evening's excess. She saw Mike approach but did not respond as he sat down next to her. "Tiffany, Mike Fanning from the Washington Record. Remember me?" He handed her his card.

Tiffany took the card in a disinterested way and dropped it on the bar. "Yeah, I remember you." It seemed she was only enthusiastic when she had an audience to play to.

Mike waved to Sam then returned his attention to Tiffany. "I've got a few more questions for you, if that's okay?" Sam arrived and Mike spoke without giving her a chance to answer. "I'll have a Heineken thanks." Then to Tiffany, "What are you drinking?"

She perked up at that. "I'll have a head slammer, no ice." Sam seemed to know what she wanted so Mike started his questions.

"I've just been speaking to the doctor. She seemed awful upset, said something about getting in trouble with the government. You know what that's about?"

Tiffany laughed, leaned forward and put her finger across her lips. "Shhh! It's all a big secret. We're not supposed to tell anyone."

This was progress compared to Shona.

"What's a big secret? The illness?"

She sat up straight and gave a mock salute. "You know, National Security. Can't talk to the press."

"You *are* the press Tiffany, so it's no problem if we talk to each other."

The conversation was interrupted by Sam with the drinks. Mike recognized his beer but Tiffany was given an oversized shot glass filled with thick green sludge. Mike threw an alarmed look at Sam. The bartender rolled his eyes skyward and walked off. By the time Mike turned back to Tiffany she had already downed the drink and banged the glass back down on the bar.

It was a good thing Mike had expenses for this job. By the time he had finished his questions there was a row of five empty glasses next to his half-filled beer. Sam did not take them away and Tiffany seemed proud to have them displayed. Like a huntress showing off her kills.

Thankfully, the expenses were worth it. By the time Tiffany's friends arrived Mike knew that Tiffany, Shona, the police and the hospital had all been visited by Homeland Security. All had been pumped for information, been given nothing in return then told to keep quiet.

That would have to do. Mike stood to leave but Tiffany grabbed his sleeve and spoke with a slur as her friends sat down "Hey guys. This is Mike. He's a friend of mine. He can buy drinks on expenses!"

Some of the friends gave Mike the 'dirty old man' look as he pulled away from Tiffany. His expenses wouldn't cover drinks for all of them and he wouldn't get anything useful out of them anyway. Besides, he had a plane to catch.

18

Tommy Sherman died late on Tuesday afternoon. Shona got the news from a distraught Mary Sherman who phoned to ask how safe were the rest of her family? From the horror in Mary's voice the death must have been every bit as gruesome as Bernadette's.

There was more bad news. On Tuesday morning a day patient at the hospital, Brad Martensen, had a tumor treated with radiation. Less than an hour later he began to cough up blood. Within two hours he had been rushed to critical care and after three hours he was raving with hallucinations. Shortly after that he also had died.

The hospital had not called Shona about either Tommy or Brad and as the primary care physician she should have been informed immediately. She was fuming about it when she left her office on Tuesday night. Mike Fanning had walked right into the middle of that one and he got it with both barrels.

Shona had spent that evening at home researching on the internet. Trawling through research databases looking for anything that might help her understand. Despite the terrible circumstances she enjoyed it more than she'd expected. There was no need for this kind of work as a town doctor and it felt good to be putting her gifts to work again.

Unfortunately even the most advanced databases were little use. Nothing matched up with the symptoms she was seeing, particularly the manner of death. It seemed whatever was killing people in Fulton, it was new.

Shona's first task on Wednesday morning was to call Alison Grove at the CDC.

"Alison? It's Shona Price here, the doctor from Fulton. I really need your help."

"Uh right, Shona. Um look, I've just arrived at my desk and I have a lot to organize today so I don't really have time for this call. Besides we've got nothing new on that. Sorry I can't help."

"What? I've got people dying out here Alison! Two more yesterday and both of them the same as Bernadette Sutton. First they start bleeding, then they go crazy and then they're dead. You're the CDC. You *have* to help."

"Well I'm sorry I can't. If you want to take this further you'll have to do it through official channels. Now please, I need to go."

Shona sat at her kitchen table in Fulton and wondered what to do next. Alison hadn't said it directly of course but it was clear she'd been told not to talk.

Shona understood the DHS might not want details of this going public, it made even more sense after the news about China. It had never occurred to her though that she shouldn't be talking to the CDC. That made no sense at all. How were they supposed to control this disease if they didn't share information?

There wasn't time to dwell. Shona had kept her day clear of appointments but there was a lot to be done. She picked up her doctor's bag, case notes and a few of the more hopeful research papers then headed to her car.

At the hospital Shona asked the duty nurse for Tommy and Brad's patient records. The nurse couldn't find them, nor could the duty doctor. After ten minutes the registrar was called.

He was a small man, dressed in a pinstripe suit and looking over the top of small round glasses that perched unfeasibly close to the end of his nose. He hurried into the hospital lobby where Shona was waiting in front of the reception desk and spoke to her in smooth conciliatory tones.

"I'm sorry Dr. Price. The records for both those patients have been mislaid." He changed to a hushed tone "Understandable I'm sure, what with the terrible scenes we had here yesterday."

"Understandable? Terrible scenes or not this is a hospital and you should not be losing patient records, especially for two patients who died here yesterday under *your* care. What's more I was *not* informed in either case. I had to find out from the relatives! As registrar I'm sure you understand this is a serious breach of protocol. Now they are still *my* patients and I *demand* to see their records."

By the time she'd finished Shona was leaning forward over the registrar. He took an involuntary step backwards and stammered slightly. "Well, uh, we don't know where the records are."

Shona kept her voice loud. "Where is the duty doctor from yesterday?"

The registrar relaxed visibly, Shona thought perhaps he almost smiled. "He's away until Friday. I don't think he can be contacted."

She reached over the reception desk, grabbed the phone and thrust it at him. "Well, let's call his number and find out."

The registrar muttered something Shona couldn't catch, but the call was made.

"Is Dr. Chowdry there?" A pause then "Uh-huh, I see. Well, thank you anyway." He hung up and turned to Shona. There was definitely a smile this time. "Dr. Chowdry is unavailable for the next few days. We'll just have to wait until Friday for those records."

Shona kept pushing. "Is it possible the records were sent to the coroner?"

"The coroner? None of the patients are having an autopsy."

"What? Three people die suddenly of an unknown illness and you're not doing an autopsy?"

The registrar pursed his lips. "The death certificates were signed by Dr. Chowdry as hospital doctor on duty at the time. The cause of death was identified as cardiac arrest following complications from massive pulmonary infection. There is no suspicion of foul play. Therefore, an autopsy is not —"

"Required. And, I suppose, the death certificates are with the patient records and only Dr. Chowdry knows where they are and, of course, only God knows where Dr. Chowdry is until Friday."

The registrar allowed himself another little smile. "I'm sure you understand that without the paperwork I can't do any more."

It was insane. Basic hospital procedures had not been followed and even commonsense had been abandoned. This annoying little man could not have been any more uncooperative.

It had to be the work of the DHS again, but why? All this secrecy was making things worse. How was National Security being protected by allowing an unknown disease to spread?

Shona stood in the lobby, wondering what to do next. The duty doctor had returned to the ward and the nurse to her station. The registrar was still smiling up at her, waiting for capitulation.

Well fuck him! If he thought this doctor was going to turn and run away at the first sign of trouble he was about to get a nasty surprise.

It was time to take a gamble, to try and turn all the secrecy to her advantage. Shona had asked the DHS man for a contact number and been refused. With luck the registrar had no way to contact the DHS either. She leaned toward him and spoke quietly this time. "Do you have *my* records?"

"Uh, What?"

He didn't have Shona's records and she knew it. She wasn't a patient and she wasn't a hospital doctor. After this conversation though it would take him only a few hours to find what he needed. She hoped that would be long enough.

"If you did have my records you would know that I have a degree in microbiology and have worked for many years as a researcher and manager at the National Institutes of Health. So I am qualified to investigate these deaths.

"Perhaps there has been some misunderstanding on your part but I assure you I am under strict instructions to collect and analyze all relevant information." She used the phrase 'collect and analyze' deliberately. The DHS man had used it and it had struck Shona as odd at the time.

"I *will* need to see those records and as soon as possible. If there is no official autopsy then I will also need to examine my patients directly, again as soon as possible."

"I can't allow that! Not without written authorization."

Shona had to keep moving forward. She couldn't let him call her bluff.

"All relevant documentation will be provided in due course. This is however a matter of the utmost urgency and your immediate cooperation is required. Alternatively, I could file a full report on your refusal to assist in this matter." It was grade-A bullshit, but the registrar hesitated when he heard it.

"Look, I'm not supposed to even *talk* to you without the right paperwork. But I don't want to impede an official investigation." There was a pause while he considered his position.

"Okay. You can start now but I will call the hospital administration to confirm your story. It won't be *my* career that's on the line. Am I clear?"

"Yes, you're clear."

"Good. I'll have an orderly escort you to the morgue. Is there anything else or can I return to my work now?"

"I will also need access to your laboratory facilities."

"We're a small hospital, our laboratory is only rudimentary."

"Well it will have to do."

The registrar disappeared back to his office to be replaced a few minutes later by an orderly who led Shona away through a door marked 'No Public Access.' They went down a flight of stairs to the basement level of the hospital where it was cold and dimly lit and the thick gray paint was cracked and peeling from the damp concrete walls.

The laboratory itself was sufficiently lit, although the fluorescent lights buzzed incessantly. Shona found a good quality microscope with slides and covers, a chiller and freezer for storing samples, gloves and masks.

One corner held a dusty wooden cabinet with glass doors and a sign that said 'Authorized Personnel Only' beneath a handwritten skull and cross-bones. Inside was a range of basic reagents and stains. The reagents would be useless; most of them had a limited shelf life. Shona hoped the stains would be adequate.

The lab's collection of Petrie dishes and beakers were stored in an air-tight cupboard and so were clean. Shona carefully numbered each of the containers and placed them in a plastic cooler.

A quick trip out to her car added a camera and her doctor's bag to the equipment. She turned to the orderly. "Okay Igor, time to go harvest some lungs."

The joke seemed to be lost on him and he followed Shona out of the room without replying.

The morgue was only a few doors from the laboratory and it was a surprisingly small room, empty except for a bare metal gurney and four metal doors along the long wall at the back. Two of them had handwritten labels the other two were bare.

Shona turned to the orderly. "We'll need surgical gowns, can you get some please." He was only gone for a minute but it felt good when he returned. Shona was a scientist with no belief in ghosts or any kind of af-terlife. Yet being alone in the stark, silent room with two dead people was unsettling even for her.

She carefully protected herself with the gown, gloves and a mask then nodded at the orderly. He opened the first door and Tommy Sherman slid out into the light on well-oiled bearings. The white sheet covering him was faintly stained where blood had seeped through from the underside.

He wheeled the gurney over and positioned it beneath Tommy, star-ing apprehensively at the blood stains. "I heard about this. They say it was bad."

Shona nodded. "Yes. It was bad."

Together they lifted the dead boy onto the gurney then wheeled him through the double doors at the far end of the morgue and out into the examination room. Shona arranged her equipment then carefully lifted the cover from Tommy.

The orderly stepped back from the gurney. "I'll wait outside if that's okay."

"Of course."

19

MS always enjoyed his visits to Senator Hanson's private office. Here they would discuss the most important matters as they relaxed into the over-stuffed leather chairs with fine cigars and the best whiskey. Safe in the knowledge that the Secret Service made daily sweeps for any microphones or cameras that might be hiding in the phones or the furniture, or even behind the ornately decorated oak panels that lined the walls.

MS had known the Senator for years and they have become good friends, but they never let that friendship stand in the way of business and today would be no different. The Senator waited until they were both comfortably settled before he spoke.

"So tell me MS, what the hell's going on at your lab?"

MS smiled. "I was hoping you could tell me. You're the one who sits on all those intelligence committees after all."

"Don't fuck with me; there isn't time for that today."

MS lost the smile. The Senator was perhaps more powerful than even MS himself. He was certainly not someone to antagonize. "Longarm might have escaped, to China. But nothing's confirmed yet."

"Ah yes, the deaths in Jouchou. They made it into one of my intelligence briefings. I thought the description was familiar."

"Yes, that's the only connection so far, but I do a lot of business in China and I have a lot of contacts there. I've given names to my lab director along with a bucket of cash for bribes. I'll let you know the moment I have something definite."

"Well I hope you've got this guy lined up to take the fall. There's more going on here than just the Chinese."

"Oh really? What's he gotten me into?"

The senator paused to sip from his whiskey. "Your head of security is missing?"

"Not *mine*, the head of security for the lab. It was reported to DHS as a matter of course."

"Yes it was, and they've been looking into it. Just a regular investigation until yesterday, when they found a terrorist plot. There's going to be an attack on a Senator."

"On you?"

"They don't know for sure yet. But I'm the only one with a close connection to your lab. So there's a good chance it's me."

"Well at least they'll be too busy with you to worry about Longarm. Can't have some crazy running around shooting at Senators."

"Not shooting MS. It's going to be a biological attack."

"Ah, shit!"

"That's right, shit! And we're *both* going to be buried in it if we don't have complete deniability on Longarm."

"But we don't know the attack will use Longarm. It would be an odd choice."

The Senator sighed. "No, we don't know, but I'm not about to take the risk. How's it going to look when the White House announces that unapproved research was used to try and kill the Senator who had it secretly funded in the first place?

"And remember I did that five years ago, under the previous administration. The party won't thank us for dragging these skeletons out of the closet just two weeks out from a Presidential election!"

MS nodded agreement. "That's true. We could kill a thousand people in China and get away with it. We could probably even survive the attack on you, if you'll excuse the irony. But we won't last a minute in this town if we cost our side the election. Not even with our considerable influence."

"Exactly!" The Senator was leaning forward now, pointing at MS. "So how do we use that considerable influence to cover our asses?"

The room fell silent as the two men drew on their cigars and considered the situation. It was MS who spoke first.

"Okay, so China should be no problem. Might even be a help if we muddy the waters by blaming them. We can say it was their guy who brought some foreign disease to the US. Hell, maybe he even supplied it to the terrorists! Then he goes home and it gets loose on him and kills a bunch of his own people.

"They'll deny it of course but they're so damned secretive about everything that no-one will believe them. So we can spin that one as much as we like, so long as they don't come out with any real evidence, and I don't see how they can. All they have is dead bodies."

When MS was done the Senator put down his cigar. "So why would the Chinese want to kill a Senator?"

"Any number of reasons. Who can guess what's going on in their devious minds? Besides, maybe it wasn't an official act. Maybe their guy was just doing some dirty little deals on the side."

"Okay, but they'll still be mighty pissed off. Plus he was here as a guest of the State Department, so any number of folks in this town won't like the idea either."

MS shrugged. "So let 'em get pissed off. It's not going to be an official statement. Just a bunch of rumors we'll get started in the press, nothing pointing back to us."

"So you can get started on that?"

"Already have, just need to tweak it for this terrorist thing."

"Good." The Senator smiled as the first part of their plan fell into place. "You'll still need to bury Longarm. If the Chinese scream loud enough then we could end up with the State Department snooping around your lab. I'm guessing you still have some of the stuff, otherwise why are you worried it escaped?"

"There's no documentation, even the lab notes were destroyed after those field trials. But we still have live cultures. I figured we could wait a few years then have another try, maybe when you guys get reelected."

"Well that's off the table now MS."

"Agreed. I'll go down there personally and make sure —"

"No." The senator waved at MS to stop. "Don't get your fingerprints anywhere near this one. Have your lab director destroy it and make sure the labs security system keeps a record. Then, if it ever goes that far, you can say he was a rogue agent and the only physical evidence will back you up."

"Worth a try, and it wouldn't be the first time that kind of thing has worked." MS finished his whiskey before he moved on. "So that just leaves the DHS investigation. I'm assuming they *will* stop the attack?"

The Senator laughed. "You think I'd be sitting here drinking with you if I thought different? Of course they'll stop it. They just won't pounce until the last minute."

"But doesn't that make them look incompetent?"

"If they fail it does. But if they stop it at the last minute then they can say well, we need more money and more secret powers if you want us to stop these things sooner. And we're all scared because a Senator nearly died so we say sure, you can have that."

A frown crossed MS's face. "Well I hope you know what you're doing. If I lose you it'll take me years to build another relationship this valuable."

"Relax MS! Like you said, I'm on all the committees and I have all the contacts so I'm well in the loop on this. Besides, there's too many careers at DHS would go down the drain if they let me die."

"Okay I'll relax, it's your funeral after all. Now tell me how we control this investigation."

The Senator leaned forward again warming to the task. "We have to stop them finding Longarm, or at least we have to stop them telling the White House about it. The way to do that is get our people in charge of the investigation.

"Shouldn't be too difficult now they've found terrorists. A lot of DHS folk turned a blind eye for us when Longarm went wrong and some of them are high up now. A bit of pressure from me, some more from you and a new team gets assigned. Everything works out except, sorry Mr.

President, we never could find out what those terrorists were planning on using."

The whiskey glasses were refilled and the men raised them in a toast. There were risks of course, but the plan was good. They spent a further fifteen minutes deciding precisely who to pressure and how best to do it. Then MS left the Senator's office with a lot of hard work in front of him, but also a growing confidence that this would all work out to his benefit.

It was well placed confidence. History had shown that most events in D.C. worked out to benefit MS somehow.

20

Shona knew that Tommy would be a mess, but she was still shocked at the sight of him. Most of the blood had been cleaned from his body and there was just a small flower of dark brown crust remaining on his lower lip. It had formed after he was covered with the sheet and a few final drops oozed out into the weave of the fabric.

The shock didn't come from that though, it came from his face. This was not the face of a ten year old boy lying peacefully after death; it was the face of a wild animal.

The eyes were not just closed but crushed down beneath the lids. The nostrils flared and the mouth was drawn back in a snarl, revealing teeth and gums. Behind the mouth his jaw was clenched shut, the muscles at its base still bulging from the effort.

Tommy had died with every muscle in his face strained to the extreme and they had stayed that way until rigor mortis had set in. Shona fished a notebook from her bag and began to write. If Tommy had been doing that through conscious effort, from intense pain say, then the muscles would have relaxed when he died. This gruesome death mask was, in contrast, involuntary and implied an unusual neurological condition.

The rest of Tommy's body was similarly distorted. He had an arched back and his hands were clamped into tight fists. The toes of his left foot were curled closed, but those on his right were turned upwards and splayed open.

Shona set down her notebook on the table then opened the plastic cooler and laid out the sample containers. From her doctors' bag she retrieved a scalpel handle and attached a new blade.

First she carefully examined the skin on Tommy's face, arms and chest. Patients had complained of body odor and a few had skin rashes. There were some discolored patches on Tommy's arms and a little around the base of his nose. Shona took samples from the arms but left the nose intact. Tommy's face was already badly disfigured and she couldn't stand to make it worse.

The skin samples were carefully placed in containers. Shona needed to record the details of each sample, but didn't want to touch her notebook or pen without removing her gloves. The examination would take forever that way so she called out to the orderly who opened the door but did not come inside.

"I need you to take notes for me." He glanced at the table then took a careful step forward. Shona had no time for his hesitation; an orderly should be used to this kind of thing. She pointed at the notebook and pen sitting on the table. "Use those. You can sit outside the door if you want. Just make sure you can hear me."

He chose to stand inside the room but turned to one side, so he was not facing the examination table. Shona returned to her work, commenting out loud on what she found so it could be written down.

She took scrapings from Tommy's nose, throat and airways, then turned him on his side and drew a sample of spinal fluid. She would not examine this herself, it would have to be sent to an outside laboratory for testing. All the patients that died had extreme muscle spasms. The infection must have reached their muscles or nerves somehow and hopefully the spinal samples would shed light on that.

Shona took a moment to rest; it was a long time since she had dissected corpses in medical school. She had not enjoyed it then and wasn't looking forward to it now.

The orderly jumped as Shona cracked the first of Tommy's ribs. "What the...?"

"I need to get to his lungs. He was coughing up blood and I think the alveoli will be damaged. Hopefully I'll find some answers there."

"His what's damaged?"

"The alveoli, they're small clusters of cells where gasses are exchanged with the blood." There were no more questions so Shona returned to her work.

There was just the slightest puff of air as the scalpel punctured the wall of Tommy's lung. She turned to the orderly. "You should probably put a face mask on now." She had been so intent on her exam she never thought to make sure he took precautions. By the time she looked back down the lung wall was slowly collapsing around the small hole she had made. It reminded Shona of one of her soufflés.

It was impossible to see what was happening in the lungs during the dissection. They sank and folded under the knife and didn't look anything like the textbook images.

Shona began to feel she was desecrating the boy, rather than examining him so when she had five samples from different parts of his lung she stopped. Each was carefully stored in its own container and recorded in her notebook by the orderly.

The collection had taken two hours, far longer than Shona had intended, but it needed to be done. She carefully placed the broken ribs across Tommy's sunken lung then folded his skin back over them. Tommy's frame had shifted slightly during the examination and now the skin did not completely cover the hole, leaving a gaping wound down the center of his chest. Shona hoped that Mary Sherman could forgive her.

"Okay, we need to put him back now."

The orderly frowned. "You're not going to sew him up?"

"I might need more samples. I'll sew him up when I know I'm done."

"Okay then."

When they got back to the laboratory Shona dismissed the orderly. "I'll be busy here for a while but I don't need any more help. I guess you can go back to the ward."

"No, I can't. I've been ordered to watch you at all times."

It made sense. The registrar was covering his butt and it didn't bother Shona if the orderly stayed to watch.

"Whatever. You better get a book to read though. Otherwise you'll be dead from boredom in half an hour." He left the room as Shona carefully arranged the samples on the laboratory bench before she gave them a first examination under the microscope.

The skin samples were all the same, showing clear damage to the surface blood vessels and possible inflammation around the nerves. Almost any skin rash would have looked the same. The damage may have been caused by the infection or maybe it was just the patient scratching to relieve itching, or maybe it was both. Shona noted what she had found then moved on.

She had concluded early that the infection was caused by a bacterium. The symptoms had so much in common with tuberculosis. So now she turned to the scrapings from Tommy's nose and throat.

Small amounts were transferred to microscope slides and colored with the laboratory stains to make the bacteria visible. Now they would appear as the familiar blobs and lines she had known so well in her research days.

The orderly returned with several copies of 'Car and Engine' magazine and sat himself at the back of the laboratory, well away from the samples.

Shona looked at her first slide under the microscope. As she had expected, it was cluttered with dead cells and myriad bacteria. After five minutes of meticulous searching she lifted her head from the eyepiece and sighed. There was nothing resembling TB. If it was present she would have seen it clearly visible under the stain.

The other slides were just as disappointing. Shona sat in front of the microscope feeling tired, hungry and cold. She would have taken a break but the thought of the registrar kept her going. He would not be able to confirm of her story and she was surprised he hadn't come down to the lab to kick her out already.

Shona stood and stretched then walked over to the chiller for the first of Tommy's lung samples. Even to her naked eye the damage was clearly visible. The flesh of the lungs, normally pink and spongy, was scarred by crusted spots of dry blood that showed where its thin membrane had been breached.

Blood had poured through those holes and into Tommy's air passages, quickly overcoming his body's ability to expel it. His blood pressure would have fallen from the sudden loss at the same time as his oxygen levels were also falling from the obstruction of air in his lungs.

His autonomic nervous system, controlling breathing and heart rate, was not designed to cope with such massive damage and would have pushed his heart faster and faster, desperately trying to get the blood pressure back up. Starved of oxygen though, his heart would have been unable to maintain the pace and before long it would have stopped.

Looking at the first sample Shona was amazed the boy survived as long as he did. The damage was so severe that any infectious agent must be massively abundant.

She took a swab from the area around one of the blood spots and prepared a microscope slide. The swab resolved into a jumble of cell fragments and other detritus, but no bacteria. Shona adjusted the focus over its full range but nothing of interest came into view. The process was repeated for the ten or so interesting regions on the slide, but still nothing.

Shona sat up and reviewed her procedures. Maybe she had forgotten a vital step? She prepared a second slide from a different sample; this time writing down each step as it was taken. Before viewing the slide she checked her notes. This time the procedure was perfect but the second slide was as barren as the first.

It simply wasn't possible for something to do that much damage and leave no trace of itself behind. Shona sat and stared at the microscope again. "Okay girl" she said out loud, "time to question your assumptions."

Maybe her bacteria needed something special. It took nearly an hour to prepare new slides using each of the five stains available in the lab, and another hour to examine them.

They were all negative. Shona hadn't found a single viable candidate organism. "Goddammit, where *are* you?"

The orderly replied from the back of the lab. "Trouble?"

"I've been working all day and I've got *nothing*."

"Oh." He went back to reading his magazine.

"Well you wait here. I'm going to get something to eat."

"Okay."

Shona walked to the lobby bought a sandwich from the vending machine. It looked dry and unappetizing, but it would have to do. She was already half-way through it when she walked back into the laboratory to find the orderly hunched over her microscope.

He looked up and asked "What is this?" He'd taken her slide out and replaced it with the Petrie dish that held the first lung sample.

"Probably a broken microscope."

He gave her a hurt look. "I didn't break it. I had one of these when I was a kid and I know how to use it. I just don't know what I'm looking at."

Shona leaned over the eyepiece and knew exactly what she was looking at. "Fuck!" She checked the microscope settings. It was on one-hundred times magnification, far too low to find bacteria, but perfect for this.

The orderly looked worried. "What is it?"

"It's a fucking fungus!"

"Is that bad?"

Shona didn't hear him. She threw the remains of her sandwich in the bin and got to work.

She cut off the smallest section of lung tissue that could be managed by a hand held scalpel, putting it on a clean slide and pressing it down beneath a small glass cover slip. By adjusting the light in the microscope she could see the surface of the tissue directly.

Even under the cover the surface of the tissue was lumpy and irregular but fungal growth was clearly evident. Shona checked a skin sample next and the fungus was there too, although not nearly as much as in the lungs.

It was unusual for an organism to populate two such different environments. Skin infections could come from almost any physical contact but the lungs implied transmission by air or airborne water droplets.

Shona returned to the lung sample and adjusted the microscope to focus on just the highest parts of its surface. It only took her a minute to find her target, a small round sac protruding up from the center of a patch of fungus. Within another minute she had counted five more.

She began to shake slightly as adrenalin was pumped into her blood and her heart beat faster than it had in a long time. When she spoke her voice was almost a whisper.

"Oh God no...."

21

Alison Grove stood at the coffee cart on Wednesday morning at her regular time; smiling at Matt as he took ninety-three seconds to make her coffee. As usual he didn't pay any particular attention to either Alison or her smile.

She picked up the espresso and walked her bike toward the CDC building. One day she would say something to Matt beyond "Decaf espresso, thanks." When she did it would be brilliant, exactly the right thing to say and Matt's handsome face would light up with yearning for her. Until then she preferred to say nothing of consequence.

"Alison Grove?"

Alison was nearly at the bike stand when a man's voice startled her out of her daydream. She turned sharply, instantly prepared to defend herself although she had no idea what she might be defending herself against. It was just that since the DHS visit she had been feeling even more vulnerable than usual.

An older man stood several feet away. He was holding one of Matt's paper cups in his left hand and a business card in his right. He extended the card towards Alison and took a step forward.

"I'm Mike Fanning, from the Washington Record. Do you have a moment, Miss Grove?"

Alison's mind went into overdrive. On Monday she was grilled by the spies, now here was one of the very people they'd been asking about. What could he possibly want? Was it a test, to see if she'd talk? Whatever the man's motive Alison did not like the anxiety he was causing, or the damage he was doing to her routine.

She should have said simply "No" and walked away, but that would have been a lie. She did have a moment, even though it was only one moment and no more.

"I do have a moment Mr. Fanning, but I'm just a researcher and not authorized to speak to the press. You should ask at reception." She looked away from Mike and began walking determinedly towards the bike rack.

Mike's voice followed her. "Just a researcher who's handling the Fulton case."

Shit! Alison's pulse raced and she was sure her face was turning red. She forced herself to look straight ahead and continued to walk until her bike was carefully propped against the rack.

Alison heard footsteps approaching as she looped the heavy plastic-wrapped cable through both wheels, the frame and finally through the bike stand. She snapped shut the oversized lock with a loud click then stood up, took a deep breath and turned to face the journalist.

He smiled and offered his card again. "Look Miss Grove—"

"You'll need to ask at reception, Mr. Fanning. There are strict procedures for communicating with the press, something I'm sure you're well aware of."

The journalist stopped smiling and put the card back in his pocket. Whether he was aware of the procedures or not, he was clearly disappointed with her response.

"Alison, I need to know what's going on. We've got the same disease popping up in Virginia, Australia and China. The Chinese stuff is all over the news but apart from me, *no one* is reporting the rest.

"People are dying right here in the U.S. and the government should be helping. *You* should be helping. Instead of that we've got Homeland Security telling anyone close to this thing to keep quiet and do nothing."

That wasn't true. Alison had been told not to talk, but she hadn't been prevented from doing further research. Her mouth opened in protest but she caught herself and closed it again. Better to say nothing and end the conversation sooner.

The journalist saw the movement and pounced. "So they have been here? Is that why you won't talk to me?"

Alison looked at his pale skin and the gray stubble on his chin, the casual jacket thrown over a worn business shirt and brown pants. *I don't need the DHS to put me off you Mr. Fanning. You're doing a good enough job of that on your own.*

She said nothing, turned away from him and began walking to the building. She could hear him following again and, of course, he didn't stop talking.

"There's a hard-working doctor up in Fulton. She's already had one patient die on her and there's plenty more getting sick. She needs our help."

That was just too obvious for Alison. She held nothing against Shona Price but she wasn't about to fight the government just for the sake of sisterhood.

Alison had reached the doors to her building when he fired his final shot. "Someone's trying to bury the truth here Alison. Tell me it isn't you."

Fuck him! Alison stopped walking and stared through the sliding glass door into the lobby. Just a few steps more and she could be inside, past the security guards and sheltered in the safe familiarity of her office.

But those few steps would have to wait because Alison would never try to bury the truth. Mike's question had set off a wave of anger that began in her chest and washed out to her extremities. She waited for it to pass but then he was standing next to her, demanding an answer.

"Well, are you part of the cover up?"

Cover up! How dare he!

"I… I don't have time to talk to you. I have to be at work."

"We'll meet for lunch then; I'll meet you here and buy you lunch."

He made it sound like a date. *Yuck!* But if she said no then it would look like she *was* hiding something.

"Okay. Here, at twelve-thirty. I'll only have twenty minutes. You don't need to buy me lunch."

The journalist smiled again and took a step closer. For a horrifying moment she thought he might be going to hug her, but he just nodded and said "Okay, twelve-thirty."

Alison sat at her desk all morning utterly unable to concentrate. Each time she checked the clock on her computer screen it had advanced only a few minutes. Questions raced through her mind at such a pace she could barely remember them, never mind answer them.

Had she made the right decision? Was this man who he said he was? What *was* the truth about Fulton, what was its connection to China and why would anyone want to hide it?

Behind it all lurked a surreal nightmare of anonymous black-suited men appearing with no warning and dragging her screaming from her chair. In the elevator they would press a small metal device to her neck. It would hiss and she would lose consciousness. Within an hour her desk and belongings would be gone. Her name would be erased from all official databases and her work colleagues, if asked, would say "Alison Grove? Sorry, there's never been anyone here by that name."

By twelve-twenty she was exhausted. It occurred to her she could stay at her desk and avoid the meeting entirely. It was tempting, but she doubted the journalist would be that easily deterred. He would soon be inside the building, asking after her and telling everyone that Alison Grove had missed her meeting.

She emerged from the lobby at exactly twelve-thirty to see Mike wandering across from the coffee cart. Alison made sure she was the first to speak. "We'll talk over here."

She led Mike around the corner of the building where there were fewer passers-by and where Matt could not see them. She didn't want him to get the wrong idea.

She spoke again before Mike had said a word. "Okay, if anyone asks, you're my uncle. I don't normally lunch with men."

"Really?"

Alison shot him an angry look in reply.

"Okay okay, I'm your uncle Mike. Can I speak now?"

Alison sat herself carefully on the edge of a concrete planter. A series of them ringed the building, to ward off truck bombs. "I have one more question."

"Okay, let's get it out of the way then."

"How did you know who I was, this morning at the bike stand?" It was one of the worries that had taken root in Alison's mind during the morning. He hadn't turned up at reception and asked for her, he'd been waiting outside and knew what she looked like.

"I'm a journalist, remember? It's my job to know who people are."

Alison frowned. That wasn't an answer at all.

"Your name was on the official entry in the CDC database. The office you work for is in this building. There's goodness knows how many websites that publish yearbook photos and I have eyes in the front of my head."

The explanation was simple, straightforward and it rang true. There was a pause as Alison considered the implications. It *felt* invasive, certainly, but all the information Mike had used was in the public domain. There was nothing she could do about it. "Okay. You can ask your questions now."

"Were you told not to talk to me?"

Alison had been looking at the ground but now her head bobbed up and her eyes scanned the surroundings. She was sure she looked like the guiltiest person in the world. "No. Well, not specifically you. I'm not meant to talk to anyone." There were no black suited men in view and she allowed her gaze to fall back down.

"Have you been told not to work on the Fulton case?" Her head shook this time and she did not look up at all. "No. They want me to keep working on that. Collect and analyze as much data as possible. If they find out you're a journalist I'm going to say I was interviewing *you*. There's no harm in me asking you questions."

Mike smiled. "Well, you better stop lying about me being your uncle then. If you're not doing anything wrong, why lie about it?"

He was right about that. Alison was surprised she hadn't seen it herself. She said nothing and waited for Mike's next question.

"What are you meant to do with the information you collect?"

"Nothing."

"Surely you have to forward it to someone."

"No. It's all in the database anyway. I'm sure they can access any of our computers if they want to."

"So let's just be absolutely clear. You *do not* have a contact name or even a phone number?"

"No." Alison kept her eyes away from Mike. The question made it seem obvious that there *should* be someone to contact.

"So what if you find something vital? What would you do?"

"Well, I'd just put it on the database. Like I said, I'm sure they're watching."

"But you'd *tell* no-one?"

"No! I'm not supposed to talk to *anyone*, and like you said, I don't have any contact details even if I wanted to." The conversation was making her feel stupid.

The journalist seemed to be thinking out loud now. "It seems like an odd way to set it up, don't you think? You find some vital information but you don't tell anyone. You just have to trust that the right people are spying on you so thoroughly that they find out for themselves."

"Well, aren't they? You're spying on me and you're just a reporter. DHS have resources you can't even imagine."

He laughed as he spoke, which made her feel worse. "They're not supermen. They'd like you to think they are, but trust me. They're wandering around in the dark a lot of the time just like the rest of us. If they thought you had anything useful you'd have been given a contact number."

Alison's face was flushed and she looked Mike directly in the eye. "Well what's the point then? Why would they do this to me?"

"I'm not sure. I need more information to figure it out, but just for confirmation, are you sure it was the DHS who came to see you?"

"Of course I am! Who else would it have been?"

"Did you see any ID?"

There was a long pause while Alison reviewed that meeting in her mind. "No, I didn't." Again she felt stupid.

"So they just said they were DHS?"

"Dean said. He's my boss."

"And did Dean see any ID?"

"I don't know, and I'm *not* going to ask him." She looked him in the eye again, to make sure he'd understood.

"Okay. You don't have to ask him. But Alison, I do need you to tell me everything you know about this. I—"

"No! I've said enough for today and I need to get back to my desk. People will notice if I'm late."

"But I need to know this now."

Alison surprised herself by grabbing his arm. He was obviously surprised too and jumped a little at the contact. She spoke quickly, eager now to end their meeting.

"You don't need to worry. I've spoken to you once so I've already broken the rules. Doing it again won't make any difference. I'll send you your information but I have to go now. Don't contact me again."

She stood and walked away. For the first time that day Mike didn't follow her.

22

The orderly looked at Shona, then at the microscope. "Oh God what?"

"Spores!"

"Spores? You just said it was a fungus."

"Yes, and spores are its reproductive cells."

"And they're bad because?"

"Because they get released into the air! So this thing that's been killing people so brutally, it's in their lungs, in their *airways* and it's making *spores.*

"Tommy's lungs are riddled with spore sacs and each one can release *millions* of spores. That poor boy spent the last few days of his life gasping and coughing and breathing out *billions* of spores. Hell, we've probably breathed in millions ourselves, just from cutting him open."

The orderly took a step back. "You mean I'm infected? For Christ's sake you could have been more careful with—"

The panic in his voice was obvious but it was too late to change things now and anyway, this was far bigger than just their personal safety. Shona spoke quietly but deliberately.

"I mean the *whole town* is infected. There's more folk sick in Fulton than just Tommy and they've all been breathing out these spores for weeks. So it doesn't really matter about today, we've both breathed in plenty already."

The orderly calmed a little but his next question was still delivered in an angry tone. "Well I guess, but if that's so then why ain't we all sick already?"

Shona paused. It was a good point.

"I don't know. Bernadette Sutton died fast but she was old. Others have been mildly ill and most of us aren't sick at all. Tommy had it and he was doing OK, then he went swimming. Brad Martensen was OK then he had radiation therapy and died within hours."

"So radiation makes it stronger, like in the movies?"

Shona laughed. She had seen those movies too, it had never occurred to her anyone might take them seriously. "No. Radiation doesn't make anything stronger, but it does make people weak and that seems to be the trigger for this thing. Healthy folks are fine, but if they get weak it just takes over and kills them."

The orderly looked worried. "So what happens when I get a cold? And what about other folks? If some virus comes into the town we could all die."

It was a chilling thought. Shona went to her bag and got out the prescription pad, writing out a sheet and handing it to the orderly. "This is for fluconazole. It's an anti-fungal. Start taking it as soon as possible and if you even *think* you're getting the sniffles you call me so I can get you on antibiotics straight away."

"Okay." He nodded and stuffed the paper into his pocket.

"So now you know it's a fungus what are you going to do?"

What indeed? There was the CDC of course, but they were being uncooperative. The NIH might be useful but had they been warned off too? Then of course there was Homeland Security. They had been very clear that Shona was not to release any information to *anyone*. But if the infection was able to spread as she suspected then it *was* a matter for Homeland Security. If the fungus became widespread in a major city it could overwhelm the hospital system in a matter of days.

It was only then that Shona realized the absurdity of her situation. The DHS man had been very clear that *they* would be in touch and had left no contact details. What was the point in that? She had vital information now and there was no one to give it to.

It was nearly seven o'clock when Shona arrived back at her office. She put Tommy's samples in the fridge and unpacked her bag, putting the used equipment into an autoclave for sterilization. Then she washed her hands although it occurred to her there was little point. The fungus or its spores were already in her respiratory tract.

By seven-fifteen she was ready to call Homeland Security, an organization that had specifically told her not to make contact. She had no number so she picked up the phone and dialed the operator. An automated voice said "Name and Area please?"

"Homeland Security, Virginia."

There was a brief pause then a click and another voice said "Department of Homeland Security, how may I direct your call?"

She cleared her throat. "I am Dr. Shona Price, from Fulton in Virginia. I'm trying to contact an agent who visited me recently. It was regarding a disease outbreak in the town."

The operator took a few seconds to digest all this. "Certainly ma'am. What was the agent's name?"

"Um, like I said, I don't have a name."

"You don't have a name?" The operator framed the question as if Shona was the first person who had ever called without a name.

"No, he showed his ID but I didn't get time to read it. He refused to leave contact details."

Again there were a few seconds of silence before the operator replied. "I can't put you through if I don't know who you're calling."

Shona did not want to fall at the first hurdle. "Well, can you put me through to whoever deals with diseases?"

"Hold please." With a click the operator was replaced by a voice intoning severely above the sound of a military drum-beat. "…and terrorists could be anywhere! If you see a suspect individual or unusual behavior then your information could be vital to national security. Call the Homeland Security tip-off line. All calls are strictly confidential." The voice continued with examples of exactly what a suspect individual or unusual behavior might look like.

Shona waited for around five minutes, learning about numerous threats to the security of the United States and her role in thwarting them as a Patriotic Citizen. The voice eventually stopped, to be replaced by a much softer male voice and blissful quiet in the background. "Duty officer."

Shona repeated her story.

The duty officer sounded perturbed. "A disease outbreak?"

"Yes, there have been about ten people fall ill in Fulton and three have died. I've identified it as a fungal disease and it is important you should know. It could be spreading very rapidly." Shona had expected an excited response to her news, but there was only silence. "Hello? Are you still there?"

"Why do you think this disease is a deliberate attack on the United States?"

"What? No. I don't. It's a fungal infection, probably rare. I didn't say—"

"Then why are you contacting Homeland Security? Surely there are more appropriate departments to handle this."

Shona sighed. "I called them. I mean, I sent a notification to the CDC. That's the correct procedure. But after that I was visited by your agent."

The duty officer was having difficulty with the story. He spoke louder, stressing each word. "At what point did you contact Homeland Security."

Shona did not appreciate the change of tone and copied it for her own reply. "I did *not* contact Homeland Security. I contacted the CDC. After that an agent from Homeland Security came to see me."

"The CDC is not a part of Homeland Security."

Fuck! Why won't this idiot listen to me? It would only get worse though if she abused the duty officer so she kept her voice constant.

"I know that, they're part of Health and Human Services."

Another long silence followed. "So I'll just run through this. You have sick people in your town and you're worried about an outbreak. You contact the CDC, who are part of DHSS. Then you are visited by an agent of Homeland Security."

Finally! "Yes, that's exactly what happened."

"Well it sounds highly irregular. What was the agent's name?"

Oh God! Here we go again. "I'm sorry I don't have a name."

"Did you lose his card?"

"He didn't give me a card. I asked for contact details but he said I should wait until he contacted me."

"Hmm… That's not our procedure at all." He was beginning to sound as frustrated as Shona. "Did you see his ID?"

"Yes, but I can't remember the name."

"Was it a legitimate Homeland Security ID?"

How the fuck would I know that? Shona paused for a breath. "I thought so at the time. I had no reason to doubt him."

"Yes, but can you be certain it was a legitimate ID?"

"No. I can't be certain. It's the only one I've ever seen. He flashed an ID at me and I believed him. I had enough on my mind at the time."

The officer seemed satisfied with this and his voice relaxed. "Thank you for reporting this Dr. Price. It is a very serious matter if someone is impersonating a Homeland Security officer. I will file a report and—"

"No wait! I have important information about a disease outbreak. I need to know who I should contact."

"I thought you had contacted the CDC?"

Fuck fuck fuck!. "I did, but they won't talk to me! I thought DHS had told them not to."

"I doubt that happened."

Shona could not shake the image of those spore sacs in Tommy's lung. Something had to be done and this call was achieving nothing.

"So Homeland Security has no interest in this matter?"

"It would take some time to confirm that."

"How much time? People are dying here."

"Alright then doctor, will you be on this number for the rest of the evening? I will need to call you back."

"No, I'm going home. You can call my mobile."

Shona willingly gave the duty officer her mobile phone number, making sure to get his name and the number for his direct line. She locked up the office then drove back to her house where she fell asleep wondering if fluconazole really would be sufficient to keep the fungus in check.

The thin digital tones of 'That ole devil called love' startled her awake a short time later. Her first thought was that someone else had died so it was a relief to hear the duty officer.

"I can tell you officially Dr. Price that the Department of Homeland Security has no interest in the medical situation in Fulton. We strongly recommend you contact the relevant authorities with your information. We will however be investigating the identity of the officer who spoke to you."

Shona didn't care about the officer. "So I can talk to anyone I like about this?"

"About the medical situation, yes."

There had been enough trouble with bureaucracy for one day and Shona was determined not to leave herself vulnerable. "Can I get that in writing?" The duty officer seemed amused but asked for a fax number and promised to send confirmation right away.

Shona no longer felt tired. She grabbed some food from the fridge and drove back over to her office where the gentle whirr of the fax machine greeted her as she walked in. There, as promised, was a letter from the Homeland Security stating that Shona was free to contact whomever she chose regarding the disease in Fulton.

With the fax copied and filed away, Shona left a detailed message at Alison Groves' office number. Then she sent the same information in an email to Alison, to Martyn Fortescue and to the official CDC email address.

With that done she sat back in her office chair. The evening's discussion with DHS had been frustrating at the time, but now it left her disturbed. It was good to have the written okay to talk, but then why had the agents who visited the town been so determined that she should keep quiet?

Perhaps the duty officer made a mistake. Was it really possible to check with the entire DHS that quickly, and outside of office hours? Perhaps they had investigated already and found nothing sinister? But then, what if they found something so important it was being kept secret even within DHS?

Shona didn't have the answers and she couldn't act on unknowns. She had the fax and that the best way forward was to get as much information to as many people as possible. She copied the CDC email to all the academic and medical contacts in her address book. Then it was time for the leap of faith.

23

Marion was making the most of her last week in D.C. Tonight was dinner at Grinaldi's where the sign outside said 'Finest Jazz in D.C.' and Marion agreed. The place had been in business for fifty years and it was known around the world.

At the back of the restaurant, hanging from the ceiling behind the small music stage was a big old TV in a wooden cabinet. When the music started it would display psychedelic patterns in time with the beat; an electronic legacy from the sixties. For now it blared out the news and Marion watched.

She was surprised to see the situation in Jouchou still getting airtime, there was no new information and no new images. The most horrifying images were repeated but tonight the coverage concentrated on reactions to the story.

Immediately after the first U.S. broadcasts the Chinese government had issued a statement strongly denying the reports and attempting to discredit them. The Jouchou Peoples Special Medical Laboratory was a research facility; it would not have taken ill patients. The video was unreliable, having been made by 'unauthorized persons' and its release was a breach of Chinese law. Western governments and news agencies must cooperate with China to track down those responsible.

The State Department had released a travel advisory. Precautions should be taken when traveling to China and, if possible, travel to Jouchou should be delayed until the situation was more clearly understood.

There was the usual speculation too. What kind of research went on at the laboratory? Was it genetic engineering and had some super-bug escaped into the local population? There were rumors of military involvement so perhaps it was a weapon or worse still, a terrorist attack on a weapons facility. The Chinese refused to answer these questions, which only heightened the suspicions they had something to hide.

The matter would have probably ended there if it wasn't for the impending election and the President's foes added questions of their own. What was the President doing to protect the US from an outbreak like this? Why wasn't the White House releasing its intelligence on Jouchou or, if they didn't have any, why were they so incompetent? It was nonsense of course, but the barrage was noisy, emotional and continuous.

In response the White House issued a dry press statement. Yes, there had been a disease outbreak in Jouchou. No, there was no intelligence to suggest any kind of terrorism or intentional release. This appeared to be a natural event and it was an internal matter for the Chinese government to deal with.

Marion turned away from the TV and took out her phone and dialed. Dale answered on the second ring.

"Hey Chief, how's the big city?"

"The city's doing fine Dale. It's my little town I'm worried about."

"Oh, how so chief?"

"Just been watching the news. Any more reporters sniffing around after that guy you told me about last weekend?"

"You must be psychic chief. I heard he was around yesterday morning, talking to Shona, but I don't know what he said."

"Dammit Dale you find out. We'll get the same treatment as that town in China if those damned vultures think they can make a story out of it. You go have another word to Shona. Tell her to keep this quiet for a few more days; just until the facts are known and they can move onto something else. Thank God we've only had one person die."

Marion picked up her glass and savored the last of its whiskey. There was a long silence before Dale replied.

"Ah, well actually Chief."

The glass returned to the table fast enough to knock a chip out of its old varnish. "Actually what Dale?"

"Tommy Sherman died yesterday afternoon, and Brad Martensen not long before him."

"And you didn't *tell* me? Fuck Dale!"

"Now hold on Chief. I didn't find out myself until an hour ago. They both died up at the hospital and it's being kept real quiet, so I don't think you need to worry about reporters."

"But *I* should have known Dale, Straight away." Marion was shouting into the phone and now some of the other patrons staring at her. She took a moment to stare back then waved to the waiter for another drink as Dale replied.

"I wasn't ready to call yet chief. Like I said, I only just found out and I wanted to talk to Shona first but she's not answering."

"Well did you check her house?"

"Just about to chief when you called but I don't think she's there. Marcy from her office said she was going to the hospital this morning. I called but the shift has changed since then. The evening folks said Shona wasn't in the ward but they wouldn't tell me who was on the morning shift."

"For Christ's sake Dale you're a cop! Who the hell do they think they are and why aren't you up there right now kicking their butts?"

Marion could hear Dale mutter something before he replied. "Look chief, give me a break. If you hadn't called I would've been to Shona's house already and I'd be on my way to the hospital right now to check the rosters. I don't need to be reminded I'm a cop.

"The hospital has its rules and I guess those folks were following them. I'll find Shona soon enough. When I do I'll get the story from her and then I promise you'll be the first to know. Now does that sound like I'm doing my job?"

Marion allowed herself to smile. "Yes it does Dale. Sounds like you've got it all under control."

With the call over Marion sat alone in her booth at Grinaldi's and started on her second whiskey. Dale was doing what was needed. If he didn't have the situation under control then he soon would have. She could relax now and enjoy her evening.

Except that she couldn't. Tommy and Brad had died, Dale couldn't find Shona and the hospital was being uncooperative. They were all things to worry about but it wasn't any of them that stopped Marion from relaxing.

It was the diplomat Du and the nagging thought that somehow there *might* be a link from Fulton to what was happening in China.

24

The next morning Mike Fanning settled comfortably into a chair at the White House press conference and wondered how many years had passed since he was last in this room. Successive administrations had become frighteningly efficient at controlling these events and Mike had simply stopped coming. But today would be different. Today he was holding all the best cards in his hand.

The conference room was full when the White House spokesman walked to the podium. He was five minutes late and looked flustered, but managed to open with a relaxed and confident voice.

"Good morning Ladies and Gentlemen. I want to start today by talking about a situation that has arisen in the last few hours. I'm sure you have all seen by now reports in this morning's Washington Record of a disease outbreak in rural Virginia. I wish to stress that these reports are, at the present time, completely unsubstantiated. It is important for the public and the press to exercise restraint. This is *not* a widespread disease outbreak and there is no need for undue concern.

"The news reports suggest a connection between this disease and the recent outbreak in China. I must stress however that this is based only on comparison of symptoms by people with no medical training. There is *no specific evidence* for such a link.

"Notwithstanding this the President wishes to assure the American people that everything necessary is being done to ensure their safety. Federal officials are investigating and this office will be releasing regular news updates to keep the public informed."

"Moving on now we have—"

It was hopeless of course. His statements were like dangling a baby seal over a shark tank. The waiting journalists drowned him out with a deluge of questions which he refused to answer in anything but the most general terms.

Mike waited for the chaos to settle enough that his voice would be picked up clearly by the TV. "Mike Fanning, Washington Record. Why has the government taken no action on this matter when the CDC was informed about it a week ago?" The other journalists fell silent. The Record hadn't published anything about the CDC so this was news to all of them.

The spokesman hesitated. "Uh. I have no knowledge of that personally. I'll have to check and get back to you." It was the first drop of blood hitting the water and to the press it meant one of two things. If the White House genuinely had no idea about the CDC then they were asleep at the wheel. Alternatively they were awake, had spent the last week trying to hide the CDC connection and had not expected to be found out.

Mike didn't pay much attention to the answer. The point of the question was to raise the profile of the story and it had worked. He moved on.

"Credible sources have independently confirmed to us that agents of Homeland Security have been investigating the outbreak since it was reported to the CDC. Furthermore, those agents have told people with important information that they are not to talk. Is the White House aware of this operation and is there any terrorist threat to the United States?"

The blood was gushing now and the sharks would churn their tank into a maelstrom. Mike did not need to speak for the remainder of the conference.

The spokesman had to wait for a full three minutes before he could be heard above the noise. "As I said before, everything necessary *is* being done to ensure the safety of the American people. This office will keep you fully informed as new information comes to hand. Beyond that

I have no further comment at this time." There was a further barrage of questions but the spokesman held his ground and refused to answer. Eventually the news conference was steered back to matters more acceptable to the White House.

Mike had followed his plan to the letter. He had not mentioned that Homeland Security denied any involvement. He had not mentioned that the Record had a copy of Shona's fax from Homeland Security that confirmed their denial *in writing*. He also had not mentioned that the Record quite deliberately did not contact Homeland Security for a response.

When he returned to his office he was met by the editor. "Great job Mike, just like the old days. Can't wait to see what kinda hornets come swarming out of this nest!"

25

Marion had not enjoyed the second-to-last day of her DHS training. This was no surprise as she hadn't enjoyed any of the other days either. She drove towards Joe's house looking forward to the end of it all and her return to Fulton.

Marion entered the front door to be met by Kathleen who rushed out of the living room to hug her and cry out. "Oh Marion, I'm so sorry!" Marion had no idea what was upsetting Kathleen or why sympathy was required. She was also still holding a shopping bag in one hand and she said to Kathleen "Can I put this down now?"

Kathleen let her go but continued to stare. "Haven't you heard?"

"Heard what?"

Kathleen took her arm and led her into the living room guiding her to the couch and sitting down next to her. Joe was parked in his chair with a beer. He looked up at Marion and said only, "It's Fulton."

The TV was showing footage from a White House news conference. The spokesman was trying to answer a question but could not make himself heard above the din of journalists shouting questions at him.

The image switched back to the studio before Marion could comprehend any of what she saw. The anchor read breathlessly from his teleprompter "That was the scene at this morning's White House press conference. We'll be back after the break with more analysis and of course we're waiting for the President's address to the nation which should be in about five minutes time."

It was then that Marion noticed the banner across the bottom of the screen, 'CRISIS IN VIRGINIA' and her mood switched from confusion to alarm. "What the hell is going on?"

Kathleen managed to look even more sympathetic than before but it was Joe who spoke. "It's Fulton. They're saying it's got the same disease as China. It's in the air and people are just breathing it in."

It was only twenty-four hours since Marion had spoken to Dale. He had told her that Tommy Sherman and Brad Martensen were dead, but said nothing about the situation being this far out of control. He certainly hadn't mentioned China or the disease being airborne.

There was no point in waiting for the promised analysis after the ad break. Marion stood up, went straight to the kitchen and called Dale. The number was busy. She waited a minute and tried again but it was still busy. She tried some other Fulton numbers but they all returned the same busy tone, even her own. She returned to the living room with the phone and sat down. Joe looked at her curiously so she said "Can't get through."

The President's address was due any moment and the TV was showing a reporter standing outside the White House. The reporter had no real information of course. His job was to fill in the gap until the address began. Guessing at what the President might say until the President showed up to actually say it.

While she waited Marion dialed Dale's cell phone again and was finally rewarded with his voice saying "Hello? Is that you Marion" at exactly the same time as the President's face appeared on the screen.

"Wait a minute Dale, don't hang up though." Marion tried to concentrate on the President but she found herself distracted by the background noise coming from the call. It sounded like Dale was at the truck races with the drone of heavy engines and shouting nearly drowning out his voice.

Dale shouted down the line at her. "Can't wait chief. I only got a second … you have to come … chief this is … National Guard are here…" He was interrupted by the voice of a second man. "Officer Reynolds, we need you over here" and with that the call clicked off.

Marion's attention returned to the TV just in time to hear the President saying "…have set up a quarantine perimeter around the affected area." She felt a sudden chill in the pit of her stomach on hearing her town described as 'the affected area.'

The president continued. "There has been much speculation today about the possibility of a terrorist attack, both in the press and from some members of the House and the Senate. I must stress that at this time there is no reliable evidence that the disease outbreak in Virginia is anything other than an unfortunate natural occurrence. I must also stress that at present there is also no evidence to confirm a link between this outbreak and recent events in China.

"It would, however, be remiss of this administration if we did not fully investigate the situation. You may rest assured that we have instructed the Department of Homeland Security and other relevant agencies to carry out those investigations and to take whatever action is necessary in response.

"As we face this time of uncertainty I ask the American people to remain calm and to stand with me in support of the brave men and women of the National Guard and the people of Virginia. We are a great nation and it is times like these that test our commitment to one another as Americans. I am sure that we will find the strength to work together and pass that test."

With that the President ended his speech and was immediately replaced by an ad for anti-bacterial soap, "because everywhere you go, germs go too."

Marion stood and said "I have to leave."

Joe stood also. "Will you be OK? Do you need any help?"

"I'll be fine Joe. I'm a cop after all *and* I'm Fulton's Chief of Police. My place now is back with my town."

A minute later she was standing in the hall holding her phone, gun and badge. She said goodbye to Joe and Kathleen and walked out to her car.

Marion approached Fulton by the main road from the east. She had tried to call Dale several times on her drive but could not get through. She had not been able to contact anyone else in Fulton either and she was getting more concerned the closer she got to the town.

It was well after dark and about two miles from Fulton when Marion arrived at the roadblock. She stepped out of her car expecting to be greeted by familiar voices from the local police departments but a voice she did not recognize said "I'm sorry Ma'am you can't go any further."

Marion scanned the scene. There was not a single police officer in sight. The voice spoke again from behind Marion. "Ma'am. This area is under quarantine. You'll have to go back."

Marion turned to see a very young man dressed in Khaki. She walked over to him and held out her badge. "I know about the quarantine. My name is Marion Quirke, I'm the Chief of Police in Fulton and I need to get back to my town."

The guard hesitated. "Our orders are that nobody goes in or out."

Marion didn't feel like being bossed around by a teenager even if he was in uniform. "Well who gave you those orders? Can I speak to them?"

"Wait here." The guard walked over to one of the military trucks parked in the middle of the road. He spoke on the radio for a minute before coming back. "Sorry, you can't go in." "Who did you speak to?"

"The commanding officer in Fulton"

"Okay, let me talk to him."

"It's 'her' ma'am, and I don't think—"

Marion stepped past the young guard and strode towards the truck. He had to run to catch up with her as his comrades sat by the side of the road and laughed among themselves. They were enjoying the show.

Marion grabbed the radio handset and held it out to the guard. "Call her." The call was made but it didn't change anything.

"I'm sorry Chief Quirke, it's a medical quarantine and we can't allow anyone in or out. I'm sure you understand."

Marion really didn't understand. "I'm not going to do any harm if I come in. I'm not infected now and I'm happy to stay in the town. It's my home dammit, I won't be going anywhere." There was a pause then a man's voice came from the radio. "The orders are clear Chief Quirke. No one is to enter or leave. This is a matter of national security."

"And who the hell are you? I thought I was talking to the commanding officer." The man replied "You were Ma'am. I am a senior field operative with the Department of Homeland Security."

Marion was sure she must have misheard. "You're with which department?"

"Homeland Security Ma'am."

26

The Chan Yen Institute was not like any place that Du Rui Kuang had been before, either in China or outside it. On the outskirts of the Shenzhen special economic zone it was a place for the Chinese government to send its irreplaceable troublemakers. Those people who thought or acted so far beyond the norm their mere presence was a disruption; yet who were so useful they could not be discarded.

From outside the most notable feature of the institute was the eight foot high fence around the perimeter. Within the fence however the neat rows of buildings and carefully tended gardens could have been mistaken for a university campus.

The rules of behavior too, were more like a university than a prison. Research and creativity were actively encouraged. Information from the outside world, even the world beyond China, was allowed to flow in with little restriction. With the inmates so well contained it was considered safe to give free reign to their creative, questioning and disruptive urges.

Du was not contemplating any of this as he sat quietly in the gardens of the institute. It was his life beyond the fence that consumed him.

He would never again be allowed a position of responsibility in China. As a Senior Party Official it had been his responsibility to maintain control. By failing in this duty he had become persona-non-grata in his own country. Summarily dismissed from all his party roles, if he ever returned to Jouchou he would find his businesses in other hands too.

A voice pulled him out of his daydream.

"Du?"

He turned to see a man in a white lab coat and carrying a small leather case in his hand. He was the first person Du had recognized since arriving at Chan Yen.

"Fen! What are you doing here?"

"Probably the same thing you are Du. Wondering if they're ever going to let me out."

"I do not wonder about that Fen. I am disgraced and I will never leave. I only wonder why they sent me here and not to a harsher place."

"You are still of use Du. I asked for you to be here, so I can continue my research."

"So you are working here. You are not a prisoner?"

"Oh no, I am a prisoner. But I am also the most qualified scientist to investigate this illness. I have taken samples from the workers at Jouchou and now I must ask you for the same."

Du turned so he could look directly at Fen. "If you have samples from the workers then you have returned to Jouchou. Do you have news of my wife and daughter? Did they reach Fujian? Are they safe?"

"I am sorry Du, I have no news. My samples were taken before I left Jouchou."

Du sighed and slumped forward, putting his head in his hands. "I must find out Fen. Even if I never see them again, I must know what happened."

Fen did not reply. Instead he placed his small leather case on the ground and opened the lid. Inside were a syringe and several small glass vials. Fen withdrew the syringe and sat down next to Du. "I am allowed to do my research here Du but I am as powerless as you. Still, I will ask the chief of security if there is any news and I will let you know the moment I hear anything."

"Thank you Fen." Du looked up and saw the syringe. "You need my blood?"

"Yes. I will also need the fluid from your lungs, but that must happen later, at the laboratory."

Du rolled up his sleeve and held his arm out. He gave a small flinch as the needle punctured his flesh but relaxed as Fen began to draw the blood. "So tell me Fen. How is your research? Can you tell me what has caused all our troubles?"

"Not yet, but I have only just begun. I am still doing the most basic tests and collecting information. What I can say is that we have something very unusual here. It does not follow the course of a normal infection at all."

"It seems to be transmitted easily and in the majority of cases there are no symptoms at all. Yet in a small number of cases the symptoms are severe enough to kill."

Fen finished filling the last of the glass vials and handed Du a plaster for his arm. "There is one more thing Du. They have given me a list of all the places you went in America. So far there is no illness in any of them but, did you visit a place named Fulton?"

Du sat up again and took a deep breath. "What has happened in Fulton?"

"People have died. Like your workers, but only a few. Did you go there?"

"Yes. I was searching for my great-grandfather."

Fen seemed pleased. "So, it is connected, it means—"

"What are they saying about me? In America?"

"They are saying nothing about you Du. They do not even know who you are. Their news is full of speculation, not facts. They rush to the most extreme conclusion and blame terrorists."

"I am no terrorist!" Du's face was red now and he stared at Fen.

"That is true, but maybe you were a target."

"It is preposterous Fen, what would terrorists want with me?"

Fen closed his case and stood up. "What do they want with anyone Du? To cause terror. Still, it seems unlikely to me at the moment. It is only one of the possibilities I am studying and I should not be alarming you like this."

Fen headed back toward the buildings leaving Du alone to stare at the gardens in silence.

27

Mike Fanning sat at his desk on Thursday night feeling hung over. Not that he'd been drinking. It was the events of the day that left him tired and disoriented, a day that had been the busiest of his entire career.

He had one last task before he went home and that was to open the nondescript cardboard box sitting on top of his papers. It was the kind available from any stationery store. The box had a preprinted panel for handwriting the address but this was neatly covered by a laser printed label. Apart from the label the only writing on the box was the postmark: Bismarck, North Dakota.

The box was stuffed with bubble-wrap and inside that were a computer memory stick and another laser-printed label with the message: 'From our mutual friend A.' Mike concluded that Bismarck was the last place he would find the sender.

He inserted the memory stick into his laptop and was preparing to examine its contents when a window opened automatically in the middle of the screen. An animated gorilla strode restlessly within the confines of the window, turning when it reached the edges but always staring out at Mike.

The gorilla seemed to have nothing at all to do with the male voice that was speaking. "Do not panic, we have taken control of your computer." This was followed by the hiss of a soft drink can being opened and the first gulps being swallowed.

Mike was struck with a sudden appreciation of Alison Grove. She had done what she promised and contacted him. She had also done it in a very unexpected way. That strange, anxious little girl must know some interesting people.

The voice behind the gorilla continued "Welcome to the world of truly secure communications. On this disk you will find a program named 'sec inst dot exe.' Run this program to install access to your new super-secure blog."

There was a pause for another gulp of drink during which it occurred to Mike he didn't have a disk. The thought was cut off as the man continued. "For verification you will be asked for the name of our mutual acquaintance. Then you will be asked for a password. This must be at least *twenty* characters. English words and repeating characters are not permitted. You will only have one chance to enter the password so make it count. If your password contains any material that can identify you then you're kinda stupid and we're all wasting our time."

Mike had never made the effort to pick up more than basic computer skills and he found the jargon annoying at the best of times. He began to scribble down the instructions in shorthand, desperate not to miss anything.

"Your password will be encrypted and logged with the super-secure site. It will not be stored anywhere on your computer and you should not write it down. You may access the super secure site via the portal www. showshovel.759046.com. The portal address will change with each access so make sure to track the changes."

Mike hoped he had written down what he needed. The gorilla leapt across its virtual cage as another gulp of drink was taken. "This disk will self-destruct in five seconds."

Mike tore the memory stick from the side of his laptop and threw it into the nearest rubbish bin. The stick made a loud metallic clang on the bottom of the bin just as the voice began to laugh. "Don't panic dude, it's a joke. Hope you didn't dump your laptop into the bathtub! Trust only the gorilla. This truth is out there. Information wants to be free."

The gorilla disappeared and was replaced with a simple form with the prompt "Verification Key." Mike typed in 'ALISON GROVE' at which the prompt changed to "Password." Mike thought for a minute then entered "wshngtnrcrdcngfcktslf." The form disappeared and Mike's laptop was back to normal. He retrieved the memory stick from the bin and checked its contents, but it was empty.

He sat and looked at his computer, wondering what to do next when he noticed a gorilla icon down in the corner of the screen. He clicked it and re-entered his password, which was refreshingly easy to remember. Within seconds he was connected to the 'super-secure blog.'

There were two messages from Alison and the first was surprisingly relaxed for her.

"Mike. Welcome to our little secret. Sorry about the cloak and dagger stuff but I like my job and I don't want to get into any more trouble than is necessary. The gorilla says this site is utterly secure even from the government and he should know (but if I told you why I'd have to kill you ;). Check out his public site www.gorillaoftruth. com. You can say what you like on this blog and nobody will ever see it except me. Gorilla says don't ever copy anything off the site. Leave it all on here where it is safe :)"

The second message was dripping with Alison's usual anxiety and was time-stamped only half an hour ago.

"Mike, what's going on? Even *I* saw the news. I got a message from Shona Price. She's found a fungus with airborne spores but much more work to do before we know if this thing is dangerous or not. Quarantine seems premature, infection isn't spreading that fast. I saw you on TV. What have you done? What have you been saying to people?"

Mike gave himself time to consider before making his own entry in the blog.

"Alison. I understand your issues. Shona called me when she found the fungus. She said you wouldn't talk to her. She was visited by Homeland Security and told not to talk to anyone. When she found the fungus she called them back. They denied everything and said it was OK to go public. The paper got hold of the story and made the most out of it. White House was caught off-guard completely.

They have to look like they're in charge so they sent in the National Guard. Then again, if Shona's right a quarantine is necessary right? Send me another one of your special memory sticks. I'll have to figure out a way to get it to her. Will keep you posted."

Mike didn't consider he was lying in his reply, but he carefully minimized his role. He was sure that Alison would refuse to talk to him if she knew how deliberately the Record had gone about inflating the Fulton story.

He was, on the whole pleased with himself and planned to get a good night's sleep then turn up late for work tomorrow. He shut the lid of his laptop, spun around in his chair and stood up just in time to see the editor walk in.

"You've done great work Mike. Here's your next assignment." Mike's face began to protest long before he opened his mouth. The editor caught it and cut him off. "I know you're tired Mike, but we can't have you relaxing just yet. This story is getting bigger by the minute and you're in the middle of it."

Mike sat back down in the chair. "Bigger?"

"Yes, bigger. The White House has just announced some kind of investigation into Fulton. They're calling it an 'Inter-Governmental Panel.' Gonna have the Chinese on it as well as us. It's supposed to figure out what's going on.

"I want you to find out who's on this panel and where they'll meet. Also, get me some background from the town, Fulton. You know the people there and they've got to have some stories by now. Living with the terrible threat of disease. Life under quarantine, etc, etc." The editor threw the White House press release onto Mike's desk and walked away.

It was of course one of the oldest tricks in politics when things turned ugly: form a committee. It gave the appearance of action but it didn't actually *do* anything and by the time it produced a report the public had usually forgotten the original problem even existed.

So it wasn't surprising that the White House had formed a committee. What was surprising was that they had involved China. What did they know that they weren't telling? Sure the Chinese weren't happy about all the media attention and this would help to smooth the ruffled feathers. But there must be more to it than that. The China connection was still just speculation as far as he knew.

Mike took out a fresh notepad and picked up the phone. It was going to be another very long night.

28

Two weeks of being lectured by the DHS had been quite enough for Marion. Now they were trying to keep her out of her own town. She yelled into the radio handset as the young guardsman waited.

"Well Mister Senior Field Operative, who's in charge there, you or the National Guard? And what the hell is the DHS doing at a medical quarantine anyway?"

The voice came back patient but firm. "The National Guard has full responsibility for this operation Ma'am under direction of the President. Homeland Security is involved also at the direction of the President to ensure any security threat associated with this outbreak is contained."

"I'm not a fucking security threat you idiot, I'm the Chief of Police! So stop interfering and put me back to the commanding officer." The other guards weren't laughing now. They were watching Marion and reaching for their rifles.

There was no reply from the radio and it was the young guard who spoke next, his voice anxious but loud enough for his comrades to hear clearly. "Ma'am we can't change the orders, and this channel is for operational personnel only. I'll have to ask you to leave." With that he flicked a switch and the radio went dead.

Marion scowled at him and stood her ground but two of the other guards stood up and walked towards her. Their weapons were pointed at the ground, but their fingers were close to the triggers.

"Okay you win." Marion hung up the radio handset and put her hands up beside her head where they were clearly visible and clearly empty. "I'll leave, but you can bet your ass I'll raise hell about this tomorrow."

She walked slowly back to her car, making sure her hands stayed in plain view the whole time. The guards kept their eyes on her and their guns at the ready until she had the car moving slowly away from the road-block. She watched them in the rear-view mirror and didn't relax until they turned away from her and headed back to the side of the road.

She still could not understand why it was a problem for her to *enter* the town. Well, whatever the reason they'd got her good and mad now. There was certainly no point going back to Joe's house to sit around being useless.

She drove about half a mile from the roadblock then turned left onto the dirt road leading to Sherman's farm. The Sherman's place should have been quarantined too, but there was no activity. The house was dark and those inside most likely asleep.

Marion parked her car behind the old barn so it would not be seen from the house. It was far enough away that even the dogs wouldn't hear. A minute later she set off across the fields in the direction of the town. Her badge and gun securely in her jacket pocket and a police issue flashlight in her hand.

There is nowhere quite as dark as the countryside at night. City dwellers are used to being bathed in a constant background glow from the streetlights, houses, cars and advertising. Beyond the city limits however nighttime without the moon is truly dark.

Marion made slow progress with her flashlight turned off, but if she'd used it out in the fields it would have been visible for miles around. She relied on her local knowledge and used the light only when necessary, shielding it with her hand and keeping it pointed towards the ground whenever it was on.

She headed out northwest across Sherman's farm. This would cause her to miss the town entirely, but she also needed to avoid the Buchanan's farmhouse which was squarely in the middle of the direct route.

Marion reached the fence between the Sherman and Buchanan farms by walking straight into it. She had been sure it was still a few yards away, but she bounced off it and fell heavily to the ground. Her flashlight fell onto the top wire of the fence then tumbled onto the other side, making a loud metallic twang and turning itself on as it connected.

She lay still for a moment, catching her breath and listening carefully, but there was no response. No dogs barking, no shouting, no lights probing in her direction. She stood up and hoisted herself over the fence, landing awkwardly on the other side.

Once the flashlight was retrieved and turned off she stopped again to listen for sounds of alarm but the night remained quiet and dark.

The route changed after the fence as Marion headed due east. This track would take her about half a mile to the north of the town's outer boundary and it was the best place to aim for. The northern part of the town had the school and a large fishing reserve so it was sparsely populated. Also she would eventually hit the river, even if her aim was way off. Once at the river she only had to turn south and follow it into the town.

It took a couple of hours before the lights of the town came into clear view. Marion only had to cross the school grounds without being seen and then it was a couple of houses further on to Dale's place. The plan had worked perfectly so far and Marion was congratulating herself when she stopped dead in her tracks and cursed beneath her breath.

The school was a blaze of lights with well-armed young men and women giving, taking, and carrying out their orders in a bustle of activity. It was an obvious place for the National Guard to set up their headquarters and she should have thought of it sooner.

Marion cursed again then headed off along the riverbank, following the edge of the road. When the school was well in the distance she crossed the road and made her way into the streets of the town.

There was no chance of staying hidden amongst the neat rows of houses but she was in the town now, no longer sneaking into it, so hiding wasn't necessary. Marion took a moment to pin on her badge then turned on the flashlight and walked down the street like she was on a regular patrol. It was two-thirty in the morning when she tapped carefully on the bedroom window of Dale's house.

A light came on inside and Marion heard her deputies drowsy voice say "What the hell?" from behind the curtain. This was followed by the outside light turning on and the squeal of the back door opening on its un-oiled hinges. The sound echoed through the still evening air but Marion's luck continued to hold and there were no signs of life from the neighbors.

She hurried over to the opening door as Dale's head appeared around the frame. "Jesus Chief!" She put her finger to her lips as he spoke again, more quietly this time. "You better get inside before I arrest you for breaking curfew."

Marion followed him into the house and through to the kitchen. The bedroom door was shut but she saw Tiffany's bright pink phone on the kitchen counter as she entered the room. She'd always suspected – but there was no time for that now and she pretended not to notice as Dale slid the toaster along the counter to hide the phone.

"Coffee Chief?"

"Thanks Dale. I don't have much time but I am getting kinda sleepy. Better make it strong."

Dale put some coffee and water in the machine and switched it on. "I'm guessing you didn't drive in on the main road?"

"Nope. The DHS have it blocked, out by Sherman's farm"

"It's the National Guard running the roadblocks."

"The hell it is! The Guard might be holding the rifles, but it was the DHS that told me I couldn't come into my own fucking town!"

Dale put his finger to his lips. "We're trying to be quiet here Chief, remember?"

Yes, we wouldn't want to wake up young Tiffany. Marion let the thought pass as she listened to Dale.

"So, I don't know what happened to you at the roadblock but the official line is that the National Guard is in charge, DHS is just investigating. I haven't tried to figure it out beyond that. Us local cops aren't supposed to ask any questions. Just shut up and do what we're told. Tell you the truth though, I think this whole thing was done so fast nobody really knows who's in charge."

"Well whoever it is they've established the quarantine, we know that. But why is there a curfew? And what exactly are the DHS investigating? Oh and why couldn't I get in on the phone?"

Dale held up is hands in mock defense. "Hold on there chief! One at a time. The curfew is part of the quarantine. Folks have been told to stay in their houses and only go out if it's absolutely essential. Sam's is closed and all the food places. The supermarket is allowed to open but only for two hours a day and folks have to phone ahead for what they want then pick it up from outside. The hospital is off limits except to the doctors and nurses. No one's allowed to leave the town *or* come in, as you found out."

The coffee machine began to sputter and while Dale tended to it Marion added more questions. "So what are you and the boys actually doing? Were you given any official orders?"

"Like I said, don't ask questions and do as we're told. They really don't want us involved so we're just helping the Guard with local knowledge and trying to keep peace with the townsfolk."

"That's it? No orders from the DHS?"

"Nope. They've asked a few general sorta questions but that's it."

Marion shook her head. "Shit Dale! You must have some idea what they're up to."

"Well I don't! Weren't you listening? I'd be the last to know. They're not exactly calling me up every ten minutes to keep me in the loop. Besides, what's your beef with them? They're just doing a job like us you know."

Marion paused to drink some coffee. "I don't know what my beef is Dale. Except that when I tried to get past the roadblock it was a DHS guy that said no. I saw the President's broadcast and he made a point of saying the DHS were here because of all the silly rumors about terrorists. But something doesn't smell right. What about the phones? I couldn't call in today, to anyone."

"Guard cut 'em off. But the lines were overloaded anyway. Relatives and news crews all trying to call the town at once. Folks here all trying to call out. They say we'll have limited calls by tomorrow, but they'll be kept to a few minutes each and they'll all be monitored."

"Monitored! Who by, and why?"

Dale just shrugged "Dunno who, dunno why, rumors about terrorism I guess."

There was little else for Marion to learn from Dale. He was doing exactly what he should be doing; cooperating with the quarantine and keeping the town in order. "Anything else I should know?"

"Nope. Apart from the quarantine and the curfew and the Guard and Homeland Security and you showing up in the middle of the night with all your questions it's just a regular day."

Marion stood and headed for the back door. "By the way Dale, do you know where Shona Price is?"

He furrowed his brow. "They had her over at the hospital all day, but I think she's back home tonight."

"Okay then, time for me to move on." She stood and walked over to the door. "Thanks Dale."

"No problem Chief, but you take care. You don't want to get shot sneaking around in your own town after dark."

She heard Dale lock the back door as she walked away, followed by Tiffany Masterson whining "Dale, who *was* that?" The man had definitely bitten off more than he could chew.

It took about ten minutes to reach Shona's house by the back streets of the town. A thick hedge ran along beneath the bedroom window and Marion was forced to tap on the kitchen window instead. It was three minutes before there was a muffled noise from inside followed by Shona's uncertain call of "Who's there?"

Marion cupped her hands against the glass. "It's Chief Quirke." She whispered at first but she could not be heard inside the house so she stepped back and turned the flashlight on her face. There was a startled "Oh!" from inside followed by "Marion!" A few seconds later the doctor opened the door.

Shona drew the blinds in her kitchen then turned on the light. The two women blinked awkwardly in the sudden brightness as they sat down at Shona's kitchen table.

"What's going on Marion? I thought you were in D.C."

"I was, but then all this shit hit the fan. I tried to come in on the road but they wouldn't let me. So I walked across the farms."

Shona's eyes widened. "Why?"

"Because it's *my* town dammit! I should be here and in charge. Not sitting helplessly in D.C. How can I help when I don't even know what's going on?"

"It's a medical quarantine. They can't start making exceptions."

Marion sighed. "Maybe you're right. But I don't like the way they treated me at the roadblock. Something wasn't right about it."

"Yes but—"

"No buts Shona. I'm here now and that's that. So please tell me, what the hell is going on? I spoke to Dale on the phone yesterday and everything was under control, now suddenly the President is making speeches and my town is surrounded by kids with rifles."

Shona avoided Marion's eyes, staring down at the table instead. "Uh, would you like a coffee?"

"No, thanks, had one at Dale's house."

"Something stronger then?"

Marion's face brightened. "Well now, maybe some of that medicinal whiskey you doctors always have."

Shona left the room and returned a minute later with two glasses of dark liquor. Marion tossed hers back then sighed in deep satisfaction, "Good medicine. Thanks." Shona sat and took a small sip, placing the glass gently on the table.

"I panicked Marion. It's all my fault."

Marion couldn't imagine Shona calling the President and demanding he send in the National Guard. "What's your fault?"

"The news, the President, the quarantine, the Guard. *All* of it."

"Okay Shona, one step at a time. We started with a few sick folk. When did it get beyond that?"

Shona told the whole story. Once she began it came in a rush. She told about the frustration of being shut down by the DHS, how not even the CDC would talk to her. She told of examining Tommy, finding the fungus and the spores. The shock of realizing the illness might be airborne. She told about her call to the DHS and their denial of ever being involved.

She showed Marion a copy of the fax. "I've got copies of it all over town. You keep this one." It seemed melodramatic, but Marion took it without comment.

"So when I got this fax, that's when I made my big mistake. I'd found the fungus and the spores. It was vital to get it checked immediately by a proper lab, but it was so frustrating. No one would listen to me. So I called the journalist."

Marion answered with a knowing "Ah-ha." Shona hadn't mentioned a journalist yet, but getting the press involved usually made a situation worse, rather than better. "You called Tiffany?"

"No! She's not a journalist. I called that Mike Fanning guy from the Washington Record. He's been snooping about ever since Bernadette died. I thought I was being smart, that I could use him to get my information out. Then they'd have to pay attention, you know, come here and do some proper tests."

Shona made a point now of looking directly at Marion. "I never expected this. *Honestly* Marion. It's a total overreaction. I wanted this thing to be taken seriously, but they've turned it into a circus. I just hope to God they've brought in some qualified researchers along with all the soldiers. I mean—"

Marion held up her hand. "Hold on there doctor! That's enough for now." Shona was heading off into self-justification and that wouldn't help anyone. "You go get me another shot of this and then I have some questions for you."

Shona looked concerned. "You're not going to drive tonight are you? You shouldn't be drinking anyway when you're so tired. Your brain function is already impaired. Drink any more and you'll start making some really stupid decisions."

Marion laughed. "It's too late for that Shona, I'm already here." The doctor didn't move though and probably she was right. "Okay then, I'll go straight to the first question."

"Okay." Shona had relaxed noticeably now that her confession was over.

"You found this fungus and it has spores, right?"

"Right."

"And spores can travel in the air?"

"Yes. They're incredibly small and light. They can float on the smallest air currents."

"Okay, so you're naturally worried that the sick folks are breathing out these spores all over town, and the rest of us are breathing 'em in?"

"Yes, but—"

Marion did not want her train of thought interrupted and she held up her hand again. "And we all know how nasty this thing is. So if folks all over town are breathing it in and they could die horribly, why do you say this quarantine is an overreaction? If you're right then surely it's the proper thing to do."

Shona took a deep breath. "Yes I found spores and yes they're airborne. So it is a serious matter and *definitely* needs to be investigated. But look at the other evidence."

"What other evidence?"

"People *aren't* dying in the streets. The whole town must have been exposed by now, including both of us. The only people getting sick are the ones who have other health problems. Bernadette was old, Brad was on chemo. I'm not so sure about Tommy but he went swimming, probably got water into his lungs."

"But you're saying we're all exposed. So maybe it'll just take longer for the rest of us."

"Possibly, but these things are never so simple and *that's* really my point. The politicians and the journalists are painting this like its all been decided, like we know for sure there is some terrible airborne killer on the loose. But we don't know that at all. What we need is thorough, proper research, not politics and headlines."

Marion frowned. "But while all this research is being done, more people could die, surely."

"I'm not saying precautions aren't necessary, but they shouldn't be taken blindly. I admit I panicked when I saw the spores but now the government is doing the same thing. If we go off in the wrong direction chasing an airborne infection we could be missing something really important.

"This fungus has definitely killed people and it definitely has spores. But something about it doesn't add up. It doesn't *spread* like an airborne infection. That's why it needs urgent research, but careful research and *proper* research. Not some overblown political cover-up."

Marion pounced on the last two words. "Cover-up? In less than five minutes you've gone from overreaction to cover-up. Why do you say that?"

"Well, what did you mean about the roadblock? You said something wasn't right."

"Oh that. Well it was manned by the Guard right? But I got pissed off and demanded to talk to the commander. Well it was a DHS guy who came on the radio and told me to get lost, not the National Guard."

Shona nodded agreement. "You're right. The Guard swept in here with all their trucks and lights and command posts and what-have-you. They *are* doing the guarding but they're definitely taking orders from Homeland Security."

"Definitely? So you have some evidence then? All I've got from the roadblock is my suspicions."

Shona continued. "Homeland Security turned up at my house at six-thirty this morning, long before the quarantine started. Long before it was even announced. I doubt more than a few hundred people had even read the Washington Record by then.

"They took me up to the hospital. Made me show them the bodies, asked a *lot* of questions but not the right ones. Asked who else knew about my tests, who had examined the bodies, that kind of thing. They took all my samples from the hospital. Took the bodies. Took my notes. Said it was National Security and I shouldn't talk to anyone.

"I was trying to tell them what I'd found, what needed to be done next. I thought I'd be talking to medical researchers, helping them with the investigation. I am fully qualified after all. But they didn't want to know anything useful. They just took all the evidence away."

Marion knew that sometimes being provocative was the best way to get to the truth. "Maybe you're just pissed off to be out of the loop Shona. You found this thing and now they're taking it away from you?"

"No! Listen! They didn't ask about the fungus or the spores, or symptoms or transmission or anything medical. They asked who else knew about it. Then they took it all away and told me to keep quiet. And remember, last night, they sent me that fax saying they had no interest in the matter and I could tell anyone I wanted."

It was strange, but Shona had no hard evidence of a cover-up. Maybe the agents sent to question Shona were simply not trained in medical matters and didn't know what to ask. Maybe they were keeping things quiet to avoid panic. Maybe the samples were in a proper laboratory right now, being analyzed by the finest minds in the country.

It was disappointing that Shona didn't have anything better to offer. Marion stood up to leave. "Well, you could be right, but we'll need a lot more evidence to convince anyone and I don't think we can sort it out tonight."

"So what will you do now?"

"Go back to D.C. I can't stay in town, no matter how much I'd like to and no matter how much sense it makes. That'll just get me arrested and I'm no use to anyone sitting in my own damned jail. Guess I need to sneak back out again. Try to get back in by official channels."

Marion glanced at her watch. "It's four o'clock. I better leave now if I want to be back at Sherman's before dawn.

"Thanks for your time Shona and sorry to get you up in the middle of the night." She was half-way out the door when Shona called out "Wait! There's one last thing. They didn't get *all* my samples."

"What do you mean?"

"I put some of Tommy's samples in the fridge. I was going to send them on to the CDC for analysis."

"What fridge? You said they took everything."

"From the hospital, yes."

"So where are Tommy's samples?"

Shona pointed at the refrigerator in the corner of her kitchen. "I was keeping them at my office, but I decided they'd be safer here. Don't tell anyone else though or I'll lose them too."

"Uh… right, of course. Thank you again Shona."

After years in her job Marion thought her hide had grown fairly thick, but she found it unsettling to know that diseased parts of a dead boy had been so close to her.

As she walked back across the farmland she thought about Shona and spores and cover-ups. She didn't know Shona well enough to judge if her ideas were sound or not. She certainly seemed guilty about going to the press. Maybe she was looking for a way to justify her actions?

If it was a cover-up then what was being covered-up? When the DHS arrived on Shona's doorstep in the morning there hadn't been time for them to test the fungus and find out what it was. So they didn't know what they were dealing with anyway. Yet if they were trying to hide something they *must* already have known what it was.

There was no point trying to hide the presence of the fungus or its airborne transmission. Both had already been announced to the world by the Record. On the other hand, if Shona was right and it *wasn't* airborne then why hide that? What was to gain by making this illness seem far worse than it really was?

Dawn was breaking by the time she reached the fence between the farms. Before long she would be clearly visible. She prayed the Guard wasn't patrolling beyond the roadblock as she ran toward her car in the half light.

29

Michael Stonehouse arrived at the Senator's office long before Marion made it back to her car. The Senator was waiting for him but unlike the last visit there were no cigars or alcohol. MS was still walking across to the chairs when the Senator closed the door and fired off his first question. "Well, what's going on with this damned thing then?"

MS had first got news of the Intergovernmental Panel from a contact with links to the White House. That had been yesterday morning and he'd not stopped for a minute since. He gave himself time to sit before answering. "It starts on Monday morning."

"Fuck! How can the White House move so quick?" The Senator seemed genuinely impressed by his opponent's performance.

"They've had the shit scared out of them, that's how. Damned Washington Record ambushed 'em with stories about deadly spores spreading through the air and they had to quarantine a whole town! When was the last time something like that happened in the US?

"Then of course the Record's making a fuss about China and it didn't take the State Department long to check their records and confirm *that* connection. So yeah, this damned panel starts on Monday." He paused for a moment and smiled. "Mind you, the schedule has its preliminary report being released a full two weeks *after* the election."

The Senator laughed. "Yes, hedging their bets there. But I have to admit they're proving to be a worthy adversary on this one. Are the Chinese definitely in?"

"Oh yeah, they're resolute. I don't know what they're sitting on but I guess they think there *is* a connection to Jouchou. They want to be in control of this thing as much as anyone and there's no way they'll be talked out of it."

"Okay then, do you have any good news for me?"

"Sure. You must have lit a damned good fire under your people at DHS. When they heard about the panel they went straight to the White House insisting they should be in charge of security."

"So they can be in control the panel's information."

"Exactly. Anyone starts sniffing around where they shouldn't and DHS can just invoke national security. The Chinese don't mind provided their security services get to attend the actual meetings."

The Senator nodded. "That's good. The more security there is on this panel, the less likely it is to reveal anything. No one's going to want the other side to see their dirty laundry. But the White House agreed to this?"

"You bet! They've got no idea what they're dealing with yet, they just know it's out of control. The slower this panel moves the more chance they've got of getting back in control before anything goes public."

"Well they're going to be disappointed then. We've been discussing the terrorist angle on our side and it's just too good not to use it before the election, it'll hit them just as hard as the Fulton story. We're just waiting until DHS has the last of the bad guys rounded up."

MS raised an eyebrow. "Some of them are still at large?"

"Yes, and it's an uncomfortable feeling, I can tell you. But I can't just sit here worrying until they're found, there's too much to do. So why don't you tell me who else will be on the panel."

"Okay." MS wasn't surprised by the Senator's reaction. He'd have done the same thing himself. "They've kept it small, about five or six members which will make it easier to control. Unfortunately there will have to be genuine scientists, and you never know what side of the fence those guys are on, but so far the list is looking favorable.

"The Chinese are sending a couple of scientists but they'll both be party members and of course Chinese security will be there to keep them in line. Australia's sending one guy who specializes in tropical diseases.

"There's going to be one more scientist from the U.S. but I don't have a name yet. The White House are pushing for someone from the CDC because it'll look good to the public and of course the CDC are already involved so they might as well be kept close.

"The other position undecided is the chair and I'm going to need your help on that one. It's down to two candidates but the best one for us is a guy from the National Institutes of Health. DHS have been using him as an advisor on bio-terror issues and he worked with the CIA for a long time before that.

"Apparently he was one of the last people to actually climb over the Berlin Wall. Hated communism and —"

The Senator interrupted. "— loved America." I've heard about him MS, and he should work out fine. So why do you need my help?"

"To make sure he gets the job, and also to make sure the DHS give him a thorough briefing."

"About what?"

"About keeping the source of this thing under wraps. If this panel gets close to the truth then it could become a matter of public fucking record! So I need your people at DHS to tell him beforehand that they *know* it's a terrorist attack, that there are grave matters of national security involved and he must do his utmost to keep the panel from revealing them."

"And if he refuses?"

"Then they threaten him. He can't take the risk of revealing state secrets."

"Hmm… well we probably *can* bully him, but what about our DHS friends? It's a big risk for them to subvert the process of this panel."

MS stared at the Senator. "Are you kidding? They got themselves put on the panel's security *precisely* to subvert its process, and remember they should have informed the White House about the terrorist threat the moment they found it.

"So they're in it up to their eyeballs already and they can't afford leaks any more than we can. You won't get any trouble from them."

"Well then." The Senator stood and walked over to his desk. "We seem to have done rather well."

MS stood too. "Yes we have." He shook the Senator's hand then headed for the door. "I'll be in touch." It was the last time the two men would ever meet face to face.

30

Marion returned to Joe and Kathleen's house at seven-thirty on Friday morning. Joe had already gone to work and Kathleen was in the kitchen, tidying up before she took the twins to school. She stared at Marion with wide eyes. "Oh my God! What happened to you?"

Marion was tired and hadn't given much thought to how she looked or what she would say to Kathleen. One thing was certain though, she couldn't tell the truth.

"Those Goddam idiots wouldn't let me into my own town! I had to spend the night in my car. I'm very tired, didn't sleep well."

Kathleen remained wide eyed. "What about the training? Today's your last day."

"Well I guess I'm going to miss my last day then." Marion climbed the stairs to her room and fell onto the bed, grateful for its comfort.

She woke only two hours later, fully dressed and smelling of body odor. She shook herself awake, taking a moment to remember where she was and why she was in such a condition.

The house was empty now apart from herself, and blissfully quiet. She longed for more sleep but Kathleen and the twins would arrive home late afternoon and there was much to do. A shower, clean clothes and a coffee helped her to feel more alive.

The first order of business was to find out who was in charge of the quarantine. Calls to the National Guard in Virginia and Washington D.C. proved fruitless. The quarantine was considered to be an 'operational matter' and as such no information could be given out on the phone.

The State Police headquarters in Richmond were no more help. Liaison was not yet established with the National Guard and was not expected to be in place until 'early next week.'

Marion sat herself in front of Kathleen's computer and began to search for anyone who might be able to help. She called the National Institute of Allergy and Infectious Diseases. She called the National Center for Preparedness, Detection, and Control of Infectious Diseases. She called the American Medical Association.

After only an hour she was lost in a maze of bureaucracy and organizational buck-passing. Her calls were forwarded, redirected, sometimes lost but most often, put on hold. The people she spoke to were sympathetic, but knew no more than Marion herself. After more than three hours of calling she was no further forward and it was time for a different approach.

She was already using Joe's computer to find phone numbers so now she Googled 'fungus' to see what would come up. What she got was an overwhelming list of research papers and educational sites, information on growing mushrooms and ads for fungus treatments.

Marion read a few of the articles but it would have taken her days to find anything helpful. Besides which, she knew nothing specific about Shona's fungus and wouldn't have recognized relevant information even if she had stumbled across it.

A search on the word 'spores' was equally disheartening and 'quarantine' returned mostly news sites. Thanks to the President's intervention the plight of her little town was now one of the world's top news stories and the first page of links were all references to Fulton. Marion checked them but they said nothing new, so she clicked through to the next page of links, hoping to find something more useful. In amongst the news sites a single entry caught her eye.

The summary read "… Fulton is no surprise. *I predicted this 2 years ago. The government must not…quarantine is bogus…*" Marion clicked it, wondering who could have predicted the Fulton outbreak so far ahead. She found herself drawn into a world that she had always avoided until now.

The website 'spindlefoldandmutilate.com' was written by someone named 'spiracyjunky12' who typed exclusively in capitals and without the aid of a spell-checker. The gist of their prediction was repeated in the latest entry.

"THE ARMY IS MAKING DISESES TO WIPEOUT TERRORIST SCUM. GO ARMY BUT U WATCH OUT. DISESES WILL GET LOSE AND KILL THE INNOCENT. I SALUT THE *INNOCENT**DEAD**HEROES*. IT IS A $$ WE MUST PAY."

Marion smiled at the way spiracyjunky12 could emphasize something written entirely in capital letters. Updating for current events, they had added: "NOW U SEE. ARMY HAS OUTSORCED DISESES TO CHINA BUT THEY CANT DO NOTHIN RITE CUS THERE LIVIN IN THE DARK AGES. THERE GUY GOT INFECTED COMIN HERE AND IT WAS RELESED."

The blog was stupid and racist but it made more sense to Marion than she cared to admit. There were no facts amongst the ranting, but combined with what she knew, it couldn't be refuted either.

She had always dismissed conspiracy theorists as crazy and was horrified to find herself giving this rubbish any credence at all. Yet despite her distaste Marion followed more links on the blog, hoping there was perhaps something useful amongst the dross.

She had visited dozens of sites, read hundreds of blog entries and even viewed a few online movies, simultaneously fascinated and repelled by what she was reading.

These people were vehement, yet their theories were supported by only the flimsiest of evidence, if there was any at all. Though not all of it was as appalling as the babble of spiracyjunky12.

Marion even found some information that seemed well-reasoned, logical and calm. Yet even the more rational-seeming sites relied mostly on conjecture when their arguments were analyzed.

In a couple of hours at the computer Marion had discovered that the U.S. government or its army or the DHS or the NSA or space aliens or the Masons or … somebody; were either in league with, controlling, controlled by, out to destroy, suppressing the existence of…; space aliens, the drug companies, the Columbian drug cartels, genetically engineered zombie soldiers, the Soviet Union (which apparently still exists in a basement room of the Kremlin), the oil companies, the TV news, … etc, etc, etc.

She found it easy to start constructing theories of her own. All it took was to ask a few questions. Why had Homeland Security told Shona not to talk and then denied it? Was it even the DHS? What was the relationship between the DHS and the National Guard? Why had they taken Shona's samples and what had happened to them? Where had the fungus come from and why weren't *more* people dying if it was spreading through the air?

Faced with her questions Marion could construct any number of ad-hoc answers. With the lack of information available from the relevant authorities, none of the answers could be dismissed. Even if 'they' weren't covering-up one of her theories, it began to feel like 'they' must be covering up *something*. Otherwise, why all the secrecy?

Clearly this was all nonsense, yet the events of the last few days had provided so few real answers that she could understand how a conspiracy theory might become accepted. Humans like to have explanations for events and a conspiracy theory at least provides the *sense* of an explanation.

Marion was glad when her phone rang and forced her back to reality.

"Chief Marion Quirke."

"Hello Chief Quirke. My name is Mike Fanning; I'm a reporter with the Washington Record."

The introduction wasn't needed, she'd heard enough from Shona on Thursday night. She said nothing and waited for Mike to get to the point.

"Hello?"

"I'm still here."

"Okay. Chief Quirke, can I just confirm that you are the chief of police for Fulton?"

"Yes."

"And what is your reason for being away from the town at this time?"

"Who says I'm away from the town?"

"You answered your phone Chief. I've been calling Fulton all morning and I can't get through. It doesn't take a genius to figure it out."

"Well regardless of your genius Mr. Fanning I don't see it's any business of the Washington Record where I am."

"On the contrary, you are the police chief of a town that has just been placed under quarantine by the President. Yet somehow you manage to be outside the town. That interests the Record very much."

Marion was still not about to answer the question. "Look. I've seen what you did to Shona Price. There's fair reporting of the facts and then there's sensationalism and exploitation. I think you know which side you fall on."

The reporter didn't let it slow him down. "Is that an official comment from the Fulton Police Department?"

Marion took a deep breath. "No, that comment was strictly off the record." Hopefully the magic phrase would save her skin. "And in fact, Mr. Fanning, I have nothing at all to say *on* the record."

"But you might have more to say off the record?"

Again, Marion did not reply and waited for him to continue.

"Look Chief Quirke, there are things I want to discuss with you that shouldn't be said on the phone. I have some disturbing details I need to confirm and you might be able to help. Like I said before, I can't contact anyone in Fulton for comment. It's like they've pulled the plug on the whole town."

In regular circumstances Marion would have refused the journalist point blank, but events now were far from regular and after all, it was his job to gather information just as it was hers. He might be able to help her put things into place.

"Okay then Mr. Fanning. Strictly off the record. No notes, no recorders."

Even over the phone the relief in his voice was obvious. "Great! Where should I meet you?"

"You can meet me at Grinaldi's, tomorrow morning at eleven."

"You're in D.C.?"

"Now I didn't say that. But I will be at Grinaldi's tomorrow. And Mr. Fanning?"

"Yes?"

"Expect to pick up the tab." Marion shut off her phone before there was time for a response.

It was only a few minutes later that a riot of shouting outside the house announced the arrival of Kathleen and the twins. The two boys raced past the door to her room calling out "Hi Aunt Marion" on the way. Being called Aunt made Marion feel old and she gave an involuntary shudder.

She found Kathleen in the kitchen unpacking groceries. Amongst the usual items were face masks, anti-mold spray and athlete's foot ointment. Kathleen held it up like it was a prize. "Can you believe it? This was the only anti-fungal treatment left on the shelves."

Marion laughed out loud. "Christ Kathleen! This thing isn't killing people through their feet you know."

Kathleen shot her a hurt look. "Well of course I know that."

"Uh right... I'm still tired from last night Kathleen, I just meant, well, we don't really know anything about this disease and it's nowhere near D.C., so don't you think this is kinda overdoing it?."

"Maybe it is Marion, but I'm no expert on spores and neither are you. What I am expert on is my two boys up there. They're my *children* Marion. I'm not going to take chances and neither are any of the other mothers out there.

"Do you know there were only three boxes of face masks left at the store? This morning people were buying whole cartons. They've put a limit on now or I would have too. I can't afford to wait until the shelves are empty before I do something to protect my family.

"It's okay for you, being on your own. If you want to risk your life, well there's no one to stop you. And don't forget, you're *from* Fulton. We're lucky you didn't bring that damn thing with you."

Marion had been so caught up in helping the town that she'd never thought about the risk to Kathleen and her family. A stab of guilt struck her at the thought of the twins dying the way Bernadette had.

"I'm sorry Kathleen. I forget the pressure that parents are under."

Kathleen sighed. "Well I'm sorry too Marion. We're all stressed out at the moment. I know you must be worried sick about the town." There was a pause then both women laughed at Kathleen's use of the phrase 'worried sick.'

Kathleen kept talking as she put the shopping away. "I don't know what your plans are now Marion, your training's over but you can't go home. Joe thinks you should stay here..."

Marion thought about the twins again and what Kathleen would have said if she knew about last night's trip to Fulton. "Well it was great to stay here for the training Kathleen but I'll be busy as a one legged man in an ass kicking contest from now on. So don't worry, I'm going to get myself a hotel."

Kathleen could not hide her smile. "Thank you Marion. You can stay tonight of course."

But Marion didn't stay. Within a half hour she had packed, said good-bye to the twins and was in her car driving away from the house. Even if Shona was right and the spores weren't that dangerous it was a risk she should never have taken. If anything should happen to those boys...

31

Mike Fanning worked all Saturday. He doggedly tried every Fulton number in the directory but none of his calls were answered. Cell phones too were unreachable and even emails to Fulton residents remained unanswered.

There was no progress either with the intergovernmental panel. He knew it was being rushed into existence over the weekend but none of his contacts were high enough in the government to be involved. The Record had other journalists who knew some of the right people, but even they were unable to get answers. It seemed that many of the important decisions were yet to be made.

By five that evening Mike was hungry, tired and disheartened. He packed up his notepad and laptop and headed out the door, planning to grab a sandwich and a beer at the little bar down the road then head home and forget about work until the morning.

He was halfway across the road outside the Record offices when a voice called out behind him.

"Hey you!"

Glancing over his shoulder he saw a disheveled woman standing on the sidewalk behind him. She stared directly at him and called out again. "Yeah that's right, you!"

When he reached the far side of the road he took another look, just long enough to see that she was dressed in several layers of filthy clothing. A rusted shopping trolley stood behind her, piled up with God knows what kind of junk.

Mike had given up on D.C.'s homeless people a long time ago. If he gave this woman money or even attention then she'd be waiting there every day, pestering him. The Record printed a standard 'you should feel guilty about the plight of the homeless' article every Thanksgiving and it was usually Mike's job to write it. That would have to suffice. He turned away from her and continued walking.

"I've got something for you, Mister Mike Fanning asshole." The woman's voice was loud enough to echo from the buildings. Mike stopped and turned back. She was holding up an envelope and now she waved it at him. "Special fuckin' delivery."

Mike looked both ways along the street, not sure what he expected to see. There was no one though except a few passers-by who ignored him and the woman in the practiced way of city people the world over.

He crossed back over the street and the woman smiled at him as he got close, but it was a predatory look. He made sure there was still a good six feet between them when he stopped.

She waved the envelope again. "A guy said this was for you. I get fifty bucks just for handing it over."

"What guy?"

The woman looked at him with contempt. "I dunno, some guy with fifty bucks. You want your fuckin' letter or not?"

"Yeah, silly question." Mike hadn't expected a useful answer, but he'd asked, just in case. He stepped forward and reached out for the envelope but the woman snatched it away and tucked it under her arm.

"You gotta sign for it."

"What?"

"The guy said you gotta give me a signature. No signature, no fifty bucks." She gave him the predatory look again. "You can put it on a hundred if you like, I don't take no checks."

Mike took out a business card and signed the back. He held it out to the woman with one hand and stretched out his other hand towards the envelope. She eyed him suspiciously and snatched the card away. When she was certain it was signed she handed over the envelope.

"Nice doin' business asshole. Thanks for the tip." With that she grabbed her trolley and walked away. For a moment Mike considered following her, to see who had put her up to this. The moment passed however and still feeling vulnerable out on the street, he decided to skip the bar and go straight home.

Fifteen minutes later Mike sat at his dining room table laughing. The envelope, so determinedly delivered to him in the street, contained a single A4 page. It was folded in half and when Mike opened it he found a message made in old-fashioned movie fashion, with letters cut out of newspaper headlines.

Mike had never seen an actual letter like this before. Anyone wanting to send untraceable mail these days used a laser printer or an ink-jet. In contrast to its format however, the contents of the letter were entirely topical.

FULTON IS JUST THE START. THEY KILLED US WITH THIS IN IRAQ AND NOW THEY WILL PAY. SEARCH THE WEB FOR IRAQ BIO WEAPON DEATH. WATCH THE VIDEO. MORE TO COME.

It didn't take long for Mike to find the video on the internet. It had been posted only five hours earlier but the description read "Death from U.S. gov bio-weapons in Fallujah Iraq. Long before Virginia." There was no firm date but Mike guessed the video was made a couple of years ago at least. The U.S. had withdrawn most of its troops from Iraq back then.

The images were low quality and the camera swung wildly about, showing as many shots of the ground as it did of the action. What it did show though was horrifying and fascinating.

Mike sat riveted as the soldiers burst from their Humvee and forced their way into a house only to find the occupants lying dead amidst profuse quantities of dried blood.

He watched a second time and then a third. Trying to make sense of what he saw. It was clearly Iraqis who had died, and they were probably a terrorist group of some kind. But who had posted the video and how did they get hold of it when it was clearly made by the U.S. soldiers?

It seemed unlikely that the men who made the video had suddenly become bothered by the deaths of terrorists. Then there was the threat of 'more to come.' More what? More video, or more deaths like those portrayed?

There was only one thing that did make sense to Mike. The deaths in the video *were* remarkably similar to those in Fulton and in China. More of that was a chilling thought indeed.

32

Marion took her seat at Grinaldi's at ten-fifty on Sunday morning. She was ready for a drink but decided to wait and make that damn reporter pay. It would be something expensive too.

The TV was switched off and recorded music was playing. It sounded like Paul Bley's 'Japan Suite' but Marion couldn't be sure. She let herself relax and disappear into the music, staying happily lost until a shadow fell across her face.

Looking up she saw a man in late-middle age with bad hair and pale skin. He was smiling at her and holding out a business card. He was not far from what Marion had imagined an irritating journalist would look like.

She took the card and glanced at it. "Hello Mr. Fanning. I'll have a whiskey thanks, neat, and make sure it's Irish."

He gave a little mock bow and without having said a word wandered off to the bar, returning with the whiskey and a beer for himself. He put them on the table and sat so he was facing Marion. "Well Chief, any news for me about Fulton?"

"You're the journalist Mr. Fanning. You're the one who's supposed to have news, so why don't you tell me what's going on?"

"How do you think I *get* the news Chief? Anyway, you're a cop and you're supposed to know more about what's going on than I do."

Marion was determined not to give the journalist anything that might come back to haunt her later. "This is all off the record – right?"

"Yes, strictly off the record."

"OK then. My understanding is that the Fulton infection was implanted in the human population by space aliens who want to release spores that control the minds of government officials to hide the existence of the former Soviet Union."

Mike snorted uncontrollably into his beer. A wedge of foam splattered across the table with a few flecks landing on Marion's shirt. "Aw shit! Why'd you have to go and say a thing like that?"

"Listen Mike, I've been doing research on the internet. They were right you know. The truth really is out there. It has to be, there's so damned much of it." With that Marion let herself relax.

"Goddam, Marion Quirke. You're one tough customer." He paused to sip from his beer before continuing. "A word of advice though. Don't give *any* credence to *anything* you read on the internet. Half of what gets printed in the paper is crap, and you might not believe this but we really do have researchers and editors and rules about sources.

"Now the internet has *none* of that so ask yourself this. Do the people who write that stuff know any more than you do? Were they there? Were they witnesses to anything?

"You bet your ass they weren't. The only difference between us and them is they're happy to put their fantasies on any damned website that'll take them and we aren't."

Marion couldn't let that pass without comment. "Nice speech, but total hypocrisy after that bullshit you printed about Fulton. You seem quite happy to put some of your own fantasies out in public.

"Bio-terrorism! You should be ashamed for getting folks all worked up over nothing. Saying there's terrorists just because you *want* it to be true. Just because you could sell a few more papers that way."

"Oh, so you think this whole thing is above board and hunky-dory then?"

"I didn't say that. But you shouldn't be pointing the finger at folks for making stuff up when you've been doing it yourself."

"Okay then, I'll take that one on the chin. But if you *don't* think everything's okay, what is it that you're worried about?"

The journalist was fishing now and Marion put her guard back up. "Nothing I can put my finger on Mike, its just all happened so fast. One day I had a few sick folk, the next I had a full-blown national emergency."

He shrugged. "Okay. So even off the record you're not going to talk. Well if you want me to buy more drinks you've got to say something, so tell me how you ended up being Chief of Police in Fulton,"

Marion sighed "OK Mike, you get me another whiskey and I'll tell you all about it."

Once the drink was ordered she began her story. "My mom died when I was seventeen. Got hit by a train crossing the tracks behind our house. I never knew my dad, he took off the moment mom got pregnant and never showed his face again.

"I was young and it was the late sixties, so I just hit the road. Plenty of other kids were doing the same thing.

"I drifted for a few years, working in kitchens and bars. Doing the kind of stuff mom had done but I hated being poor so I went up to the gold mines in Alaska."

Marion downed the last of her whiskey. The sound of jazz drifted across from the bar as the journalist waited.

"They paid good money up there and the work was okay but it didn't take long for trouble to find me."

Mike leaned forward. "What kind of trouble?"

"Gee Mike. I was a twenty year old woman working at a gold mine in the middle of God knows where. Some asshole wouldn't take no for an answer so I broke his wrist. Problem was, he was some big deal engineer and the company couldn't replace him. But they could get another cook from anywhere.

"They wanted to throw me in jail but the lawyers said I'd get off on self-defense and it would just cost them a whole lot more money. So I got a bus ticket home and a stern lecture about what would happen if I ever went back."

Mike smiled. "I was right then, you *are* one tough customer. But how'd you end up in Fulton?"

"Well I didn't want to drift again and I didn't want any more trouble. I looked around for somewhere small and quiet and Fulton was perfect. I got an office job at the Fulton police and it didn't take long before they asked me to be a cop, turns out I'm very good at it.

"And now, mister nosy journalist it's time to change the subject."

"OK then, answer me this. How could the Fulton fungus have traveled to Iraq?"

"No Mike! Don't sit there and try to feed me fucking crap like that. If there's any connection between my town and *anything* going on in Iraq then you just tell me straight. If there isn't then you stop wasting my time and tell me something I might want to know."

"Okay."

Mike described what had happened with the homeless woman and the old fashioned note made from cut out letters. Then he took out his laptop and showed Marion the video.

She waited for the end before commenting. "Christ Mike! You've got my attention, but how can you be sure it's the same disease?"

"Because, as you astutely pointed out earlier, I'll sell more papers that way."

Marion made a disapproving face.

"Okay. So really, I don't think anyone's sure it's the same disease. Well, no one who's talking anyway. But the symptoms are so similar. It would be a huge coincidence for people to start dying like this all over the world from *different* causes."

"Now you sound like all those conspiracy theorists Mike. You have a few facts and you're creating an ad-hoc explanation. Maybe people die like this all the time, from all sorts of causes. It's just that now we're all paying attention."

"I dunno Chief."

"Exactly, you don't know. Do you, in fact, know any more than I do? Were you there? Were you a witness to anything? No."

The argument had run its course. They both fell silent and returned to their drinks. It was Marion who broke the silence. "Just out of interest, in the video, what did it say?"

"You heard. It was just the soldiers yelling at each other and talking about the bodies."

"No Mike, the *banner*, on the wall in that first room. What did it say?"

"Death to America I guess. It was Arabic. I didn't really think about it."

"You're being lazy Mr. Fanning. If that was *my* crime scene, I'd get the banner translated as soon as possible."

Mike sighed and made a phone call to the Record, asking to have an expert look at the banner. When the call ended he pointed at Marion's glass and asked "Another?"

"Thanks Mr. Fanning, but I think it's time for you to feed me."

Mike shook his head in mock disbelief. "You're lucky the paper has a budget for this story Chief Quirke."

After they had ordered Marion asked "So what are these disturbing details?"

"You mean that video wasn't disturbing enough?"

"It was plenty disturbing Mike, but Friday on the phone you said you had disturbing details. That was *before* you got the letter, or the video."

"Oh yeah, Right." Mike took out his notebook and leafed through the pages for nearly a minute. "Okay, here we are. Agents of Homeland Security purportedly visited Fulton well before the quarantine and told everyone to keep quiet. How did you assess those agents? Did they seem genuine to you?"

"Dunno Mike. I never met them. I know they spoke to Shona and to Dale, my deputy. But they never came to see me."

"Don't you think that's odd? They visited the town and only interviewed the deputy?"

Marion was pleased to catch him out. "You haven't been doing your homework Mr. Fanning. I haven't been in Fulton for the past two weeks. I've been here in D.C. on a mandatory training course, given by… Homeland Security." There was some grist for the conspiracy mill!

Mike ignored the bait. "But they didn't interview you here in D.C. either?"

"No."

"Why do you think that was?"

"I wasn't in Fulton when the disease broke. No point interviewing someone who wasn't there."

"I guess that's cop logic huh?"

"Yep."

"Alright then, but here's the strange thing. The DHS has denied, in writing, that it ever interviewed anyone at all. What do you make of that?"

"They're a huge department. It doesn't surprise me if one hand doesn't know what the other one is doing. Hell, even Dale and I—"

"So you don't think it's at all strange?"

"Of course it's strange, this whole *thing* is strange. But who knows what's really going on inside the DHS? Shona didn't think they were asking the right questions anyways."

"When did you speak to Shona?"

Fuck! That was a stupid mistake. "Uh, I spoke to her yesterday, after you called." It was a lie but Marion didn't have time to think of anything better. She felt like one of the criminals who ended up in her jail. Trying to talk her way out of a bad situation but only making it worse.

The journalist sat back and put his hands behind his head. "There's been no phone contact with Fulton since the quarantine was established. Even the cell phones are out. I spent all yesterday trying to call the town and I didn't make it through once."

"I guess I got lucky."

"Jesus Chief! You're talking to a journalist here. I write bullshit for a living. You think I can't smell it from a mile away? Besides, you blushed."

Marion could still feel the slight redness on her cheek. "Off the record or not Mr. Fanning, I think I've said enough."

The food arrived but the awkwardness remained. They ate in silence and Marion had nearly finished her meal before Mike spoke again. "Look Marion, I'm not the enemy here. I need to get to the bottom of this as much as you do."

Marion put down her knife and fork and looked directly at Mike. "Like I said before. I phoned Shona on Saturday. I was very lucky and I got a connection. I guess the signal must have bounced off a satellite or sunspots or a passing U.F.O. or something."

"Okay sure. You talked to Shona on Saturday, by *phone*. Now please will you tell me what she said?"

Marion relayed Shona's comments about how the DHS were careful to ask who knew about the fungus but didn't ask any medical questions. How they took all Shona's notes and samples. How it seemed that they were trying to hide the fungus, not investigate it.

When she finished Mike challenged her. "But you don't *know* they're trying to hide it, do you? Maybe they're just trying to avoid a panic. Maybe all of Shona's stuff will turn up at this intergovernmental panel. It's hardly a cover-up when three countries are cooperating to do exactly the investigation that Shona wants."

"Well that sounds reasonable Mike. And I have to admit I have no hard evidence to support a cover-up. Any ways, I can't see what it is they're covering up. The President has announced this thing to the world. Unless of course they're trying to make it look worse than it is."

Mike frowned. "How can it look worse than it is? People breathing spores then dying in pools of their own blood is bad enough, even for me."

"Yes, but what if it's only a *few* people? Shona is a trained researcher you know. She says she found spores alright, but when she looks at the *pattern* of the illness, it's not like an airborne disease at all. It doesn't make sense to me, but then it doesn't make sense to her either."

"So she's saying this thing is spread by spores but at the same time it isn't?"

"She's saying something doesn't add up. More research is needed but the White House and the DHS have jumped the gun and gone all Red Alert. Now she's worried the research won't be done. If this thing isn't airborne then how *is* it spreading? We could be missing something vital."

"Now *that's* something I could write about, but of course, I'd need to speak to the source."

"Well you have a phone Mike."

"Yes I do, but it doesn't seem to be as lucky as yours and I was just wondering—"

"I thought we'd agreed about that."

"Yes, yes, we agreed. But the Record has a bunch of high-tech satellite phones, one's that can't be cut off, even by the government. If there was a way to get one to Shona then I could talk to her direct, get some real information."

The suggestion was met with an angry silence from Marion. She could see how this would benefit Mike but did he really expect her to take the risk of breaking the quarantine again? The anger subsided however at the thought of returning to Fulton and maybe doing something concrete to help. "Keep talking."

"Uh, that's it actually. I'd like to get a satellite phone to Shona. We can talk to her and she can access the internet with it too. I'm just hoping you might know how to get it into the town."

"Well sadly I don't. The town is in quarantine and I've spent the last two days being denied permission to return. Even if I could go back I'd need to know how big this phone is, and how heavy."

Mike described a small box shape with his hands. "They're not heavy these days. Even I can carry one."

"And what would be in it for me?"

Mike laughed. "You get what I get. You get a line into the town."

"Not good enough. You've been digging around this story for a while. I want to know *everything* you know."

Mike did not laugh at that. "Flat out no. If I share my information with anyone the Record will fire me immediately. If I share it with a cop they'll make sure I never work in journalism again."

"Then I guess that fancy phone stays where it is."

"Maybe not. Do you have access to a computer while you're away from Fulton?"

"Yes."

"Then I think we have a solution. I've established communication with Alison Grove at the CDC in Atlanta. We have a secure blog and if we can get that phone to Shona then she can join in. So long as you can get to a computer then you can join in too."

So it was that Marion came into possession of a KCT-7041 digital satellite phone, extended life battery kit, recharger and instruction manual. She wondered if being caught breaking quarantine with this device would be enough to have her labeled a terrorist. Probably it would, police badge or not.

She was about to leave when Mike's phone rang and he glanced at the screen. "You wanted to know that the banner said?"

"Yes."

"America killed these martyrs with germ warfare. America will pay."

33

The first meeting of the Intergovernmental Biosecurity Emergency Investigative Panel began at nine the next morning. An entire floor of a downtown government building had been requisitioned for exclusive use by the panel. This wasn't as grand a gesture as it first seemed, the building was being refurbished and was otherwise empty.

The work on level seven was complete except for the fittings and replacement of the carpet, which was stained from years of use and paint-splattered by the recent work. Its musty smell was nearly hidden by the strong odor of the new paint.

What wasn't hidden was the sound of the work still in progress on the level below and the muffled noise of power tools provided a continuous and irritating distraction.

Security guards were stationed in the downstairs lobby of the building, at the elevators and fire escapes on level seven. All people entering the building were checked and anyone going to level seven was accompanied by at least one guard.

At seven fifty Alison Grove stood in the elevator behind her appointed guard and beside a painter who was heading up to level six. The elevator was lined with dirty plastic sheets and every movement caused it to squeak and rustle alarmingly.

It had been a busy weekend for Alison, starting on Saturday morning when her boss Dean had called her at home. She had argued of course but it was no use. She suggested Shona Price should be on the panel, but Shona was in quarantine. She suggested Dean, or even his boss should go, but the orders had come from the White House itself. He was to send whoever had been dealing with reports of the Fulton illness, and that was Alison.

The next two days passed in a frenzy, equal parts obsessive organization and crushing anxiety. She spent Saturday at her desk, collating what little information she had. Sunday morning she got up early to pack and by mid-afternoon it was time to head for the airport.

So it was that on Monday morning Alison found herself standing in a dimly lit plastic-lined elevator beside a painter who could contain his curiosity no longer. He leaned over and whispered at her. "What's going on up there?"

Alison said nothing and took a step away. He leaned closer but she was saved by the security guard who turned around and flashed his ID.

"Sir, you have been instructed not to communicate with anyone in this building except your direct work associates." Before he could say any more the elevator stopped and the painter stepped out.

At level seven Alison was met by another security guard who checked her ID then handed her a four page document headed "National Security Non-Disclosure Agreement and Waiver of Civil Rights."

Alison didn't like the title at all and began reading slowly, determined not to miss the smallest detail. She had only made it through the first paragraph when the guard interrupted her.

"Just sign it."

"I'm not going to sign a document waiving my civil rights without reading it!"

The guard however had other plans and he grabbed the paper from her hands, turned to the last page and held it up against the wall in front of her. "You're already in the building lady. You don't get out until you sign." He held out a pen towards Alison then pointed at the page. "There, on the line."

Alison took the pen and signed. Her signature was shaky and curved awkwardly on the page, partly because she was writing against the wall, but mostly because she was scared.

The guard took the paper away then pointed to an open door down the corridor. "Now you go in there."

Alison didn't move. "I'll need a copy of that, for my official records."

"Yes ma'am I'll get right on it but you need to go to the conference room *now*." The guard held out his arm and shepherded Alison down the hall.

A conference table and chairs occupied the center of the room and a portable whiteboard and overhead projector were stuffed into one corner. Apart from these basics the room was bare. There were phone jacks but no phones. There did not seem to be any internet connections, just bare cables hanging from holes in wall. On this first day there were not even extension cords for the panelist's laptops.

Two Chinese men and a woman stood by the window, talking quietly to each other. Next to the whiteboard were two men, one of whom was definitely DHS. He was dressed in the same style as Agent Johnson's silent accomplice had been; a black suit topped off with the seemingly essential earpiece.

The other man was younger and wearing a suit jacket that didn't quite match his pants. He clearly wasn't used to the formality and fidgeted with the sleeve of the jacket, smoothing out imaginary creases.

Alison had seen this look before. It was how the scientists at the CDC dressed when they applied for grant money. They were perfectly at home with the most difficult ideas and abstract concepts, but ask them to deal with bureaucracy and they didn't even know what to wear.

Alison had stopped in the doorway. Now she smiled cautiously and said "Hi" in a quiet voice. The Chinese glanced at her then looked away. The DHS man did the same but his companion smiled back and replied in a loud, cheerful voice. "Hi there, I'm Dave Walters, Australian Department of Health and Ageing." He walked over to Alison, holding out his hand as he did so and Alison noticed that he was quite a handsome man.

She was grateful for the welcoming response and allowed her smile to broaden as she shook Dave's hand.

"Hi Dave. I'm Alison Grove, Centers for Disease Control."

"Oh hey, you guys are great. I wish we had your resources back home."

Alison had never thought of the CDC as well-resourced. She was about to comment when the final panel member arrived. A tall thin man in late middle age, he introduced himself in a strong east European accent. "Hello everybody, I am Doctor Vencel Fodor. I am a senior administrator at the National Institutes of Health and I have been appointed to chair this panel. I see we are all here so perhaps we can take our seats now."

Vencel strode to the head of the table and sat down. The DHS man immediately positioned himself at the other end where he was joined by the Chinese. Dave had already arranged his papers on the same side which left Alison with the near side of the table to herself. She sat carefully at the halfway point between Vencel and the DHS man, looking across at Dave.

Vencel spoke as they were sitting down. "You know who I am already. The two gentlemen at the far end of the table are representatives of the U.S. and Chinese security services. They are here to represent the National Security interests of our respective governments and will not be participating in the panel's deliberations. The Australian government elected to send only a scientific representative."

Alison wondered why there was any security at all. In her mind this was a scientific panel. Issues of security would only be relevant *after* the panel had reached its conclusions. Once again the spies seemed remarkably interested in this particular disease.

Vencel continued to speak. "Perhaps the scientific delegates could introduce themselves now."

It was one of the Chinese delegates who spoke first. "I am Dr. Tai Sheng." He gestured to the woman sitting next to him. "This is Dr. Xing Shi Lun. We are from Jouchou Peoples Hospital. I must make it clear that the hospital is *not* part of Jouchou Peoples Special Medical Laboratory." Vencel waited for more but the pair sat in silence so he pointed to the Australian.

Dave looked around the table and Alison felt a tinge of embarrassment when his gaze fell on her. He spoke in a nonchalant voice, as if he was introducing himself at a party. "Hi, I'm Dave Walters. I'm a research scientist with the Australian Department of Health and Ageing. I specialize in tropical diseases so when anything strange comes along they give it to me and hey, I couldn't say no to a free holiday in the States!"

Dave obviously thought this last comment was funny. Unfortunately it was lost on the Chinese and Vencel too sat stony-faced.

Alison thought it was flippant given the occasion, but now it was her turn to speak. She felt the familiar heat growing on her cheeks as the other panel members looked at her. "Uh, I'm Alison Grove, Centers for Disease Control, Atlanta. I'm a researcher. I collate data relating to disease outbreaks. I have brought all the data I have relating to Fulton although its quality is not nearly adequate yet." Her eye accidentally caught Dave's as she finished and her cheek burned.

Vencel took back control of the meeting. "Before we start I must stress the importance of security. Given the degree of media speculation and the possibility that misrepresented information could lead to widespread panic, members of the panel must refrain from speaking to the media at any time. All press releases are to be made through the proper channels by relevant government authorities in each country. Panel members are prohibited from speaking directly to members of the general public for the same reasons.

"I will now distribute our terms of reference. These were negotiated at length between the participating governments and we are therefore required to adhere to them strictly." Vencel handed out copies to the panelists. The security men already had copies of their own.

"We shall take a thirty minute break. Please read the terms during this time then sign the form at the end indicating you agree to be bound by them."

Alison read the cover page of the document. It was headed 'Intergovernmental Biosecurity Emergency Investigative Panel. Official Terms of Reference.' Beneath this and in larger type were the words

"FOR PANEL MEMBERS AND AUTHORISED GOVERNMENT REPRESENTATIVES ONLY."

She was about to start on the details when Dave called across to her.

"Hey Alison, you want a coffee?"

"Uh, sure."

The walked down the hallway to the small lunchroom. There was instant coffee on the counter and a machine to make hot water. Alison looked in the fridge for milk as Dave spoke.

"So what did you make of all that?"

Alison prepared her coffee as she answered. "Make of all what?"

He looked surprised. "The security."

"Oh, I don't know. I've never done anything like this before. I don't know how much security to expect."

"Yeah, neither do I but it seems overdone. Did you get a grilling?"

"What do you mean?" Alison put her coffee on the small table in the middle of the room and checked her watch, aware of the deadline for reading the terms of reference.

The Australian furrowed his brow. "I arrived yesterday evening, right? The news is full of talk about spores and airborne transmission and there's even a quarantine. But anyone with half a brain can see this thing isn't airborne. The epidemiology just isn't right."

Alison nodded agreement. More people would be dead over a much wider area if the fungus was spreading by air.

"So straight off the plane they sent me to a meeting with the security guys. They ask me about my background. Am I a radical, who do I give money to, that kind of stuff. I guess it makes sense but then they bring in their medical guy and I'm thinking great! We can start doing some real work.

"He asks me what I think is going on and I say it can't be airborne. Well he just goes berserk. Says I haven't seen the data and I can't call myself a scientist if I rush to conclusions with no evidence; says he'll take me off the panel if I'm going to undermine it from the very start."

Alison looked past him into the hallway but there was no one there. "My God! What did you do?"

Dave shrugged again. "Oh I told him to back off. I've seen the data from Miltonah, there's no evidence of airborne transmission there and I haven't seen any come out of the 'States either. But if the panel has good evidence then of course I'll go along with it."

"And what did he say to that?"

"He said I better remember to keep an open mind. I said sure, no worries, and he left."

The kitchen fell silent and Alison realized she was staring at Dave. He had a nice smile, a lot like Matt from the coffee cart back in Atlanta. She coughed nervously. "I think we better get back to the meeting room."

He smiled at her again. "Oh yeah sure. Better find out what's in those terms we're agreeing to."

34

Du Rui Kuang found himself coming repeatedly to the place where a row of trees stood behind a small pond. If he sat for long enough and let his mind wander he could almost believe he was in the countryside around Jouchou.

It was a gentle respite from recent events as memories of family outings drifted through his mind, his wife's smile and the laughter of his daughter, splashing in the water and trying to catch fish with her bare hands.

The daydream was interrupted by Dr. Fen coughing gently beside him. "Ah Fen! I see they've finally let you out into the light."

Fen smiled as he gazed at the pond. "Yes. I have made good progress."

Du sensed there was more to come and waited for Fen to speak again. When he did not, Du prompted him. "Please, sit next to me. Tell me about your good progress."

Du had always maintained a careful distance from the staff of the institute. Too much familiarity with the troops and discipline would be undermined. As a result though, Fen and Du knew nothing of each other beyond their formal work relationship.

Fen sat but did not speak immediately. When he did his voice was almost a whisper.

"Du, it is not your fault." He kept his eyes on the reflections in the water.

"What is not my fault?" Fen was clearly treating him with a great deal of respect and this conversation must be important to the scientist.

"The illness Du. It did not come from your laboratory. You were not responsible."

In earlier times Du would have reprimanded Fen for even suggesting he might be responsible. Now though, he appreciated the news. Perhaps he would see his family soon.

"Thank you, Fen. I have been wondering what went wrong. I thought the staff, or maybe even you, had been careless." It was a small mercy. Du knew that his career was still over. The debacle at the laboratory would ensure that whether the illness was his fault or not.

"Tell me Fen. If it is not my fault then why did the illness follow me from America to Australia to Jouchou?"

Fen coughed and stared deeper into the pond. "It did not come from the laboratory, but I am sorry, it *must* have come from you. That is the only way it could have followed you around the world."

"Then it *is* my fault."

"No! You were infected but it is not your fault. You had a fungal infection, on your skin. It is a mild one that you would not even notice. Perhaps a light rash or body odor, but maybe nothing. A fungus like this could live on your skin for the rest of your life and do you no harm."

"Yet people die when I am near them? You are not making any sense Fen. They say the fungus makes spores and travels through the air. I have seen the news from America. They have quarantined the town where my great-grandfather lived and we both saw what happened in Jouchou. But you say I have bad skin."

Both men fell silent for a moment at the memory of those workers dying so horribly but Fen was sure of his reply. "The Americans are wrong and I can prove it. Yes, this fungus infects the lungs as well as the skin, something that the natural strain doesn't do, and during the latter stages of illness the fungus does form spore sacs in the lungs and it does release spores. The infected person certainly breathes out the spores and others will breathe them in. But, the spores themselves are sterile."

Fen paused to let that sink in. "I have been testing them right here at the institute. The spores *will not* grow in the lungs or on the skin or in a dish of agar. I cannot get them to grow anywhere. The lifecycle is all wrong. This fungus lives on the skin and it doesn't spread through the air, it spreads by contact."

Du turned to look at the scientist. "But Fen, if the spores do not grow then how does this fungus get into the lungs at all, and why do people die like that?"

Fen paused. "I do not know how it gets into lungs, I am still studying that. Once it is there though, in *some* people, it reproduces rapidly. There is complete pulmonary breakdown and the person dies.

"It seems perhaps it is only lethal in people who are weak, or sick already. Your factory workers had lungs full of cement dust. Some of them were dying anyway. That's why it took them all so fast. You have had the fungus for over a month. I don't think you have felt ill at all."

It was true that Du had not experienced any symptoms except perhaps for the stronger body odor he had noticed in America. It was also true that many of his workers were already sick from the cement dust, but there were others to consider. "What about my family in Australia, and what about the people in America where I visited? None of them worked in a cement factory."

"It doesn't *have* to be concrete dust Du; many things can make a person weak and vulnerable. You must remember also, I am still studying. There could be some other trigger I have not found."

The answer was of no use to Du. Maybe Fen was right about this fungus, but that didn't change Du's situation and he feared the answer to his next question. "Then what about my family? Are they safe?"

"I do not know. I have asked for them to be given the same drugs we took when we arrived here. The drugs should kill it in a few days."

Du sighed. "Thank you Fen. I know you can do no more while you are kept in this place."

Fen stood and bowed. "I must return to my work now Du." He turned to leave but Du called out.

"Wait! You said before, the natural strain doesn't infect the lungs. What did you mean by that?"

"Ah... what I meant was... we have the natural strain in the laboratory at Jouchou. We have tested it on animals and even on ourselves. It is safe. Irritating at best. The one you brought from America did not come from us."

"We have it in Jouchou? As director of the laboratory I should have known. Why were you studying this fungus Fen? Why did you withhold it from me?"

"You knew about the army contracts, and you knew they were secret. I was instructed to discuss the details only with those who absolutely needed to know. You agreed to that Du."

It was true. The army contracts were lucrative and Du had not cared if the army kept its secrets. "If the fungus is so harmless, why does the army study it? And why do you call it the natural strain?"

Fen took a step back. "I cannot say Du, you know that. Perhaps I have said too much already but I wanted you to know that you are innocent in all this."

The scientist walked away and left Du to his thoughts. They quickly returned to his wife and daughter and the hope that Du's drugs had reached them in time. He would leave Fen to deal with the army and whatever curse it had visited upon Jouchou.

35

Alison sat at the conference table of the Intergovernmental Panel reading its terms of reference and the further she went the less she liked them. They seemed designed to *prevent* the panel from reaching a conclusion.

She looked around the room. The Chinese had flicked briefly through their copies then signed them. Vencel had left the room with his which left just Alison and Dave. He sat across the table from her deep in concentration, making margin notes and searching back and forward through the pages.

Two minutes before the half hour deadline Alison still had two of the appendices to read. She was scanning the first one when Vencel walked into the room accompanied by a DHS man. Vencel took his place at the head of the table and looked around the room.

"We're all here so let's get started. We shall begin by hearing an oral summary from each delegation of the information they have brought to the panel."

Alison's anxiety increased. She really should say something about the terms but Dave's story about his security briefing was still fresh in her head and she kept her mouth shut as Vencel went on.

"I'd like to begin with—"

"Wait a minute!" It was Dave, rescuing Alison from her dilemma.

Vencel looked sternly across the table at him. "Yes, Mr. Walters?"

"Well there are some issues with the terms of reference we should sort out now. Surely it's important that we all start out with a clear understanding?"

"*What* issues Mr. Walters?"

"Well, the terms don't allow the panel to undertake its own investigative work, but I'd like to know what that means. We'll have to start by reviewing the current information of course, but that will raise questions. If we can't investigate those questions how will we ever get to the bottom of this?"

He paused for breath and Vencel opened his mouth, but Dave was too quick. "For instance, we'll need to interview medical personnel who've actually dealt with this thing, and there will have to be a lot more lab tests done just to identify the organism. When do we get access to samples from this town, ah… Fulton?"

"As I said before the break Mr. Walters, these terms were agreed by our respective governments. It's not our place to dispute them."

Dave ignored the answer. "And some of the underlying assumptions are wrong."

"*Wrong*, Mr. Walters? I thought I had explained. These terms were decided after careful negotiation at the highest level. How can you call them wrong?"

Alison watched in amazement, Dave didn't seem at all bothered by Vencel's response.

"The terms of reference *assume* there is a single common disease agent for all three of the known outbreaks. Now that may be the case but it's something we should establish as fact. Otherwise the rest of our deliberations may be pointless."

Dave looked at Vencel, waiting for the next challenge. This time though, Vencel only sighed and motioned to him to continue, which he did with gusto.

"The terms of reference are also in the *wrong sequence*. Here's what it says in the summary. The primary purpose of the panel is to provide our member governments with the optimum procedures for containment and eradication of the disease. Secondary to this is the identification of the disease organism. Tertiary, is the identification of the origin of the disease organism and its method of reproduction and transmission.

"But how can we identify procedures for containing this disease if we don't know what it is? Our *primary* purpose must be to correctly identify the disease organism, or organisms. That step alone may be sufficient. If it is a known organism then the methods of eradication may also be known.

"If it is a new organism then we will have to identify its method of reproduction and transmission *before* we can figure out how to eradicate it. Which brings me back to my first point, it's highly unlikely that all the information we need exists. We won't be able fulfill any of our objectives if we can't do any investigation."

Dave scanned the room, but the other panelists sat passively. Alison agreed with him, but again the thought of being bullied by Vencel stopped her from speaking up.

After a few seconds silence Vencel answered. "I take it you are finished Mr. Walters?"

"Well actually, one last thing. It says here the panel is *not* expected to produce a final report. That ah… Individual members will communicate the panel's conclusions to their own governments in due course. That seems highly unusual, don't you think?"

Vencel glared down the table at him. "You're finished now?"

"Ah, sure, all done."

"Good then. I would point out first that this is a highly unusual situation. It takes time for a panel such as this to produce a report Mr. Walters and time is something we don't have. For our conclusions to be of use they must be communicated to our governments immediately.

"As for the sequence given in the terms of reference, it is one of priority rather than chronology. But I must reiterate that it is absolutely *not* our purpose here to question or re-draft the terms of reference. I really do suggest Mr. Walters that you read the terms in their entirety before raising any more objections.

"Now, does anyone else have a comment?" He raised his eyebrows and looked pointedly at Alison then the Chinese delegates.

She noticed Vencel had said nothing about the panel's inability to investigate. It was clearly the most restrictive part of the terms. She hoped that Dave would raise it again but it was Dr. Xing who spoke.

"We are representatives of our government and as such we are happy to comply with whatever terms of reference have been negotiated on behalf of the people." The doctor cast a glance at the Chinese security man and he nodded his approval.

Vencel sighed with satisfaction and put his copy of the terms to one side. "Moving on then, we will now hear summaries from each delegate of the information provided to the panel by their government."

The summaries went on until two that afternoon. When they were done Vencel spoke about the quarantine and the need to take the possibility of airborne dispersal seriously. There were significant issues for public buildings and transport, particularly air travel.

Alison thought it was odd as none of the summaries had mentioned spores or airborne transmission. She remembered Dave's comment: "they've already decided."

The meeting ended with Vencel handing out the written submissions each delegation had brought to the panel. They were to be read before the panel resumed the next morning.

On the way out of the conference room Dave asked Alison if she wanted to meet for dinner. She would have loved to spend an evening just looking at him, but coping with the panel was enough and she declined the invitation.

Instead she walked directly back to her hotel with one of the panel's security guards walking silently beside her. When they reached the room he warned her not to leave without him then sat down on a chair directly outside the door.

On her own in the room, Alison found it much easier to feel angry about the panel. The situation was wrong and *something* had to be done. It was clear though that she would get nowhere if she fought openly and she didn't have the stomach for it anyway.

There was only one way out. Alison plugged in her laptop and left a message for Mike, confident that even the DHS would not be able to break into the Gorilla's encryption.

"First day was USELESS. Too much POLITICS! DHS and Chinese security are in the room with us all the time. They say there is a terrorist connection but won't say anything about it – National Security.

Terms of reference are all wrong. They do not allow us to investigate so we are reliant on whatever we are fed. This is a serious problem. We have little hard data and what we really need is some quality analysis of actual samples from infected individuals. Like Shona did in Fulton but in a real lab with proper resources.

The Chinese had nothing really new, nor did the Australians. The Australian guy thinks it's all a set up and the politicians have already decided what will happen.

I think I agree with him. If things don't change the panel will not come up with any useful findings and the politicians will be able to say what they like."

She started on her reading and it was nearly six o'clock before the sound of an ape screeching alerted her to a reply from Mike.

"Don't be surprised about the politics. It's a government committee after all. DHS took all of Shona's samples from Fulton. Thought you would have access to them. Are you getting an analysis of them? Thanks for keeping me informed. Will talk again tomorrow. Mike"

Both Alison and Mike were disappointed with the exchange. Mike had hoped for better information from the panel. Alison had hoped for better support from Mike. Her heart sank at the thought of what she'd gotten into. How on earth could she make things right?

36

Joe Sullivan was comfortably relaxed as he sat in his usual chair, waiting for the TV news. He was wearing his favorite sweater, the one with holes in the sleeves that Kathleen was constantly telling him to throw out. His dinner was half eaten from the plate on his lap and a cold beer sat on the small table next to him. His only concession tonight was to put the beer on a coaster. He always did that; it was easier than listening to his wife complain yet again.

Kathleen too was relaxed. The twins were upstairs with their computers and would stay there until it was time for bed. Dinner had been made and Joe would eventually clear it away. The rest of the evening was hers. She sat in her chair next to Joe and let the TV take her away into a daydream.

Kathleen's reverie was interrupted by the arrival of the news. Tonight it began with a reporter standing outside the White House and the 'BREAKING NEWS' banner.

"Rumors are spreading this Tuesday evening in Washington tonight that New York Senator John Hanson has died. The Senator was rushed to hospital this afternoon and was immediately admitted to an intensive care facility which a short time later was put under quarantine.

"It is believed the Senator was suffering from the same infection responsible for the quarantine in Virginia. Sources close to the Senator would not comment this afternoon except to confirm that he was hospitalized and receiving medical care.

"There have also been reports of intense activity at the hospital by agents of Homeland Security and this has fuelled speculation that the Senator may have been the target of a terrorist attack. We have been unable to get any confirmation however and Homeland Security has refused to comment."

The image cut back to the anchor. "As you heard there, Senator John Hanson has fallen gravely ill today and may possibly have died."

The anchor put one hand to his earpiece and paused for a moment. "I'm getting word now that there is to be an emergency press conference at the White House. Apparently the President's press secretary will be reading a prepared statement."

The image cut to another reporter. This one was standing outside the hospital where Senator Hanson had been admitted. The reporter spoke about Fulton and the quarantine and what might happen now at the hospital. She moved on to the subject of the Senator and whether he was already dead but was cut off in mid-sentence as the White House press room appeared on the screen.

Technicians were still setting up cameras and microphones as the Press Secretary walked to the podium and began to speak over the noise.

"It is with great sorrow that I have to announce the death earlier today of Senator John Hanson. This has come as a great shock to all of us in Washington D.C. as I'm sure it has to everyone throughout our great nation. Our thoughts tonight are with the Senator's wife and family."

This had been expected. It was the next comment that got a reaction from the gathered press.

"I am able to confirm that the Senator's death is the direct result of activity by a terrorist cell operating in the Washington D.C. area. Evidence of this cell has only recently come to light and unfortunately the security services were unable to obstruct its plans to attack the Senator."

Questions were shouted at the press secretary but he ignored them and raised his voice.

"Several members of the cell have been detained over the past few days in a covert operation however some members, including the leader, have managed to evade capture. It appears those individuals were responsible for today's attack."

The press would wait no longer and the room erupted in a barrage of questions. The secretary held up his hand and shouted above them: "Quiet please! I will not be deviating from the prepared statement and will not be taking any questions." He stood silently until the press accepted he meant it and settled down.

"The captured terrorists had infiltrated the food service industry and we believe that is how the Senator was infected. There is no evidence to date that security has been breached at either the Capitol building, the White House or any other government buildings or that the infection has been released to the public in any widespread way."

The press secretary picked up his papers and glanced to his right, behind the curtain at the edge of the stage, clearly waiting. When nothing happened he turned back to the room. "Ladies and Gentlemen, if you could please remain in your seats for a few minutes there will be a further announcement." With that he turned and left the stage.

The noise peaked as every cell phone in the room was activated. A voice-over on the TV coverage said "We will return to this White House press conference as soon as there are any developments." The scene at the press room was replaced by a woman drinking coffee.

"Mmm… I don't want to live without my Holdvieg's Roast—"

Joe hit the mute button, leaned forward and shouted at the TV. "Fuck! A Senator!"

Kathleen scowled at him. "Joe Sullivan! You keep it down. You don't want the boys to hear language like that!"

He leaned back in his chair. "Well what am I supposed to say? God dammed crazies killed a Senator!" He sat watching the ads in silence and fuming.

Kathleen waited for a minute then asked "What do you think Marion will do?"

Joe smiled at the thought of his cousin. "She'll do whatever it takes. I've never seen her run away from a fight yet. Wouldn't want to be those terrorists if *she* gets hold of them."

"But she was so convinced there weren't any terrorists. She kept saying there was no evidence."

"Well maybe she had to say that honey."

"What do you mean?"

"Well think about it. Some diplomat goes to Fulton and causes a fuss. Then folks get sick. What does Marion do? She comes to D.C. and spends two weeks with Homeland Security."

"Yes, but that was training."

"She *said* it was training. I bet she's known about this from day one."

"Well then why did she find out about the quarantine on the news and why couldn't she get back into the town?"

"I dunno honey. I just can't believe she'd let something like this go on in her town and not do anything about it. Besides, she was gone all night so maybe she *did* get back to the town. Makes more sense than sleeping in her car."

Kathleen stared at her husband. "You think she might have gone back?"

"Well maybe. If she's hunting terrorists then anything's possible. She sure wouldn't tell us about it."

"But she came back here Joe!"

He shrugged. "Yeah, I know that."

"After the quarantine, and the spores! She came back here."

"Oh God! I didn't think of that." Joe stared at his wife. "Well then I guess she didn't go to the town. She wouldn't risk our lives like that. I'll say one thing; she's sure got herself mixed up in a heap of trouble this time."

Kathleen did not relax but the ads had finished and Joe turned up the volume.

The seal of the President of the United States appeared on the TV screen. It wobbled slightly as the camera zoomed out to reveal the podium and stage at the White House press room. There was no time for a voice-over as the President walked onto the stage and stood behind the podium.

"My fellow Americans. As you have already heard our nation has suffered a tragic loss today with the death of Senator Hanson. I am sure that the American people join with me tonight in offering sincere condolences to his wife Abigail, their son Matthew, and their two daughters, Julie and Pamela.

"You have also heard that this terrible event is the result of a direct terrorist attack. An attack that has been launched on the very heart of our democracy.

"This administration became aware of a terrorist cell in the Washington D.C. area only very recently." These words were carefully chosen. The White House knew they would be blamed for not stopping the attack.

They also knew the DHS had concealed its knowledge of the terrorists for some time. They were livid at being put in this position but nothing would be said for now, not before the immediate crisis was resolved.

After that though there would be a day of reckoning. The DHS would be investigated and it would be found wanting. Heads would roll. Reputations would be lost. Until then nothing must be said to contradict that future outcome.

The President continued. "I immediately ordered detention of all individuals connected with this cell. Unfortunately, as you have already heard, some have managed to evade capture and have carried out this terrible attack. I wish to assure the American people that I have ordered the security forces to launch an immediate and full investigation and to redouble their efforts to apprehend those terrorists still at large.

"This is, however, an unprecedented situation in the history of our great country and the authorities are faced with a mammoth undertaking. In addition to finding those responsible they must deal with a disease outbreak in the heart of our capital city.

"At the present time there are still many things we do not know but as President it is my responsibility to act on the best information that I have at hand."

Some of the assembled journalists exchanged curious glances. Presidents never admitted to being ill-informed before they announced their plans.

"It is highly likely that the disease used to kill Senator Hanson is the same disease that has recently been found in Virginia."

A murmur spread through the room. This had been rumored of course, but to have the President say it was something else.

"This disease is spread by airborne spores, which makes it extremely dangerous and difficult to contain. To assist the authorities with their critical task and to ensure the safety and security of the government process and the people of Washington, I have tonight signed an executive order to bring into force the following emergency measures.

"All hospital facilities in the metropolitan D.C. area are to be placed under strict quarantine. This is to ensure that these facilities do not become compromised. Only authorized staff and registered patients will be permitted access to hospital facilities.

"We know the terrorists have been targeting food service facilities and consequently, all commercial premises where food is served in public areas are to be closed. Premises with drive-thru facilities and those making home deliveries will be allowed to continue operating. Staff at these premises will be thoroughly vetted in the coming weeks."

The original wording of the Presidents order had simply shut all public food outlets. It was changed however after enormous pressure from the fast food industry who argued they were an essential public service. The White House did not know who had leaked the news to them but that was another matter that would have to wait for later.

"To reduce the risk of spreading airborne infection any persons exhibiting symptoms of pulmonary illness will be prevented from traveling by air. Other forms of public transport will remain open but the public is urged to avoid these where possible. All residents in affected areas are requested to stay in their homes where possible and avoid all public gatherings."

These were extreme measures and the President had considered deeply before agreeing to them. To help him decide the experts from the DHS had shown him detailed maps and computer animations. Patterns of wind drift and human movements were overlaid by large swathes of color that grew with alarming speed.

The outer yellow region was labeled 'manageable' and inside that was an orange band for 'epidemic'. At the center of a large red area were the words 'medical overwhelm.' It was speculation of course, and it was the worst-case possibility for a highly airborne, highly infectious disease but it could not be ruled out. It was that, combined with the terrorist attack, which forced the President's hand. It would simply have been irresponsible for him to take the risk of not acting.

The President paused and for once the reporters remained silent. The news was too much even for them. "As of this moment the White House is closed to all but those authorized personnel who are absolutely necessary to its function. Likewise, the houses of the Senate and Representatives and their administrative offices are closed to the public until further notice.

"I appreciate that these are unprecedented measures and that they impose severely on the normal rights and freedoms of U.S. citizens. We are, however, facing a crisis the like of which we have not seen before. These are not actions to be taken lightly or without due deliberation and I can assure the American people that I have undertaken that deliberation with all care.

"I know these measures will cause great disruption for many and there will even be hardship for some. But I could not in all conscience allow our capital city and those people most vital to our democracy be exposed to this terrorist threat. I must stress these measures will only remain in place until that threat has been removed.

I thank you all for your cooperation in this matter. May God bless America."

37

Vencel Fodor looked pale and tired as he sat in the back of the limousine. MS thought perhaps he was shaking too, but maybe it was just the motion of the vehicle. The DHS agent certainly wasn't shaking. He sat next to Vencel and waited impassively as they headed off from the curb with nowhere in particular to go.

MS was irritated at having to see either of them, and particularly at having to do it in the back of a Limousine. But the DHS man had been insistent and the car was simply the most discreet place to hold the meeting at short notice. No one would see them together and the driver, if asked, could be relied on not to have seen who they were.

It after nearly midnight now and MS wasn't in any mood to waste time.

"Well Doctor Fodor. You are concerned about the situation at the Intergovernmental Panel?"

"A Senator is dead!" The shaking was definite now. "The panel has been meeting for just two days and a Senator is dead from the same disease we are supposed to study. Of course I am concerned!"

"We are all concerned doctor." MS delivered the words at a measured pace. "This is a terrible event, and it makes your work at the panel even more important than it already was."

"Precisely!"

When Vencel didn't add to his comment MS prompted. "So your concern is?"

"I have been a bureaucrat long enough Mister Stonehouse to know when something isn't right."

"And that would be?"

Vencel sat forward. "It was explained to me before the panel started that terrorists were involved, although no evidence was provided." He glanced at the DHS man, but there was no response. "It was also explained that, because of national security, I must keep the origin of this disease a secret.

"I am a patriot, so if that is truly necessary then I have no problem with it and I have done my best at the panel until now. But when the Senator died I asked for more information." He looked at the agent a second time and again was ignored.

"If Homeland Security knew about the attack then surely they have information useful to the panel, information about the disease. But instead of giving me an answer they told me to be quiet. I must continue as if nothing has changed. Then when I said I would take the matter back to the White House they brought me here, to see you!

The shaking had stopped now and some of the color had returned to Vencel's face. As he spoke he gestured with enough force that the DHS man bounced slightly on the seat next to him

"I have heard the stories about you Mister Stonehouse but I have never really believed them. That a man who has never been elected, who has never even run for office, could have such influence in a democracy - it is unacceptable. Yet here you are and now I am certain there is something wrong with the panel!"

MS let him calm down before replying. "You should not believe the stories you hear doctor. This town loves its rumors more than it loves a free lunch. As for my influence, do you really think I can control the Department of Homeland Security?" He cast a glance of his own at the agent, who still did not respond.

Vencel hesitated. "Well —"

"I'm here doctor because I am a good friend of Senator Hanson. He was instrumental you know in having you appointed to the panel."

"That can't be true. I was appointed by the White House."

MS sighed, as if explaining something difficult to a child. "Yes you were, but don't be naïve. Your panel was established in a matter of days, to deal with a national crisis. Nothing happens that quickly in D.C. without the approval of both sides. So of course there was cooperation and the Senator, being the target, was brought into the loop by DHS. It is their duty to protect him, after all."

The doctor did not look convinced. "None of this was mentioned at the White House briefings. Not the Senator or the terrorists. If it is so important why didn't they tell me and why do I have to keep it secret even from them? It should be in the panel's terms of reference."

A snort erupted from MS. "The terms of reference are a public document! The White House can't allow them to expose matters of national security. Besides, if you read those terms, the one's the White House gave you, you'll see they're quite prescriptive."

Vencel nodded agreement. "Don't remind me. That idiot from Australia wasted half the day arguing about it. He wants to go out and do his own field work!"

"Well I doubt the White House would thank you for that."

"That is true. But still I must raise these matters with them, for clarification."

"No!" The shout from MS was so loud that Vencel raised one arm involuntarily in self-defense. Even the DHS agent jumped. "You must *not* mention this to the White House."

"But —"

"They're *politicians* doctor. There are some things they can't afford to know, not directly anyway. So they rely on people like us to know those things for them. They rely on us to do the right thing, as patriots, for the greater good."

The doctor hung his head in thought. When he looked again and spoke his voice was quiet. "I thought it would be different here, in America."

MS had not been expecting that and could manage only to say "What?"

"I grew up behind the Iron Curtain Mister Stonehouse. I've heard lies before, I've heard distortions and half-truths and disinformation used to keep the powerful in power.

"You tell me to keep secrets from my government because I am a patriot, because it is for the greater good? You take me right back to that world Mister Stonehouse, where I can trust nothing and no-one. So stop playing games and tell me what you want, tell me how I'll suffer if I don't comply then let me decide."

MS relaxed back into the luxury of the limousine, allowing just the faintest trace of a smile to appear on his face. "If this meeting becomes public our friend here will back up my version of events one hundred percent. Understood?" He pointed at the DHS agent but kept is gaze on Vencel.

"Understood."

"Good. Then I am here to offer you a job."

It was Vencel's turn to say only "What?"

"I've heard that you are under a lot of stress at the panel. You're nearing retirement and I'm worried it might all be too much for you. As a patriot I appreciate your service to the nation and I want to help. So I'm offering you a job."

"In exchange for my compliance."

"In exchange for the sacrifice you are making doctor, on behalf of our great country. I'm only suggesting that, when this is all over, you might consider a position at one of my research laboratories or pharmaceutical companies. They all need good advice and you're just the kind of man to give it to them. It's the kind of work that wouldn't take much of your time but it will pay handsomely."

Vencel hung his head again. "And the threat, Mister Stonehouse?"

"Do I need to threaten you?"

The limousine stopped at precisely the spot where Vencel had first got in. He opened the door and stepped out, followed by the DHS agent. MS grabbed the agent's arm. "You keep a close eye on him." The agent nodded then was gone.

MS took out his phone and made a call. He'd need as much dirt as possible on Vencel. If the doctor changed his mind then he would have to be brought down as quickly as possible.

38

Marion Quirke was thoroughly pissed off. Since her meeting with Mike on Sunday she had worked tirelessly to get official authorization for her return to Fulton. Now it was Tuesday evening and the last two days had been an utter waste of her time.

She had lost track of the number of calls she'd made and the number of forms she'd filled out. There must be over a hundred officials who had promised to call her back but never did. No matter what she tried, the answer was always no.

Dinner that evening was at a small family run pizzeria where Marion sat staring at the menu but found herself still thinking about Fulton. The daze was broken by a stream of fast, loud and angry Italian words that spilled from the kitchen out into the little restaurant.

Marion looked up but there was nothing to see. The lone waiter looked worried and he started walking back towards raised voices until he was almost knocked over by an older man coming out through the small swing door at speed.

Still shouting and waving his arms wildly he called out to an elderly man sitting near the window. "Hey Mr. Kensington. You gotta go back into politics!"

The elderly man smiled. "What is it now Papa? What's the government done to you this time?"

"It's not the government Mr. Kensington, it's the *President*! He says he's gonna shut us down. We been selling our pizza here for over twenty years and nobody gets sick. Now the President says we got the spores and we have to stop."

Marion dropped the menu and stared at Papa. She couldn't imagine the President had any idea this place and its 'beautiful' pizza even existed.

Mr. Kensington looked equally surprised. "Hang on there Papa. Just take it easy and tell me the story one piece at a time."

By the time Papa finished his explanation Marion was long gone. Every official in D.C. would be swamped by tomorrow morning and she would never get her authorization. The city held nothing for her now and there was no point getting trapped in it. She jumped into her car and started the long drive back to Fulton.

Avoiding the roadblock she drove directly to Sherman's farm. There was a small side-road close by that went down to a stream and the car would not be found for weeks if she left it there.

It took Marion less time to reach the school than on her previous visit but from there on she was more cautious. She had been explicitly denied permission to enter the town many times in the last few days. That and the satellite phone she was carrying would ensure her a tough time if she was caught.

At Shona's house she picked up a small stone and bounced it off the bedroom window. It brought back memories of her school days. Sneaking out at night and waking her best friend exactly the same way so the two girls could smoke her father's cigarettes.

Three stones found their target before the back door opened followed by Shona's voice in a hoarse whisper "Marion! Get inside." Just like the last visit the two women blinked awkwardly in the bright light of the kitchen. "I didn't expect to see you back here again"

Marion explained. "I've been trying to get official permission to come back to Fulton ever since my last visit but they're not letting *anyone* in. Now there's all this trouble in D.C. well, that'll only make it worse. I'm sure they're convinced that terrorists are running around here too."

"You think that Chinese man was a terrorist?"

Marion shook her head. "I don't know what to think Shona. The more I try to understand all this, the less sense any of it makes."

"So why are you back?"

"For this." As she spoke she took the satellite phone out of its bag and put it on the kitchen table. "It's a thank you gift from the Washington Record and of course our mutual friend, Mike Fanning."

Shona gave a knowing look. "Ah, you've met him then."

"Yes and he's one slippery customer, but he's been more help to me than anyone else since the quarantine was imposed."

Shona pointed at the phone. "So what's it for?"

"None of us on the outside can make any contact with the town. Land lines, cell phones, internet are all down. I've tried to find out why but I'm just told it's for security. I haven't heard from Dale so I'm guessing no one on the inside can get out either."

Shona confirmed. "We haven't been able to call out since the quarantine. But we can call each other. Some folks were taking their cells up to the top of the church tower but the Guard put a stop to it. Said it was a safety risk."

Marion patted the phone. "Well they can't shut this down, it's a satellite phone." She spoke with satisfaction now that she'd managed to get the damned thing all the way to Fulton. "As used by fearless journalists the world over."

"Yes, but what's it *for* Marion?" Shona asked again. "I doubt you took the risk of coming here so we can catch up with our relatives."

"True enough. I'm afraid this phone is only for talking to Uncle Mikey. I told him what you said about the pattern of infection, how it doesn't make sense and maybe the spores aren't spreading it through the air. That got him all excited and he's been wanting a chat ever since."

Shona gasped. "You told him you were here? That you broke the quarantine?"

"Like I said, he's a slippery customer."

They spent the next fifteen minutes installing the phone and getting it working. They connected it to Shona's computer and Marion handed over the memory stick so she could access the secure blog.

They also discussed where to hide it if the Guard came to visit. Mike had said the signal was hard to trace because it went 'straight up' to the satellite, but there was no point in taking chances.

It was just after one-o'clock in the morning when they finished with the phone. Marion suggested that Shona call Mike immediately. Not because there was anything to report, just to wake him up. It worked perfectly and within thirty seconds Shona was chatting to a suitably irritated journalist.

After five minutes she put down the phone and winked at Marion "You were right, he was fast asleep!"

"Well then, my work here is done."

"Not quite." Shona spoke softly, holding Marion's arm so she did not leave the kitchen. "Mike wants you to do him a favor."

"Goddam! I've done enough favors for that man already. What does he want me to do now? Go down to Mexico and bring back some drugs for him?"

Shona didn't answer immediately but she gave Marion a curious look as she began searching through the back of her cupboards. After a lot of rummaging she produced an insulated drink cooler bag and with no further explanation went to the fridge and carefully retrieved several sealed plastic bags stored in an old baking pan.

The bags were slowly transferred to the cooler along with whatever ice Shona was able to find. When all this was done Shona presented the bag to Marion. "These are the only remaining samples from Tommy Sherman. You need to take them to Mike so they can be analyzed."

Marion had been watching the activity in silence.

"Fuck Shona! I can't believe you still have those in your fridge."

Shona wasn't concerned. "There's no real risk. The bags were properly sealed before they went in there and anyway, you could eat a pound of this stuff without doing yourself any harm. Your digestive juices would kill the fungus in five minutes and they'd kill the spores even faster."

Marion refused to take the bag. "Sorry but I'm not taking those anywhere, even if they are safe. Smuggling a phone *into* the quarantine is one thing, but if I'm caught smuggling this stuff *out* they'll put me in a little dark room somewhere and throw away the key."

Shona put the bag down. "I hadn't thought of that. I don't think Mike had either."

Marion was sure that Mike *had* thought of it. She ignored Shona's apology and stayed angry. "What the hell is Mike going to do with these anyway? He's a journalist not a scientist. Shouldn't they stay with you?"

"Not any more. Mike told me he has a contact on the intergovernmental panel, the new one that's investigating all this."

"Now I *am* impressed with that."

"His contact says the panel is only allowed to read documentation forwarded to them by their governments. They aren't allowed to do any research of their own. They don't have any test results from Fulton and they *don't* have any samples."

"But what about the samples they took from you? Surely they're being analyzed right now in some government super-lab, and the results will turn up at the panel all nicely printed on watermark bond?"

"I hope they do, but Mike isn't so sure. He said his contact *asked* for samples. She says the terms of reference make it look like the panel is a whitewash."

Marion took a leaf from Mike's book. "But can she be *sure*? Does she have any real evidence?"

"I don't know, call Mike if you want. I know I can't force you to take the samples and I'll totally understand if you don't. You've taken enough risks already."

Marion let her mind run once again through all the facts, the absence of facts, the conjecture and the wild fantasies that surrounded the Fulton outbreak. Yet again she could not make sense of it.

Ultimately though, her decision was simple. If she took the samples and got caught she would spend the rest of her life in jail. If she left the samples in Fulton then the truth about the fungus might never be known. Her town would be forever at the mercy of the politicians and the media, used by them for whatever dubious purpose suited their ends.

Taking the samples was at least another chance to act. A chance to get this mess cleaned up so life in Fulton could get back to normal.

The risk would be enormous, and perhaps she was overestimating her ability to avoid the National Guard. But after all the thinking what finally drove her action was the simple fact that Marion Quirke was desperate to do something, *anything*, to help her town.

She lifted one corner of the cooler bag and looked in. The pink flesh of Tommy's lungs was gray and desiccated from its time in the fridge. She picked up the bag and did her best to sound relaxed.

"Oh well you said I can eat a pound of this stuff so if they catch me I can always claim its jerky."

Shona walked her to the door and gave her a gentle hug. "Good luck Marion."

"Thanks Shona, I think I'm going to need it."

39

The sky outside the conference room was gray and drizzling but the weather was the last thing on Alison Grove's mind. The entire country was in turmoil and the epicenter was Washington D.C. The President had been forced to act quickly and there was no time for a planned introduction of the quarantine measures in the city.

Some hospitals were implementing their own quarantine while others were waiting for official notice. The Maryland National Guard, given no warning at all, was only just beginning the process of calling up its reserves and drawing up logistics for the quarantine. As yet there was no formal list of quarantine sites or instructions on how the quarantine was to be carried out.

People were frightened by the death of Senator Hanson. They were frightened by the thought of terrorists on the loose. Most of all they were frightened by the thought of spores, drifting through the air and spreading disease wherever they went.

Airports across the country had started ad hoc security measures to screen passengers for illness. There were, of course, no proper tests available so it fell to the regular security staff to do a job they were not trained for.

Most airports were relying solely on the passenger's appearance. At some, each passenger was being asked to cough as they passed through the metal detector at the gate. At others they were forced to walk past a heat sensitive camera. Regardless of the methods employed, no passenger with any obvious symptoms of illness was permitted to fly.

The situation at food premises was equally confused. Many of the smaller businesses had opened as usual. The owners did not see themselves as terrorist targets and they could not afford to be closed. Even outside D.C. however they stayed mostly empty as the public avoided them and went to supermarkets instead to buy frozen, shrink-wrapped or microwaveable food.

The franchise chains were flooding the politicians with a deluge of complaints. The exceptions they had negotiated for home delivery and drive-thru were not working. The phones did not ring and the lanes stayed empty. The industry calculated that in just the D.C. Metropolitan Area the ban would cost them thirty-million dollars a day.

In contrast to the food premises the nation's roads were choked beyond capacity. The number of cars had doubled as all but the poorest people abandoned public transport for fear of breathing contaminated air. There was hardly a rental car left and rates were soaring.

The morning commute was now immovable gridlock in cities all across America. Millions of extra cars sat packed on the roads, their windows shut tight and their air-conditioning switched firmly to recirculation.

Alison stood at the window and watched the endless line of cars jam the street outside. It was nine-thirty and the conference room held only her and the Chinese delegates. Even the daytime security contingent had not arrived and the floor was still guarded by the overnight shift.

Dave Walters arrived at eleven, having abandoned his taxi and walked to the building. Vencel arrived shortly after Dave, accompanied by a full set of security personnel. It was eleven-fifteen when he finally called the meeting to order. "Welcome Ladies and Gentlemen. You must all be well aware by now of the situation. It seems our work has been somewhat overtaken by events.

"In light of the news I think we can safely assume that transmission of the fungus has been through deliberate human dissemination. Clearly then, the requirement for us to determine methods of containment is void. That has become a matter for the security services.

"The requirement to find procedures for eradication has of course become far more urgent and we need to make that our top priority. I propose we spend the rest of the morning reviewing our combined expertise in airborne disease transmission."

Alison sat in silent amazement. She found it hard to believe Vencel was a scientist. It seemed that all his native curiosity had been sucked out and replaced by unquestioning acceptance of the official line. It was Dave Walters who spoke of course, saying the things that Alison was too scared to say.

"Hang on there mate. It's an enormous leap of faith to say that all transmission of this fungus has been deliberate. The outbreaks in Fulton, Australia and China make no sense in that hypothesis.

"Terrorists would have tried to hit much bigger targets. Now maybe the Fulton outbreak was a practice run for D.C., but you can't say that about the others. Also, this committee has no evidence at all of deliberate dispersal. All we have is a single pronouncement from a politician."

"Are you calling our President a liar Mr. Walters?"

"He's not *my* President Vencel, and he *is* a politician. This panel needs to be very careful about making assumptions not backed by real evidence. We can't rely on vested interests, otherwise what is the point?"

Vencel and Dave were just getting warmed-up and the argument would have continued for the rest of the day if Tai Sheng had not interrupted.

"Please, I must speak."

Until this point the Chinese delegates had endured the arguments between Vencel and Dave in silence and they had only spoken when asked. Vencel spat his words back at Tai Sheng. "Can't it wait? I really think we need to sort the matter out. The panel can't operate when some members are determined to undermine its work."

Vencel turned back to Dave, ready to launch into him but Sheng spoke again. "No. I must speak. I have…" he paused, looking for the right words, "…information of… direct consequence."

It was enough to stop Vencel. "You have information about the terrorists?"

Sheng cleared his throat. "I have received information from my government. One of our scientists has been testing the fungus. It is not a natural strain. It has an abnormal lifecycle and there is no airborne transmission."

They all spoke at once. Dave asked "How *is* it transmitted then?"

Alison said just the word "Abnormal?"

Vencel was outraged, though more at having his authority undermined than at the specifics of the news. He thundered down the table towards Sheng. "What do you mean it is not natural? Are you saying that terrorists *made* this fungus? That's preposterous!"

Sheng waited for them all to finish. "You must stop this disorder and let me speak. I will tell you what I know then you can return to your arguing."

Vencel took a breath. "Of course Dr. Tai. Please present your findings."

Sheng spoke for over an hour. He told them about Du Rui Kuang; how the disease had followed him from Fulton to Australia, and then on to China. He described what doctor Fen had discovered about the fungus. How it lived on the skin and was normally harmless, how the strain from Jouchou became highly infectious in the lungs of people with compromised immune systems. How it produced copious spores but that those spores were utterly inert.

When pressed on his description of the fungus as 'not natural' he had nothing to add. It was described that way in his documents, but they did not elaborate.

Dave and Alison had taken extensive notes during Sheng's presentation. His information answered many of their questions, but raised so many more.

Vencel sat silently the whole time but when Sheng finished he was the first to speak. "Dr. Tai, you must admit that much of this is conjecture."

"Some, yes. But I have copies of all relevant documents for the panel. My government has also authorized samples to be made available to any research laboratory with the facilities to do further analysis."

Alison was surprised at such openness from the Chinese. They must be sure the fungus was not their fault.

Vencel was clearly caught off-guard. "Your cooperation is appreciated Dr. Tai, but there is still a considerable amount we do not know and of course, you're information will need to be independently verified."

Alison wondered again about Vencel. This was the soundest evidence the panel had been presented with and the sterility of the spores made most of the current quarantine arrangements irrelevant.

Vencel continued. "Now, if we can return to—"

"Dr. Tai. Your presentation implies that transmission of this pathogen is in fact very difficult. So what use would it be to terrorists?" The interruption came from Dave Walters and yet again Alison found herself agreeing with him.

"Mr. Walters!" Vencel's exclamation echoed around the room, but the Australian would not be deflected.

"We can't just ignore this information Dr. Fodor. It has a direct bearing on our deliberations. Yes, I agree it must be verified but there is more substantiation in these documents that there has been in any of your assertions about terrorism. Now can we please hear Dr. Tai's answer?"

The Chinese delegate opened his mouth to speak but Vencel jumped in. "Dr. Tai did not mention methods of dissemination once during his presentation this morning. Furthermore Mr. Walters there is nothing in his information to preclude terrorism and I'm sure he would agree with me. Yes, Dr. Tai?"

Tai Sheng hesitated, but when there were no further outbursts from Dave or Vencel he spoke. "I agree terrorists could disperse this organism. But I also agree with Mr. Walters. It seems an unlikely choice given that it only causes problems for weakened immune systems. There are many better organisms to use for that kind of purpose."

Vencel cut in before Dave could speak. "Well none of us are psychologists Dr. Tai and it's not our job here to delve into the minds of those responsible for this outbreak." He turned his attention back to Dave. "Your question has been answered Mr. Walters so perhaps we can return to our agenda."

"No wait—"

"No, you wait Mr. Walters!" Vencel lifted half out of his seat and stared unblinkingly at Dave. "We have been presented with a lot of information this morning and it will take some time to digest. I can see no point in this panel allowing itself to be distracted by discussions which may turn out to be unnecessary once we have all read Dr. Tai's documents. It is nearly time for lunch so we will take a recess until two o'clock."

With that Vencel stood and left the room. Dave and Alison immediately began to question Sheng who handed them written copies of all his material.

After a couple of minutes Vencel returned and spoke briefly with the Chinese security agent. Then he announced that they must clear the floor for a security sweep and that the panel would recommence the next morning.

The information they had received was to be kept secure and no documentation was to leave the conference room. One of the security guards positioned himself just inside the door to make sure of it.

Vencel reminded them that despite Sheng's comments, a terrorist *had* been detained disseminating the fungus and a Senator had been killed. The panel members should now consider themselves targets.

Alison hurried to leave the room. Dave raced after her and calling out "Wait Alison! We need to discuss this with Sheng and Shi Lun." He was right, but she also had to tell Mike and the others. It might not be long before Vencel tightened the security further and she wouldn't be able to communicate with them at all.

She spoke in a rush as she walked down the hall. "I'm sorry Dave. You talk to them, bring me up to speed later." Dave tried using his smile on her but Alison was determined. She turned away from him and stepped into the elevator. An equally determined security guard stepped in with her.

When they reached the ground floor Alison strode through the lobby and out into the courtyard in front of the building, making a dash for her hotel.

The guard seemed surprised she could move so fast and had to run a little to catch up. He spoke through short puffs of breath. "In a hurry to get somewhere?"

Alison couldn't very well say *Yes, I'm rushing off to blab about this to the press*, so she just said "Yes, back to my hotel."

"What's so urgent back there?"

That was a problem. Alison had been trying to think of a reasonable excuse since she had left the conference table. She stuttered a little and said "Uh… feminine problem. Forgot to bring my, uh…" It was enough for the guard. He stopped asking questions but kept walking along with her.

At the hotel room he said "You probably don't want me in there, I'll wait outside." Alison congratulated herself on thinking of such a brilliant excuse. Alone in the room she fired up her laptop and added a hurried entry to the secure blog.

"To all. Chinese have just revealed their research to the panel. They say the fungus makes copious spores but those spores are ENTIRELY INERT. This means the fungus is NOT spread by air. Actually spread by skin contact. They have volumes of documentation but I don't know if I can get it out of the conference room. Vencel is going nuts and tightening up security. We're in recess until tomorrow."

Alison had only just pressed 'send' when she heard the guard putting his keycard into the lock. She leapt up and ran to the bathroom, closing its door behind her with an alarmingly loud bang.

"You okay in there?"

Fuck! The guard's voice was close which meant he was in the room, standing just feet away from the laptop. Alison had to get him out of the room before he noticed what was on the screen.

"Ah… sure, I'm fine! Could you just wait outside and give me some privacy for another minute or so?"

"Well alright, but I'm supposed to keep a close watch on you."

"I'm in a bathroom on the tenth floor! I can't run away and no-one's going to get in!" She was shouting now, hoping to drown out any noise from the computer.

There was no response from the guard but after what seemed like a full minute she heard the hotel door click shut. She stood in the bathroom and forced her breathing to return to normal. Then she stepped back out into the hotel room.

The guard was not there and the laptop didn't seem to have been touched. Alison closed the blog but left machine running, being careful not to move or change anything else the guard might have seen when he was in the room. When the blog was gone from the screen she called out. "Okay then. You can come back in."

The guard returned and scanned the room in his usual methodical way, but didn't seem to give the laptop any special attention. He settled in his chair and Alison stood by the window, looking out.

Had he seen the blog? There was no way to know short of asking him. Alison looked out over D.C. and did her best to think of something else.

40

Marion had returned from her second trip to Fulton at eight o'clock that morning, checking into a nondescript motel on the outskirts of D.C. She spent enough to get a room with a mini-bar which, once it was emptied, was just large enough to hold the bag with Tommy's lung samples. With that done, and bone tired from her nocturnal activities, Marion collapsed onto the bed and slept most of the day.

By early evening she was sufficiently refreshed to be hungry so she phoned for a pizza and switched on the TV. By the time her food arrived the news had begun and the TV was showing images of airports crowded with frustrated and weary passengers.

Fights had broken out at the departure gates. Some passengers were denied travel but insisted they were well and tried to force their way through. Others had been intimidated into leaving the lines, or even attacked, for nothing more than coughing or sniffling.

Beyond the airports a more general paranoia was beginning to spread and the media had no problem finding people with extreme responses. They spent the most time (nearly a full minute) interviewing Ulysses from New York.

Ulysses had sealed his entire apartment with packing tape, including the ventilation ducts. He proudly panned his web-cam around the room to show the world how well he'd done. Every available space was stacked with dive bottles, nearly two hundred in all.

Ulysses reassured the interviewer. "I went and got all the bottles they filled up before this stinkin' bug got loose. You wait, when the day comes and the streets of Manhattan are clogged with the dying, I'll be the only one breathing sweet clean air."

Ulysses was presented with the patronizing tone the news reserved for stories about 'crazy' people. Marion knew, however, there was a more subtle but equally powerful message.

By concentrating on the extremes, the news gave the impression that things were much worse than was actually the case. This in turn, provoked further overreaction from the public. Even in a town as small as Fulton, Marion often found herself calming folks down as a result of some alarmist nonsense in the local Echo.

She sat eating her pizza and wondered how long it would take before it was impossible to rent or buy a dive bottle in the U.S. She didn't particularly notice when the show moved on to its 'Behind the News' segment.

The newsreader spoke in a serious tone. "While some people are taking drastic measures to counter the disease outbreak, there are others who question whether a quarantine is necessary at all."

Marion sat bolt upright as a picture of Shona appeared on the screen. The picture was at least ten years old and showed a young looking Shona wearing a white lab coat. "Shona Price is the doctor responsible for isolating the infection in Virginia and discovering the airborne spores. Dr. Price was interviewed in the morning edition of the Washington Record today and raised some serious concerns." Marion smiled to herself. Mike Fanning had not wasted any time.

"In the article Dr. Price states that although she clearly observed spores, she is not convinced the infection is being spread by them. She cites as her evidence the pattern of the outbreak. She believes that far more people would have been infected if the spores were highly infectious.

"The doctor is backed up by Harvard mathematician Dmitri Gubin who has been using computer software to analyze the spread of the disease." Shona was replaced by an image of Dmitri as he began to speak by phone.

"I have developed specific computer models to analyze disease outbreaks. This disease just does not follow the pattern for an airborne pathogen. If it were airborne we would expect it to have spread much more quickly over a far wider area. Senator Hanson appears to be the only known case in Washington D.C. but if he was exposed to something in the air then so were many other people. Although it is terrible the way people have died, there have in fact been very few deaths from this disease. Somewhere in the range from thirty to fifty, and that includes those in China, although—"

The call was cut short as the newsreader returned. "In the studio this evening we have analyst Daniel Calder." The view widened to reveal Daniel sitting at the same table as the newsreader.

Marion cursed under her breath. She had never discovered what qualified Daniel to analyze anything, but he turned up on the news regularly and could always be relied on to push a right-wing line.

"Firstly, I think it is important to acknowledge that it was Dr. Price who first identified this disease and its spores. For that we should all be very grateful.

"Now I'm sure Dr. Price is a fine country doctor and I'm also sure Dmitri is an excellent mathematician. But the situation here has moved way beyond anything we've seen before." The phrase 'country doctor' seemed carefully chosen and Marion noticed that Daniel didn't mention Shona was, in fact, a qualified and experienced researcher.

"It is very important to remember that what we're dealing with here is a new organism, and one that is being *deliberately* released into our community. We can't expect it to behave like anything we have seen before.

"The White House has established the intergovernmental panel to look into all these matters. They are all experts and we really need to wait for their findings rather than speculating and perhaps causing unnecessary fear."

Marion wondered how Shona and Dmitri were causing unnecessary fear by saying the disease was *less* infectious.

"The American people need to realize we're dealing with a double attack here. We not only have to deal with the disease but we also have to identify and stop the terrorists who are spreading it. Quite frankly, anyone who questions the quarantine or our measures to combat the threat is assisting those terrorists."

Marion turned off the TV in disgust. Shona was doing everything she could to resolve a very difficult situation. Of all the people who had appeared on the news that evening Shona was the one with the most direct experience of the disease and the best qualifications for understanding it. Yet now she was being portrayed as some kind of ignorant hick by people with God knows what unspoken political agenda.

The TV remained off while Marion finished the pizza, still fuming over the way Shona and Fulton were being treated in their time of need. When the food was gone she plugged her computer into the phone line and connected to the secure blog.

The most recent message was Alison's hurried entry from the intergovernmental panel. Marion read it twice to make sure she understood. The news had not mentioned anything of the Chinese revelations but surely the White House knew. Wasn't the panel reporting directly to them? The Chinese had real evidence to back up Shona and Dmitri.

Maybe it had been decided that revealing the information now would undermine the search for the remaining terrorists, but was that sufficient justification to throw the country into chaos?

Marion could not think of an explanation that satisfied her, although she could find plenty that would sit comfortably on the internet conspiracy pages. She selected the 'chat' option and entered: **"Marion here. Anyone home?"** There was no response so she began to check the regular news sites, hoping to find a less biased presentation than she'd seen on the TV. After a few minutes she was interrupted by a beep and a reply from her favorite person.

"Mike here."

"Mike, what's going on? The news tried to make Shona look stupid. Didn't mention the Chinese info from the panel."

"Yes. The DHS and their buddies are going with the terrorist/ spores angle and won't be put off. The President has to act on the

info he's given, and that's what they're feeding him. Mind you –
someone did kill the Senator. I don't think I'd like them coming
after me, even if this thing isn't airborne."

Marion was irritated by the last comment.

"Now you sound just like the TV. Let's all panic before we know
what's really going on."

"So how was the Senator infected then? You think they walked
up and injected it into his veins? And what about the people in
Fulton. Did terrorists pick them out one-by-one and rub some fungus on their faces?"

She was even more irritated by that.

"I don't know Mike, but neither do you. None of this makes
sense until we know the truth about the fungus."

"Agreed."

"Okay, so why doesn't the Record publish what it knows about
the panel and the Chinese?"

"We'd love to but they'd know we had a spy. There's only 5 members. It wouldn't be the Chinese and it wouldn't be the Australian
or Vencel. That leaves Alison. She's too vulnerable so we'll have to
keep quiet for now."

Marion tried to think of a way out.

"What if you just said it was the Chinese?"

"Maybe, but they'd deny it and then *they* would know we had
a spy. Don't know what their motivation is. They might rat on Alison
themselves."

Marion wasn't used to the kind of maneuvering that went on in
Washington.

"Surely the panel is trying to get to the truth. Won't they confirm
the Chinese results?"

"Don't think it's going to happen. Panel now reviewing general
info about fungi. Vencel is playing along with the security guys and
won't allow open discussion."

"So what do we do?"

There was a long pause from Mike.

"We need independent verification about the spores. That they aren't viable. Did you get the samples from Shona?"

"Yes. I have them with me now."

"Good. Alison is arranging a contact for you in Atlanta - to do the tests."

Marion had assumed the samples would go directly to Mike or to some reliable laboratory arranged by the Record. That would make her one of his 'sources' and hopefully she'd be protected at least a little by that. But now it seemed she was supposed to take the damned things clear across the continent and deliver them to some total stranger. It had been a big enough risk to smuggle them out of Fulton.

The consequences of being caught forced their way back into her mind. She would be labeled a terrorist for sure. Would she even get a trial or would she just disappear? The thought of that made her angry. Terrorism was being used too often to justify dubious actions by the government and its security forces even under a 'liberal' president.

With the anger came the realization that if she did nothing, if she allowed the fear to control her, then those people would win. She thought again about Shona and Fulton and how the whole damned mess could probably be sorted in a few days if everyone just went after the truth and instead of pushing their own self-interested agendas.

Marion realized she was still in a conversation with Mike when the laptop beeped at her.

"Marion, are you still there?"

"Yes. Lost in thought for a moment."

"Will you take the samples to Atlanta?"

"Yes. But God help me Mike, if I go down, I'm taking you with me."

There was no reply to that but an hour later a message arrived from Alison. It was the address of a laboratory the CDC had used for contract work. The head of the laboratory was a friend and was qualified to investigate the fungus and the spores. Once they had the samples then confirmation of the Chinese data would only take about a day.

There was no reason now for Marion to stay in D.C. She had slept well and wasn't tired. It took her only a few minutes to get fresh ice from a machine in the parking lot and carefully re-pack the samples. A few minutes more and she had checked out of the hotel.

It was just after nine-o'clock when Marion headed off on the long drive to Atlanta, wondering if she would ever get a regular night's sleep again.

41

Alison arrived at the Intergovernmental Panel on Thursday morning with her laptop tucked firmly under her arm. Since yesterday's incident with the guard it just didn't feel safe to let it out of her sight.

Dave was already sitting at the conference table, reading Sheng's papers. He looked up and smiled at Alison. "Hey there! You need to read this stuff, it's dynamite. They're going to email it to me, just in case old Vencel the Destroyer doesn't allow us to take the documents away at all."

Alison sat down at the conference table and wrote her private and work email addresses on a slip of paper, along with Mike Fanning's and a special one that the Gorilla had given them. She was going to give the paper to Dave, but paused. What if he thought this was about more than just the fungus? It would be better to give the paper to Sheng or Shi Lun some time when the security guards weren't looking.

At precisely nine o'clock Vencel strode into the room. He began to speak before he'd even sat down. "In view of the information we received yesterday, and also in view of the excitement this has caused amongst the panel…" He paused to look pointedly at Dave. "… I have deemed it prudent to consult again with the Department of Homeland Security regarding terrorist dissemination of the disease organism.

"I have also reviewed with them the information presented yesterday by the Chinese delegates to this panel. They agree with me that this is interesting despite its speculative nature."

Alison felt a surge of anger. The information was beyond interesting and far more solid than speculation. For God's sake, the Chinese had hard data about the infection, obtained from laboratory testing on actual samples.

Vencel continued. "It is important to remember that this data is limited in its scope, being restricted to China only. The panel must review it in the light of all the evidence. Hopefully we can, with some discussion, extract the material that is pertinent. I will summarize now the most glaring omissions.

"Firstly, the Chinese contention that this organism is not a natural strain must be validated by independent parties before it can be accepted. This is particularly the case given that the Chinese delegates can not elaborate on this claim."

Alison was still angry and she began to take notes of what she considered the glaring omissions in Vencel's reasoning. No 1. Under the terms of reference this panel is not permitted to undertake its own research. So where will this independent validation come from?

"Even a small government would have the facilities to engineer an organism of this nature and there are many rogue states who would willingly supply terrorist organizations."

Alison added No 2. You just pointed out we don't know what the Chinese mean by 'not natural' but now you're calling it 'engineered.'

"Most importantly, there is no reference in the Chinese information to terrorist dissemination of the disease organism. A fact which is now established."

No.3. It has not been established that the outbreaks in China, Fulton or Australia are due to deliberate, never mind terrorist release. Furthermore, this panel has not seen any evidence that the death of Senator Hanson was due to deliberate release either. We are expected to rely solely on the assertions of the DHS who have provided this panel with no information at all.

"So, to summarize. The Chinese submission does nothing to disprove that this lethal organism is being released by terrorist agents and it does not contain any actual evidence on the origin of the organism. The panel must be cautious not to be trapped into invalid conclusions in this matter."

No 4. Vencel Fodor is highly selective and is ignoring competing hypotheses that are equally valid as his own, but fail to support his predetermined view.

Alison said nothing when Vencel stopped and again it was Dave who spoke. "Given that we now know the airborne spores of this fungus are inert, do Homeland Security see any purpose in continuing the quarantine around Fulton and the majority of the emergency measures introduced by your President?"

Vencel sighed and gave Dave the kind of look that schoolteachers reserve for their most troublesome students. "Mister Walters. The method of transmission is yet to be confirmed by independent research. That it may not be airborne is good news, but people are still dying. Need I also remind you that the organism has appeared in our capital city, has already killed a US Senator and that terrorist individuals have been detained in connection with that death.

"The method of transmission does not change the need for quarantine or relax the requirement for vigilance on the part of the US government."

Alison had thought her list was finished, but now she added: No 5. Airborne transmission was the primary justification for the quarantine. If it is not airborne then many of the President's emergency measures are unnecessary.

Vencel was not finished however. "I would remind you also Mr. Walters that this panel is an advisory body only. It is our purpose to review the information at hand and make recommendations to our respective governments. We have no authority at all to tell our governments what to do and we certainly do not have the authority to tell the governments of other panel members what to do."

Dave retaliated. "Surely though our recommendations must take into account these solid laboratory results showing the spores are not viable and therefore are no threat. Some kind of quarantine may still be required but its nature would be quite different to the current one."

There was another frustrated sigh from Vencel. "Mr. Walters our recommendations will take into account the Chinese results, but they will also take into account everything else presented to this panel and not just the data from your new found friends. I take it that will satisfy you?"

But Dave wasn't satisfied. "What about the death of the Senator? Will the panel be seeing any actual evidence of the terrorist attack? The outbreaks in China and particularly in Australia make no sense in the terrorist model.

"Those outbreaks clearly followed the man Du, who is not in any way a terrorist. Irrespective of how he got infected he has been spreading the disease independently of any intentional attack. If, as you put it, we're going to avoid being trapped into invalid conclusions then we need to know as much as possible about this."

Alison was again relieved to hear Dave say what she was thinking. Vencel on the other hand was furious and he bellowed at Dave. "Mr. Walters. The identity of the terrorists is a matter of national security and is part of an ongoing operation to detain those terrorists. If you imagine that I, or anyone else, will reveal such information to this panel then you are very much mistaken."

He paused to catch his breath and recover from his indignation. When he spoke again his voice was quieter but no less angry. "If you won't take my word for it however I can show you this."

He picked up his briefcase from the floor and retrieved a plastic file folder which he slid across the table toward Dave. "This is a highly sensitive document and I must stress that its contents may not be revealed outside of this room. Each panel member will review it briefly then pass it on until it is returned to me."

Dave wasn't listening. He'd already opened the document and was poring over it. Alison strained to read it from a across the table but it was too far away.

After a few moments of silence Sheng spoke up. "Please, for the rest of us, what is it?"

"It is the initial medical report on Senator Hanson. It shows he had the fungal infection but it also shows he had a severely depressed immune response. At his death the Senator's blood had a concentration of immune suppressing drugs well in excess of a therapeutic dose.

"The Senator was not prescribed any such medication nor was he reported to be taking any. The only reasonable explanation for the presence of the drugs is deliberate and covert exposure."

Alison agreed with Vencel this time. If the Senator had been given immunosuppressants without his knowledge then someone was very determined to kill him. It certainly supported the terrorist theory.

A suppressed immune system also made the Senator's death consistent with the deaths in Fulton and China. The catch for Vencel was that it also suggested the Chinese were right and the fungus was not particularly dangerous to the general population.

She found herself hoping that Dave would raise this point but it was Sheng who spoke again. "This is very sophisticated for terrorists. Doesn't it suggest a more, uh, scientific approach?"

"Regardless of what it suggests to you Dr. Tai, we have the terrorists in custody. There is no doubt in my mind. I am only sharing this document to demonstrate to our skeptical friend here that the danger is very real and not some fantasy on my part."

Sheng did not reply and Dave was still engrossed in the medical report. Vencel seized the opportunity. "It seems then that the matter of terrorist dispersal has been established beyond reasonable doubt. I suggest therefore it is time for us to move on."

The remainder of the session was spent reviewing scientific papers Vencel had obtained from various journals. He insisted on presenting them 'to ensure the panel had sufficient background understanding.'

The Chinese delegates were clearly not happy but they did nothing to stop him, choosing instead to spend much of their time in conversation with their own security man. As always, Alison said nothing and even Dave stayed quiet after he finished reading about Senator Hanson.

So it was that the Intergovernmental Biosecurity Emergency Investigative Panel gave no further consideration to the Chinese submission or its implications.

42

It was nearly midday as Marion walked into the lobby of a bland industrial building on the outskirts of Atlanta with a small plastic cooler bag under one arm. She had been forced to stop and rest several times during the night when her eyes began to close against her will. Now that the drive was over she felt that same heavy sensation return. She stopped for a moment and shook her head. This was no time for sleep.

The lobby was empty except for a low table and two worn office chairs. A battered phone sat on the table next to a sign that read "Lift handset and dial extension." Beneath this was a printed list of company names and numbers. All but one had been crossed out and replaced with new, hand written entries.

Marion found 'Hunter Diagnostic - 817' scrawled at the bottom of the page in almost illegible handwriting. She had lifted the handset to dial when a door opened at one end of the lobby and a voice said "Looking for someone?"

It was a young man in a light gray lab coat. She guessed it was originally a white lab-coat but years of service had left it worn and drab. She replied "Yes, I'm looking for Sanjay Ramalingam, of Hunter Diagnostic."

The young man smiled. "That's my boss! Who shall I say is calling?"

Marion had been so focused on getting to Atlanta she hadn't given any thought to what story she would tell at the lab. "Uh, tell him it's his aunt, from Washington D.C."

The young man gave her a quizzical look.

Damn! That was a stupid thing to say. It was unlikely she looked much like Sanjay's aunt. "Well, friend of the family really, not his actual aunt."

The look remained and the young man didn't move. As a cop Marion knew it was best to say as little as possible. Elaborating a lie almost always made it look less plausible. But she was tired and not thinking straight. "I knew his parents when he was little." The young man's smile returned but it was not so convincing this time. He said "Wait here" and was gone.

She had always thought the local Fulton criminals were kinda slow, their stories and excuses were so inept. Now here she was doing the same thing. It had been all too easy and she would have to be more careful from now on. Hopefully Sanjay would play along and the young man would be convinced.

Marion sat on one of the chairs and allowed her eyes to close. It took her only a moment to fall asleep, but it took only another moment for her head to fall forward and wake her up again with a start.

When her eyes opened they were looking directly at a red and yellow poster taped to the wall inside the main doors. It was issued by Homeland Security and warned her that terrorist activity could occur anywhere. She was to report suspicious activity immediately.

After five minutes alone in the lobby Marion's weary mind had combined the lie about being Sanjay's aunt, the message on the poster and the young mans' look into a vivid fantasy of arrest and detention. She had no problem imagining the squealing tires, flashing lights, guns and megaphones as Homeland Security agents surrounded the building to demand she give herself up.

A deep voice startled her out of the daydream.

"Marion?"

A distinguished looking Indian man stood in front of her, at least as old as herself, if not older. He wore a lab coat like the young man's but his was a bright white that matched the color of his hair.

The man leaned forward and shook Marion's hand. When he spoke again it was with a heavy Indian accent. "I am sorry for the delay; I was supervising some delicate work. Alison said I would have a visitor, but I did not expect my long lost Aunt!" His face broke into a smile at this last comment.

The amusement was a relief to Marion, but she was also disturbed that he wasn't better informed. She asked carefully "What did Alison tell you?"

"She had a favor to ask and someone was coming to see me." He paused. "You know, that's quite unusual for Alison. She is usually most insistent about details."

Marion's heart sank and she silently cursed Alison. She had been expecting to find a co-conspirator, ready to grab the samples and hurry them away to somewhere secure. But this man was simply a friend, maybe only a colleague, expecting to do a simple favor. Now Marion would have to explain the situation and take the risk that Sanjay might refuse to get involved or worse, might even turn her over to the DHS.

She took a deep breath, followed by a long sigh that filled the lobby. She was acutely aware of that red and yellow poster and her voice echoing in the empty space. "It may be more of a favor than you are willing to do. I can't explain it here. Where can we meet later?"

Sanjay remained amused. "Please Aunt Marion, you must let me finish." He put his hand into the pocket of his lab coat and took out a memory stick. "You see, after Alison spoke to me this arrived. So I know why you are here and I am happy to help. Now please, where are the samples?"

So, Alison had done more than just phone Sanjay after all. But she still did not know why this man would willingly take this risk.

"Why would you do this Sanjay. Do you understand the consequences?"

"Please! Time is important here."

"Maybe so, but I need to know I can trust you."

"If I am not to be trusted then it is too late already, but if I do answer will you give me the samples?"

"Yes."

"Quickly then. Your revolution was a long time ago, but in India we fought the British for our independence until nineteen forty-seven. We too remember how precious our freedom is and how it is worth fighting for.

"That is why I will take the risk. Freedom is always worth fighting for and the best weapon we have is the truth. Alison has told me what is happening to her and to your town. They are spreading lies about this fungus and people are suffering. So we must fight them with the truth. We must prove that they are lying so everyone will know. Now please, you must give me the samples."

Marion picked up the cooler bag and placed it on the table next to the phone.

"You have the samples in that?"

Marion nodded.

"Oh goodness no, let me look, quickly." He pulled the bag across the table and opened the lid. Inside the samples were still sealed in their plastic bags which were floating in a mixture of cold water and partly melted ice cubes.

"They've been like that the whole time?"

"Well, the ice got kinda melted on the drive down."

"You let them get warm?"

"It was a long drive and this is what Shona gave me. I couldn't exactly pop into the local store and ask for special equipment to carry infectious samples. Besides, the water's still cold and so the samples never got warm. The water never got into the bags either." Marion realized she was being more defensive than was necessary, but it had been a long trip in difficult circumstances and she damned well deserved a break.

Sanjay returned to a calmer voice. "Well then, that will have to do. I just hope it is good enough. If they got warm then a million other fungi and bacteria and goodness knows what would be growing in there as well."

He carefully picked up the cooler. "Do you want to see the lab?"

"Thanks but no. I need to sleep now."

"Well, this is goodbye then Aunt Marion. I will let you know as soon as I find anything." With that he tapped at the memory stick in his pocket.

"Goodbye Sanjay, and please stop calling me Aunt Marion. It makes me feel old."

He smiled as he turned and walked away to the lab. "No problem Marion. I will be in touch."

There was nothing for Marion to do now except find a hotel and sleep. She walked out towards her car, taking one last look at the Homeland Security poster on the way. As a cop of course she should be reporting her own suspicious activity.

43

Alison arrived late to the panel the next morning, having slept in for the first time in many years. She put it down to the stress of the last few days. It was the sort of thing that normally did not happen to her.

Having rushed through her morning routine Alison managed to take her seat at the conference table only ten minutes after the official start time. It was a relief to see that she was not the last to arrive; Dave's chair was still empty.

Sheng and Shi Lun sat silently at the far end of the table and did not seem to notice her. Their security man was not with them but there were more of the regular security men than usual. Vencel was in his usual place at the other end of the table from the Chinese.

He spoke as Alison sat down and tried to organize herself quickly. "Welcome back Miss Grove. I suppose we can start now." This only made Alison feel flustered and she knocked some of her papers onto the floor.

Vencel ignored her discomfort. "Today we are continuing with our review of the literature. I am sure you all understand this review is vital to our confidence that the conclusions finally reached by this panel will be robust.

"I hope we have put the dramas of yesterday behind us. Despite the wishes of *some* people to disrupt the work of this panel there is much for us to still do." Vencel stared pointedly at Dave's empty chair then at the Chinese delegates.

He distributed copies of yet another scientific paper then said as an afterthought. "Oh yes, one other piece of administrative detail. Dr. Dave Walters will no longer be joining in our discussions. Now, onto this paper which discusses the effect of host diet on pulmonary fungal growth in both pig and mouse human-analogue studies."

Alison felt a stab of pain in her abdomen. "What was that?"

Vencel looked up at her. "You have a question Miss Grove?"

"Did you say Dave has gone?"

"Yes."

"But why? He said nothing to me about this."

Vencel abandoned his reading to look at Alison. "Dr. Walters was not working out. He refused to limit his discussions to the terms of reference and was constantly disruptive. We have important work to do here Miss Grove and Dr. Walters was hindering that work. After detailed discussions between the State Department, the Australian government and myself, it was decided that he would return to Australia."

Alison tried to grasp the thoughts and feelings that raced through her head. Dave had been the only one with the courage to ask the *right* questions. Now he had been removed specifically for asking those questions.

She knew too that there was more to her sense of loss than just the work of the panel. She was suddenly embarrassed at speaking out in front of the group, even though she had stopped respecting Vencel's authority a long time ago.

Alison tried to speak again but could only manage "But—"

"I know you liked him Miss Grove, but the work of this panel is far too important to be disrupted by one man's agenda."

It's clear that the work of the panel is entirely one man's agenda. Alison did not dare let the though escape from her mouth and she kept it shut for the rest of session.

She read the scientific papers but retained nothing as she struggled to make sense of her inner world. It did not seem to bother Vencel at all that she was not contributing.

After the lunch break Sheng and Shi Lun did not return. Alison wondered how Vencel had convinced the Chinese to withdraw from the panel, but he walked into the room looking anxious with several security men close behind, stone-faced as usual.

Vencel spoke directly to Alison, his usual arrogance now tempered with a hint of uncertainty. "Miss Grove, it would seem that our Chinese friends have decided not to return this afternoon. Given there are now only two of us qualified to do the technical work I suggest we split the review of the scientific papers between us."

Alison had no doubt that the Chinese left because their contribution had been so determinedly quashed by Vencel. She wondered if they saw him as part of an American cover-up, then realized that she saw him that way too.

Vencel had been desperate to control the panel since its first day and now, thanks to that folly, it had almost completely disintegrated.

Alison desperately wanted to get away from that disintegration. She knew it was silly, but she felt that she might fall apart with it. When she finally spoke her voice was quiet. "Is there any point in us continuing? We're hardly intergovernmental any more. This work could now be carried out by regular government agencies."

Vencel looked surprised. "Of course we must continue. *Our* government still needs to understand this fungus and we were chosen to do that job." He paused then asked her "Miss Grove, do you wish to leave this panel?"

Alison ached to scream at Vencel *Yes! Yes! Yes! Of course I want to leave this stupid panel and its farcical review of scientific papers. Of course I want to leave this ugly room in this ugly building with its ugly security men. Of course I want to leave and go back to my nice safe job where I never have to feel scared or anxious or even uncertain, and especially of course I want to leave and never have to see your face or hear your voice or be bossed around by you ever again!*

Thanks to years of practice she was able to let the volcano erupt with only the slightest trace of emotion crossing her face. When she didn't talk Vencel spoke for her. "Well then. We should continue as I suggested." He threw a stack of papers onto the table in front of Alison and left the room.

44

With less than a week until the Presidential election the politicians were at the point now where they would say anything to cast doubt on their opponents. Rumors became accusations, accusations were met with denials and denials spawned further rumors and accusations. None of it was any help to voters.

Worse still, the remaining terrorists had not been caught and the fear of attacks beyond Washington D.C. grew stronger every day. Every accident, every illness, every cough or sniffle was suspicious. The news would report them all and add the phrase "authorities are yet to determine if this incident is the result of terrorist activity."

Air travel had gone from chaotic to almost nonexistent as travelers decided flying was just too dangerous, too difficult or both. Other modes of public transport were just as empty and cities across the US experienced permanent rush hour conditions.

The emergency measures had been in place for only three days but it was enough time for people to forget their initial shock and get frustrated. The President's critics were more than happy to fuel any feelings of discontent. He was at fault, of course, for allowing the disease to get loose and he was at fault for not catching the terrorists. But he was also at fault for the emergency measures and the quarantine that was causing so much chaos. Decent, honest Americans should not have to tolerate such disruption.

Spontaneous protests had erupted as people found themselves stuck in immovable traffic or denied access to buildings or other public spaces.

Joe was watching the latest protests on TV when Kathleen walked into the room. He spoke without looking up. "You gotta look at this honey. I can't believe these people are so selfish; out there protesting 'cos they can't get a flight or they gotta spend a couple of extra hours in their cars. Hell, I'm living in D.C. and getting the worst of it but I'm sure not whining about it and blaming the President! It's a goddamned national emergency and I don't care if you voted for the guy or not, you gotta stand behind him at a—"

"Joe!"

He turned to look at his wife, who was still standing in the doorway.

"What is it honey?"

"The boys are sick."

Joe leapt from his chair and ran up the stairs to the twin's room. He found them both asleep but even from the doorway he could hear an unmistakable wheezing as they breathed. He turned and walked back toward the stairs, meeting Kathleen at the top.

"Call an ambulance, now!"

Kathleen nodded and went into their bedroom for the phone. Joe rushed back to the living room and shut the door behind him. He grabbed his cell phone from the floor by his chair and searched through its list of numbers. The phone rang for nearly a minute before he was rewarded with a sleepy voice.

"Hello Joe?"

"Marion, where are you?"

"I'm in bed Joe. It's late and I haven't had much sleep the last few days. Can I call you back in the morning?"

Joe did his best to keep his voice down, but it was hard not to shout. "The twins are sick and we need your help."

There was a long silence before Marion answered. "You need a doctor Joe. You hang up and call one right now."

"Ambulance is on its way, but if those boys have the spores then don't you know someone who can help?"

There was another silence. "Why do you think they have the spores Joe?"

"Because… well I don't know if it's spores or not. But you've been in our house and you're *from* Fulton." Joe heard noise from the phone that sounded like a shout but was too muffled to hear clearly. "Hello? You there Marion?"

"I'm here Joe. You make sure you tell the paramedics when the ambulance arrives."

"Well of course I will! But don't you know someone who can help? There must be someone at the DHS who knows how to cure this thing."

"I'm not at the DHS Joe, and even if I call them they won't tell me any more than they'd tell you. I tried to get into Fulton for days, remember? They were the least helpful of anyone."

"You just spent two weeks at DHS. You must know someone there."

"It was *training* Joe. That office has nothing to do with what's happening in Fulton."

"But you must know *someone*."

Marion sighed loud enough for Joe to hear. "Okay Joe. I know some medical people. I'll get their advice and you can hand it on to your doctor."

"Why can't you just give me a number, so my doctor can talk to 'em direct?"

"Because I don't want you or Kathleen or the boys to get mixed up in what I'm doing, it's much safer for you all if you stay out of it."

"Stay out of it? Fuck Marion! You make my boys sick and then you tell me to stay out of it? You're *family* Marion. You know more about this than anyone else and you *have* to help me."

"For God's sake Joe! I'll do everything I can, but I'm neck deep in a pile of shit myself and I don't have any magic answers for you."

The wail of a siren broke into the conversation and Joe shouted into his phone. "Fuck you Marion Quirke!" He threw the phone at the wall and stormed out to meet the ambulance.

45

Mike Fanning joined the secure blog at five to nine on Saturday night. He was in his office at the Record and eager to get the lab results so he would have something to publish. By five minutes past nine all the members of his little conspiracy were online.

Sanjay began the conversation:

"I have completed my tests. The samples were degraded after their travels but I can confirm the Chinese results."

Mike replied immediately: **"Sanjay, can you be specific please. Can you list exactly what it is you are confirming."** The reply was slow in coming but as detailed as Mike could have wished for.

"1 - The samples contain colonies of a fungus. 2 – The surface of the fungus displays many fruiting bodies. 3 – The fruiting bodies are clearly releasing spores. 4 – Even with my degraded samples I was able to observe significant densities of airborne spores released by stimulated fruiting bodies. 5 - The spores released into the air and spores collected directly from the fruiting bodies are all sterile. I was unable to germinate any spores."

"So in your opinion could this fungus be transmitted by air?"

Again there was a pause. **"The spores are transmitted by air but they are not viable so the infection itself cannot be transmitted by air. It is most likely transmitted by direct contact and transfer of the mycelium."**

"The what?"

"The body of the fungus. If transferred to a new location that is suitable then it will just continue to grow."

"So an infected person has to *touch* me before I get infected?"

"That would be the most likely transmission. Or maybe if you touched a surface that an infected person touched. If it was something like a damp towel or a kitchen sponge then the fungus could live a long time. On dry surfaces it would die quite rapidly."

"How rapidly?"

"Minutes to hours. I have not done those tests."

The next question came from Shona. "Sanjay. If this fungus is transmitted by touch and not by spores, how do you think it ends up in peoples lungs?"

"I do not know. Clearly the fungus thrives in the lungs. There would need to be some transfer path from the skin to there. Perhaps the fungus can live in nasal mucus also. Perhaps there could be transfer via a handkerchief. Also, many people pick their noses. I suspect transfer from skin to lungs is quite likely in most individuals. The devastating lung infection however is very unlikely. But this is speculation. More research is required."

Shona replied. "I agree with that. It only seems to be compromised individuals who get the lung infection. Even through direct contact everyone in Fulton has been exposed by now, but the infection rate is surprisingly low."

Mike did not want the discussion to get sidetracked into technical details. The public, and his editor, would not be interested in those. He fired off his next question. "Okay it's not airborne. Sanjay, what do you think the Chinese mean when they say this thing is not natural?"

The reply from Sanjay was disappointing. "I do not know. From what Alison tells us they have not elaborated and the phrase could mean any number of things. It could even be a simple mistake in translation. They have compared this new strain with an old one they have in their laboratory. Perhaps when they say 'not natural' they only mean it's not the old one."

"But could you guess at what they mean? Is it possible this thing is genetically engineered?"

Mike was disappointed by Sanjay again. **"I would need to sequence the DNA and that would take a week at least in my laboratory. Then I would need the original strain for comparison. You are speculating on very slight evidence Mike."**

Mike was grasping now. **"So the Chinese could be talking about an engineered organism?"**

"Could be. But even if we prove the fungus has been engineered we wouldn't know *why*. You'd have to ask whoever created it."

It was Marion's turn to keep the discussion moving. **"We're getting sidetracked here. Sanjay, do you have any more results?"**

"No."

"Okay. We know the fungus isn't airborne. We know the quarantine of Fulton is unnecessary and folks just need to wash their hands. So what are we going to *do* about it?"

Mike replied. **"It's bigger than just Fulton. Most of the emergency measures in D.C. aren't needed either. Planes and buses and trains are much safer that we've been told and all this gridlock can just go away.**

"The President has put the country into panic for nothing. We have to publish everything we have. We can get ourselves a whole special section in the paper. Compare our stuff with what's been made public. We can ask some serious questions about who it is that's pushing the whole spores thing and what they have to gain."

Alison jumped on this. **"No! Just the FACTS Mike. It is clear this situation has been manipulated. But speculation about motives or espionage or genetic engineering only distracts people from the truth. Anything we can't prove can be questioned – and that means our story can be attacked. Also, if we publish so close to the election and we're not rock solid then we look just like everyone else. Like we're trying to influence the election rather than tell the truth. We MUST stick to JUST the facts and let people draw their own conclusions."**

If Mike stuck to the facts then he would barely have a single column, never mind a special section and of course, publishing before the election would make the story far more marketable. He countered Alison.

"You need to consider this carefully. After all, it is a fact that the Chinese said what they did, even if *we* can't confirm some of it. That information gives readers a context – a wider picture context for making up their minds. It also puts pressure on those in power to justify their actions. We may be wrong, but at least we'll force them to offer a better explanation than they have so far. As for the election, it's our *duty* to publish now, so the public knows what's going on before they vote."

Shona joined the argument. "Speculation does NOT provide a sound context and it's no basis for voting. You can't reach a valid conclusion based on false premises. We might as well publish fiction and ask people to choose based on which character they like the most. We have enough good evidence to show the fungus isn't airborne. We should stick to that."

Sanjay agreed. "Shona's right. The media report rumors and gossip because they can't be proved wrong and they are more exciting. There is far more to this issue than just selling newspapers. If we put spin on our story then we are no better than the people we are seeking to expose. We must stick to the truth. Then it will be obvious who the liars are."

Mike cursed them all beneath his breath. Then realizing they couldn't hear him anyway he cursed them again out loud. These people were typical of do-gooders everywhere. Well-meaning but utterly naïve about how the world actually worked.

He could publish any number of indisputable truths but if they weren't marketed properly they would be useless. People had to be grabbed emotionally if they were to pay any attention at all and Mike knew from years of experience that saying "this is true" just wouldn't do it.

If he published a calm dissertation of facts it would be swamped in five minutes by a deluge of histrionic misrepresentation and attacks from the very people they were trying to expose.

To get the story across Mike would publish as much speculation as he could squeeze from the dry facts. He would ask the leading questions and create doubt. He would suggest connections and ulterior motives.

Then he would portray his small group as noble and upright citizens. The little guys who stumbled on the truth and fought to get it heard for the sake of everyone.

They would be heroes and it would make their critics look like monsters. It would be a *hook* and most importantly it would get plenty of TV coverage. Hell, the last part was mostly true anyway. They really were the little guys who stumbled on the truth!

So marketing the story was going to be easy. Getting this group to agree to it would be much tougher. They couldn't stop him from writing what he liked of course, and maybe he would just have to do that. He knew though that if he lost their trust then he would never get anything useful from them again. He was wondering what to say when Marion weighed in.

"We've taken too many risks to chicken out now. We have to get our story out there and Mike's the only one who can do it.

"If he has to spice it up a bit well so what? There's got to be a proper investigation into all this and that's when the truth will come out.

"We're all going to end up in exactly the same pile of shit whether we publish a lot or a little. We've still all *done* what we've done.

"So Mike you publish everything you've got and let's take those assholes down."

Unfortunately Marion's comment didn't sway the others and the debate continued late into the evening. The group certainly knew some truths about the Fulton outbreak that were hidden from the rest of the world. But they were no better informed than anyone else about the wider situation.

Was the release in D.C. really due to a terrorist attack? What were the true motivations of the White House and the DHS and how would either react when the group published? Was the fungus really artificial? Was it really intended for espionage? Who had made it? How big was the risk they were each taking? What were the legal implications of their actions? Would they be treated as terrorists or as regular criminals?

By midnight they were all tired and had not come to any resolution. It was Sanjay who suggested they should call a halt and try again the next day. The others willingly agreed and a second meeting was scheduled for eleven on Sunday morning.

46

Alison sat at the small desk in her hotel room and signed off from the blog. It was so frustrating that the group could not decide how to present their information. They all knew it was important and had to be released.

The regular security guard was sitting at the window, watching the weather and the interminable gridlock. A new directive had been issued and he was now required to be within sight of Alison at all times, except when she was sleeping or in the bathroom.

Alison had turned her laptop so the guard could not see its screen but he hadn't given her more than a glance all evening.

Alison was surprised they let her use the laptop at all. One of the guards had asked what it was for and she'd said "Research. I need to check the database at work." That must have been good enough because since then they had never seemed interested in the computer again.

Alison went to bed that night with her mind churning from the discussion on the blog. The toughest question for her was 'what is the right thing to do?' Alison always tried to do the right thing even though sometimes it would distress the people around her. She didn't enjoy that, but the right thing was, well… right. It just had to be done.

She lay restlessly in her bed and reviewed the situation over and over again. Each point was considered carefully and weighed against the others.

The facts were weighed against the speculations. The personal risks were weighed against the greater good.

None of it helped. What she needed was more information, not more thinking. Eventually she drifted off into fitful, unsatisfying sleep.

It was no surprise then for Alison to realize she was awake again at three-forty on Sunday morning. It was a surprise to see the light was on and her security guard standing by the door. He was talking on his phone and didn't seem to notice she had woken.

Still groggy and confused from sleep she was about to speak when there was a loud knock. It was the kind of knock only used by those in authority, those who know they don't actually have to knock and they're going to come in anyway. The guard opened the door and walked out of the room, leaving Alison staring out into the empty hotel hallway.

She sat up in bed as three men walked into the room. Dressed in standard black suits they could have been a replacement security detail except for the way they moved. Feeling suddenly vulnerable Alison leapt from the bed, keeping it between her and the men.

The blanket was dragged part way with her but then it fell to the floor. Alison reached down and grabbed it up, pulling it around her as quickly as possible. She tried to speak but her throat was dry and she could only produce an inarticulate squawk.

The first man walked directly to Alison and stood in front of her with his arms folded. She stood and stared back at him, still not fully awake and feeling weak and disoriented after the leap from the bed.

The man was large and solidly built. He looked down at Alison from an expressionless face and she was in no doubt that she would not be permitted to leave her spot.

The second man went directly to Alison's laptop, which was on a small table beside the bed. In a few seconds it was scooped up by his gloved hands and sealed in a heavy plastic bag.

While this was happening the third man was searching the room for – what? Alison didn't know but he was being very thorough. He looked in all the drawers and cupboards, lifting up any loose objects, checking underneath and inside them. He disappeared into the bathroom just as the laptop man finished bagging the power supply and carrying case.

The third man returned from the bathroom with another evidence bag. Alison saw her toothbrush, a bottle of deodorant and a pair of panties that had been drying in the shower. There were other items in the bag but the man was moving too fast for her to make them out. His last act was to throw her gown onto the bed as he walked out the door with laptop man close behind him.

Through all this the big man had not moved and had not taken his eyes off Alison. Now he motioned to the gown. "Put it on." They were the first words spoken in the room since Alison had woken up.

It was barely two minutes after the first intrusion, but it was enough time for Alison's fear to be replaced with anger. Who were these men invading her privacy in the middle of the night with no warning, no explanation and certainly no warrant?

Losing the laptop didn't bother her nearly as much as seeing the bag from the bathroom with her personal items. What did they want with those?

Alison was steady on her feet now and feeling a confidence she didn't usually possess. The worst had happened, her fears had come true. There was no point being anxious now, it was time for self-preservation.

She looked the big man directly in the eye. "What if I don't put the robe on? What if I demand my civil rights instead? What if I demand to see a search warrant or call my lawyer? What if I run out into the hallway screaming and say you tried to rape me?"

Her voice got louder with each sentence and it felt good, really good, to be standing up for herself. Alison was so caught up the new emotion that she missed what happened next. All she saw was a strange disconnected flash that appeared in the middle of her vision then broke up into a million tiny sparks.

47

"Damn those fucking Chinese!" MS did not look at Vencel or the DHS man as he walked. In fact, he wasn't really looking at anything, his focus was drawn to somewhere entirely beyond the room by the force of his anger. "Damn their fucking scientists and damn their fucking tests and damn their fucking security team for letting any of it get to that fucking panel! What the hell do they think they are playing at?"

But MS knew exactly what they were playing at. "So they admit it was *their* guy who spread the disease around the world. But look! It's actually quite harmless and it came from America anyway so aren't they just so wonderful and open and honest for telling us all about it?

"Sure, they wanted to join us on that panel and sure they were happy with all the security and sure they wanted to keep it quiet just like everyone else. Until three days later when it suits them better to go it alone.

"Don't those fuckers know how much I'm worth to their economy? How many of their glorious workers have jobs in stinking dirty factories that *I* own? How many millions of dollars *I've* donated to their damned Communist Party or used to bribe their local government and their police and all their other greedy little fucking officials? How dare they treat me like this!"

Of course MS didn't expect the Chinese to act any differently than they had. He would have done exactly the same thing himself. He stopped pacing and his attention returned to the room.

"If the Chinese are believed then the whole spores story will be discredited. For fuck's sake Vencel, why didn't you keep this under wraps?"

"It is under wraps!" The head of the Intergovernmental Panel stood to face MS. "I have done everything you asked but I could not control the Chinese. Yes, their information is part of the panel's official records, but thanks to my intervention it is clearly flagged as unconfirmed. Now they have left there is nothing more they can add."

MS put his hand on Vencel's shoulder. "Okay okay, you can sit back down. You've just about destroyed that panel and that suits me fine." He let Vencel sit before he turned to the DHS man. "You said there was *another* problem at the panel?"

"It seems likely that information from the panel has been directly leaked to the media."

Vencel's gasp was drowned out by MS. "What the fuck did you say?"

"It seems likely —"

"I did actually hear you the first time. Now give me the fucking details." MS was pacing again, with his right hand curled into a tight fist.

The DHS man did not seem intimidated and spoke at a relaxed pace. "A member of the panel was detained by us in the early hours of this morning. She's an American, the CDC representative. She was on the panel to make it look legitimate *and* because she was supposed to be a quiet little mouse who would do exactly as she was told.

"Unfortunately someone forgot to tell her that and she's been leaking information from the panel the whole time."

MS stopped pacing. "And this went to the media?"

"It went to a group of people, but one of them is a reporter with the Washington Record."

"Fuck! So they know everything already?"

"We have to assume that although we haven't confirmed it yet. We know who she's been talking to from following her internet traffic but she's been using some very sophisticated encryption to mask the message content. Even our geeks haven't cracked it yet."

"But they will?"

"They don't have to, we'll crack *her* soon enough. She's been in detention for six hours already and the interrogation guys were mighty pissed off about her spying right under our noses like that."

At least there was some good news. MS relaxed his fist but returned to pacing. "You said there was a group?"

"Yes. As well as the Record this girl's been in direct contact with the doctor and the head cop from Fulton. Also some guy in Atlanta with a microbiology lab."

"It's not her." MS was certain of that. "It's the Record that's been in contact with those people. They've been putting together their story and now this girls gone missing they'll break it, first thing tomorrow morning."

The DHS man stayed calm. "They'll be *detained* first thing tomorrow morning. Then the story goes away – no one to back it up."

"No. If you start locking up journalists the story doesn't go away, it gets *bigger*. You can bet your ass the Record is expecting trouble from us. They'll already be leaking details to the TV and other papers.

"If you try to shut them down the whole damned story will turn up on some fucking website while they make a fuss about the government cover-up. We'll just have to fight fire with fire on this one."

MS looked across at Vencel. "I think perhaps you should sit this one out Doctor Fodor. There's plenty of magazines in the outer office." He walked to the door and held it open until the doctor had left. Then he sat behind his desk and addressed the DHS man.

"The damned Washington Record is the only paper in this town that I can't influence in some way. All the others, and the TV, I can get them to play along. So we'll have them undermine the credibility of the Records story as much as possible.

"Any chance you guys get to comment, you play the same game, okay?" The DHS man nodded agreement as MS launched into his plan.

"Now the Chinese won't be difficult. They're foreigners so we can always play the xenophobia card and say they're not to be trusted. They're just trying to hide their own culpability. They walked out of the panel too. We can spin that by saying they didn't like what it was finding so they're trying to destroy it.

"Then we have the terrorists. The Record can't just make them go away. No matter what anyone reveals about the disease they have to admit that a Senator was deliberately killed by terrorist action in our capital city. That's already scaring the shit out of the public, so if we keep that in their faces they won't be in any mood for excuses.

"Then there's these people talking to the Record. They're Americans but they're being unpatriotic. Leaking information to the press for God's sake! They might as well be terrorists themselves.

"The girl from CDC signed a non-disclosure agreement. The cop should be upholding the law, not undermining it. The doctor and this laboratory guy, they should be treating the sick but instead they're undermining the authorities who are trying to deal with the disease."

MS leaned back in his chair. "You got all that?"

The DHS man nodded agreement. "Got it."

"Okay then, you go back to your work and you let me know the moment that girl tells you anything at all."

48

Alison Grove was aware of only a thick heavy feeling in her head, accompanied by a rough buzzing noise in her left ear. A conscious effort was required to force her eyelids open but it didn't help much. Her vision was blurred and the room seemed to have become much darker.

Alison's first thought was that she had been shot in the head. That would explain the flash and her sudden descent into incapacity. Perhaps the three men had come to protect her from some crazed assassin, but had failed in their mission. Perhaps they *were* the assassins and everything had gone according to plan.

She didn't have an answer to that question and for once in her life she didn't care. The thought of dying here on the hotel carpet with her head in a pool of blood was just too horrible to consider. She wasn't dead yet and there must be something she could do for herself.

With a supreme effort Alison forced her head upright and opened her eyes again. The room was still a blur so she reached out in the darkness, trying to grab the mattress but it wasn't there.

She rolled over, trying to stretch further. Her body moved freely but her right hand refused to follow. She tried to roll again but now her hand was in the air above her head and she could not drag it down. That didn't make any sense at all. If only she could *see*. A third attempt at vision was useless and Alison let herself slump back to the floor and into unconsciousness.

There was no way to know how much time had passed. It may have been only minutes, or it may have been hours. Alison found herself worrying about it when it struck her that worrying meant she was awake and feeling better. She was still slightly dazed but definitely functioning now. She opened her eyes and this time they worked.

She was still expecting to see her hotel room, but it had been replaced by a room where the walls, ceiling and floor were made entirely of concrete. There was nothing in the room except for a stark metal chair, firmly bolted to the floor. There were no windows, just a solid metal door in the wall behind her. A grille on the ceiling provided dim light and seemed also to be the source of the incessant buzzing noise. The air was stale with the smell of sweat and urine. Alison's right hand still refused to budge but now she could see that it was handcuffed to the back of the chair. She dragged herself up off the floor and noticed for the first time that she was dressed in her robe. It fell open as she turned to sit down and she quickly pulled it closed, suddenly feeling vulnerable again.

There was no pool of blood where she had been lying and a quick inspection told Alison her head was dirty but it did not have any bullet holes in it. If she hadn't been shot then why had she been unconscious? She sat in the chair holding her jaw which ached and decided they must have just hit her.

For a long time after that Alison sat alone on the cold chair in the dim light, listening to the harsh buzzing and holding her robe tightly around her. The floor was cold and she had to tuck her feet uncomfortably underneath her on the chair to keep them warm.

Her emotions refused to settle and she swung wildly between overwhelming anxiety and white-hot anger. What was going to happen and why had she been brought here?

Alison had no idea how long she had been sitting when the door behind her squealed on its hinges and footsteps entered the room. She turned to see who it was but a man's voice commanded "Look forward!" and she did. It was the kind of voice one doesn't disobey.

From the footsteps Alison guessed there were at least two people in the room, maybe three. When no one came to stand in front of her she turned again but strong hands took her head and forced it back straight. She could do nothing but wait and stare at the empty concrete wall in front of her.

The voice spoke again. "Do you think we are stupid?"

Alison was still at least as angry as she was scared. She tried to stand this time, lifting her body out of the chair, turning it towards the voice and shouting back as best she could. "Who are you? Why am I here?"

The hands grasped her shoulders and pushed her back down. "If you do not cooperate you will be bound to that chair with wire."

That was too much. Before her fear, or the hands, could stop her Alison leapt from the chair. She would *not* be treated like this!

The hands belonged to a large man with olive skin, a bushy moustache and a very surprised look on his face. This was partly because he wasn't expecting trouble from a small woman but mostly because Alison had forgotten she was handcuffed to the chair and the leap had thrown her to the floor at his feet.

The voice came from a man of medium build standing away from the chair towards the back of the room. He wore the black suit and white shirt of security, but his status was indicated by an equally black polished leather briefcase on the floor next to his feet.

The voice did not react to Alison's sudden move at all. He just stood and watched like a bored commuter. Or, she thought, like someone who's seen this a thousand times before.

The big man with the hands responded quickly for someone his size. Alison barely had time to look at both men before he picked her up and forced her roughly back into the seat. The fall had only increased Alison's anger and she shouted now at the concrete walls.

"You fucking assholes. I am a US citizen and I have rights. I demand to be released. I demand a lawyer. I demand to know who you are!"

The echo died away and she waited for the voice to tell her off again but instead she heard the door open and footsteps leaving. There was nothing to do again except to stare at the wall again, listen to the incessant buzzing of the light and sense the presence of the hands.

After a minute or so the footsteps returned. Alison was still angry and she shouted again. "You can't do this to me. When I get out I will tell everyone. There will be an investigation and you will be exposed."

There was no reply but she heard someone approach the chair rapidly from behind. Without warning her robe was grabbed and pulled down off her shoulders then dragged heavily from underneath her. It fell to the floor except at her wrist where the handcuffs held it in place.

She had tried to defend herself but the hands were holding her firmly now and they pinned her arms to her side and against the back of the chair. A second pair of hands wrapped her with a dirty orange electrical cord.

When they were finished Alison was firmly bound to the back of the chair. Only her head and legs could be moved. She was dressed now in only the thin t-shirt and flannel pants that she had worn to bed in the hotel. The chair felt suddenly much colder and the cord was tight enough to cut into her arms and her breasts. If it was meant to make Alison feel helpless then it was working.

When it was clear that Alison could not move the voice walked around the chair and stood directly in front of her, leaning forward so his face was only inches from hers. His words were delivered with contempt. "We're not playing games here little girl."

The smell of stale coffee was overpowering and as he spoke little flecks of foul saliva landed on Alison's cheeks and lips. She tried to turn away but the hands would not let her.

The voice had a message for Alison. "It is two days before a Presidential election and terrorists are engaged in biological warfare on your home soil. Your country gives you an important mission, a way to help fight the terror, but you betray that mission. Do you really think you have *rights*? Do you really imagine you're going to get a *lawyer*?

"Even your liberal President won't save you now. He's got more of a mess to deal with than you can imagine and he's about to kiss his next term in office goodbye.

"You can forget about him and you can forget about your nice little dream world with its rules of law and its courts and procedures and checks and balances. The public is scared and the gloves are off. A Senator is dead, there's gridlock on the roads and deadly spores are in the air. We can do whatever we damned well like and we will.

"Did you really think you'd get away with chatting to your terrorist buddies right under our noses like that? Did you really think we weren't watching your every move?"

Alison's eyes widened before she could stop them and the voice pounced.

"Yes that's right. We know."

Her mind went in ten directions at once.

The voice stood and returned to his position behind the chair. "There are only two ways this can end for you now. Bad or very bad. We have a few simple questions. If you answer them to our satisfaction then you *might* get a trial and go to a regular jail. If not...."

The voice let Alison sit in silence for a while to experience whatever unpleasant consequences her mind could conjure up. "Here's a tip little girl. The CDC does *not* use ultra-secure encryption. Only people with something very, very naughty to hide use that and you've been doing it since you arrived at the Panel. That alone could keep you locked in this room until everyone you ever knew has forgotten you existed."

Again, the voice left her in silence, allowing time for the implications of what he was saying to sink in. Then he offered the possibility of a way out, just the slightest hope of redemption. "It's always possible of course that you're a pawn. A naïve idealist who got herself caught up in something much bigger and much more treasonous than she ever intended.

"We know how these groups operate. They trick you into joining. Then when it's too late you find out what their real agenda is. If you threaten to expose them they say that you're guilty too and so you're trapped – forced to betray your country when you never really wanted to. I think perhaps that's likely in your case Miss Grove. Your psychological profile indicates you are the type."

Another pause, this time to let hope take root. "So, now it's up to you. Tell us everything you know, in a spirit of cooperation and repentance and we'll do the best we can for you. Refuse and we can only assume you are a deeply committed terrorist in which case, let me assure you Ms. Grove, you will go straight to hell." The voice did not wait for her reply, leaving the room the moment he was done speaking.

Alison was truly afraid now. She knew that once she was accused of terrorist activity then they really *could* do whatever they wanted with her. She also knew though that the voice was not as well informed as she was supposed to think. She was *not* part of a terrorist group although she decided with some chagrin that Mike probably had tricked her into joining his conspiracy.

If the voice knew who she was communicating with then presumably they were already arrested too. The only hope then was that the Record would tell all to get Mike out of trouble.

If the voice didn't know, which seemed more likely, her best hope was to say nothing and wait. Mike would have to publish after her arrest and it would be obvious she wasn't a terrorist.

But what if the Record was prevented from publishing? If Mike had been arrested too then maybe all his material was already locked away and the Record didn't have a story beyond one of their journalists disappearing.

In her isolation Alison had no way to know what was the best course of action and that, of course, is exactly what the voice wanted. She sat on the cold chair trying desperately to think her way out of the predicament.

She was so deep in thought that she forgot all about the hands. It was several minutes after the voice left the room when the scraping of his shoes reminded her that he was there. He put a metal bucket on the floor next to her then left also, never having said a word. Alison looked at the bucket in horror. She couldn't even use it – he had left her tied to the chair.

49

The Sunday morning meeting started slowly but ended much sooner than any of the group had expected. By ten past eleven Marion, Shona and Sanjay were logged-in. They chatted amongst themselves, revisiting the issues from the previous day.

At a quarter to twelve Mike appeared with a terse message. **"Alison has been detained. We can all expect a visit from the DHS in the near future."**

There was a long delay as the others took in the news. It was Marion who replied for the group. **"How do you know? Nothing on the news about it."**

"I slipped a few bucks to the porters at her hotel. Just to let me know if there was any trouble. I thought she might run away or something. Wasn't expecting this.

"They're won't *be* anything on the news about it either. Not until I print it. Alison wasn't arrested. She was taken away by security from the panel. They're DHS, they don't even have to say they've got her."

There were no replies as each of the group sat wondering what to do next. Except for Mike who's mind was set. **"I'm going to publish tomorrow. We have to get this out for Alison's sake. We don't know why** they've taken her but they might try to say she's a terrorist. Getting the truth published is her best defense."

Shona replied. **"Wait Mike. We need to discuss this. There's still the matter of *what* to publish."**

Mike didn't bother to reply. How much justification did these people need before they would act? Yesterday's debate had wasted enough of his time. He was about to say just that when Sanjay replied in his support.

"Mike is right. Alison is alone now and the best thing she can do for herself is to tell them everything. So we must assume they will come for us next. If we hide the truth then they can say what they like and no one will know any better. We must publish so people know Alison is not a terrorist and neither are we. We must publish so people know the spores are harmless and the government is wrong. It is too late now to do anything else."

Mike couldn't have put it better. He logged-off immediately and walked down the hallway to the editor's office.

The editor was delighted by Alison's detention and he threw the full weight of the Record's resources into the Fulton story. Everything they knew, or thought they knew, would be printed: the unfolding of the story in Fulton, Shona's discovery of the spores and her doubts about them, the farce of the inter-governmental panel, the Chinese story and Sanjay's confirmation of it and the strange video from Iraq. All would be laid out before the public.

The front page would be reserved for Alison's detention. What had happened to her and why? The Record would admit that she had talked to them about the panel. They would point out however that Alison had not revealed any US government secrets beyond the absurd way the panel was run.

There was no time for Mike to do the writing; other journalists were called in for that as he hurriedly transcribed his notes. The editor scrutinized, ensuring every possible element of drama in the story was fully exploited.

By the time Mike was dozing uncomfortably at his desk the early edition of the Washington Record was being unleashed onto the streets of Washington D.C.

It was barely ten days since the Record had published its first article about the illness in Fulton. Since then the public had been forced to deal with the quarantine of the town, the gruesome deaths in China and the terrorist killing of Senator Hanson followed by nationwide disruption of transport and food.

All this, they had been told was brought about by tiny particles of disease that could be drifting in the very air they breathed. Contamination spread with malicious intent by enemies as invisible as the spores themselves. To leave the house, to share the air with strangers, to breathe at all, was putting them in terrible danger.

Yet now the Record, the paper that had started all the trouble, had changed its mind. Despite the deaths and the quarantine and all the disruption the threat was mild at best and there was nothing in the air to be concerned about.

The Chinese government held a hastily arranged press conference at the United Nations. They formally announced their withdrawal from the inter-governmental panel and publicly released the information they had presented.

The timing resulted from an act of marketing genius by the editor at the Record. He had contacted the Chinese to warn them of the story and to ask for comment. He was betting they would make their findings public in response. It was their best defense against any accusations Du had spread the fungus deliberately or that they had tried to cover it up. It did the Record no harm at all to have China officially support their story mere hours after it was released.

50

The President was furious. He knew he'd been manipulated but he also knew that short of a confession by one of his enemies he would never have the evidence to prove it.

With the election so close there was only one way to deal with the sudden turn of events and that was to take it head on. So at six o'clock on Monday morning, one day before the election, the President had sequestered himself with his writers and started work on the most important speech of his career.

By ten-thirty the work was done and the President stood grave faced before a crowd of carefully selected supporters.

"My fellow Americans, we are living indeed in troubled times. The events of the past few weeks have been unprecedented in the history of the United States and it has been both a burden and a privilege for me to be your President during those weeks.

"To those who might be hoping that I am ready to give up now, to run away because the job is getting tough, I say this. Think again.

"I have been your President for the last four years and in that time there have been those of you who supported me and those who did not. But I am resolute on one thing. I know that regardless of whether you supported me or not, I have served you *all* with determination, integrity and honor.

"I have worked tirelessly for the good of *all* Americans and I stand before you today still committed *one hundred percent* to that same goal. I will also tell you this America; I am committed one hundred percent to being your President for the next four years as well."

At this the crowd erupted into a deafening roar. The President beamed his most telegenic smile and waited for the noise to subside.

"I am sure that you are all aware of the information in this morning's Washington Record and the subsequent announcement by the Chinese government. I am also sure you are aware of the massive criticism I have received from my political opponents as a result.

"The thing that they forget, and the thing you must remember is this. We are dealing with the unknown. An unknown that has already killed Americans as well as those in other nations. An unknown that it is my sworn duty to protect you from. Yet just because a newspaper has tried to cast some doubt amidst all this, I have supposedly become incompetent.

"Do not allow yourselves to be deceived by my critics America. When they tell you that the quarantine in Virginia was never necessary then they are wrong. When they tell you that the quarantine in our capital was never necessary then they are also wrong. When they tell you all the other steps I have taken to contain this threat were never necessary then they are utterly wrong.

"They are also forgetting this is a direct and deliberate terrorist attack. They are forgetting that a Senator has died. They are forgetting that the best medical advice available up to and including today is that this disease is spread through the air. They are forgetting these things on purpose America, and they are hoping that you will forget them too.

"If I had failed to act as I did. If I had not imposed the quarantines or the other emergency measures well *that's* when I would have been incompetent. *That's* when I would have failed you, the American people, but I did not.

"I did what a President is *elected* to do. I took action when it was necessary. I let the buck stop here. I made the tough decisions and I stick by them!"

There was another pause for wild adulation from the crowd.

"Do not imagine though that I am ignoring this new information. If even half of what was printed this morning turns out to be true then it is significant indeed and I will act accordingly."

The President, of course, forgot to mention that if half the information printed was true then the Inter-Governmental Panel he had helped establish was a complete failure and his Department of Homeland Security was acting on its own behalf.

"I have already launched a full and thorough investigation into all aspects of this situation and I can assure you that any further necessary actions will be taken without delay.

"If it turns out that some of the emergency measures are not required then they will be curtailed as soon as possible. I will not do that however until I am absolutely certain that those measures really are unnecessary and that curtailing them will not impose further risk on US citizens.

"I can also assure you that when my investigation is complete there will be a thorough and complete public reckoning. I am confident the investigation will show that I have always acted with the highest regard for the welfare of the American people. Should it be found that there are those among us who have not, let them be warned that their deception will be held out to the full light of day."

This was not a reference to the Fulton conspirators. It was a threat to those in the DHS who had hidden their knowledge of the terrorist attack and exaggerated the significance of the spores. The President was determined to carry out that threat. Even if the election was lost he would deal severely with those fuckers before he left the White House.

"As I take my leave of you now I ask you to consider carefully before you vote tomorrow. Ask yourself about the character of the man you want to lead this great nation of ours for the next four years.

"You may have disagreed with me at times but you must recognize that through those disagreements I have always acted with integrity. I have always acted with honor. I have always acted for the good of all Americans.

"I opened today by saying that we live in troubled times. Well you know from my record America that I am the best candidate, I am the *only* candidate with the experience, commitment and strength to lead you through such troubled times.

"Give me your vote and I promise you this crisis will end and it will end quickly. I will take America through the fire and I will bring it out the other side stronger than it has ever been. Then we will all stand together. We will raise our heads up high and we will proclaim to the entire world that we are still here and we are still proud. Proud to be the home of the brave. Proud to be the land of the free. Proud to be America!"

The last words were shouted above the manic roaring of the crowd. The President flashed a final fearless smile to the cameras, waved to the crowd then strode confidently off the stage.

There was much for him to do and it had to be done quickly. If his promised investigation was to bear fruit it must begin immediately, before its targets had time to cover their tracks.

51

The twins slept peacefully beneath their plastic quarantine tents as Joe kept watch. The doctors were giving the boys all kinds of drugs and assured Joe they were doing fine; all their signs were normal and there was nothing to worry about. Joe wanted to believe them, but he had to agree with his wife. "If everything's okay then why are they keeping us here?"

Kathleen was somewhere out in the corridor taking a break from their vigil. They had been confined to a makeshift quarantine ward for the last three days, ever since Joe called the ambulance to their house.

The paramedics had rushed up to the boy's room and started checking their vital signs. They were older and obviously experienced, but they had turned almost white when Joe uttered the word 'spores'.

Half an hour later the family sat locked in the back of the ambulance watching men in hazmat suits set up a cordon around their house. They were driven away just as a sign was put up on the front lawn 'QUARANTINE AREA – NO UNAUTHORISED ENTRY.'

When Joe wasn't watching his sons he followed events on the small TV in the corner of their room. The sound was turned down low and he had to strain to hear it but he had followed most of the President's speech.

Proud to be American, well he could sure agree with his President on that. As for taking action, well that was clearly the right thing to do.

Beyond that though it really didn't matter what had been said. Joe was always going to vote for the other guy anyway.

He watched his boys breathe as the analysts dissected the President's speech. His attention was drawn back to the TV when the anchor returned. "In related news, warrants have been issued for the arrest of those named in the Washington Record this morning." Four small mug-shots appeared on the screen. "The four have been named as —"

Joe never got to hear the names as a sharp cry was followed by the sound of a plastic coffee cup hitting the floor. He turned to see Kathleen standing in the doorway, her mouth wide open. "Oh God Joe, it's Marion!"

They watched as the news revealed the actions of the Record's informants. When it got to Marion they turned the sound up just a little. "Marion Quirke, the Chief of Police for the town of Fulton is wanted for questioning but authorities say they are still trying to locate her. According to the Record article Chief Quirke broke the quarantine around Fulton twice, even smuggling out bio-hazardous material—"

"Fuck!" Joe kept his voice quiet but his body was tense and his hands had clenched into fists.

"... and authorities say Chief Quirke first visited the town on the night quarantine was declared—"

Joe turned away from the screen and rushed from the room, knocking his chair into the wall with a loud bang. He went into the men's bathroom and slammed his fist into the concrete wall, leaving a scraping of skin and a small smear of blood on its rough surface. A few more blows and his rage was gone.

He found Kathleen out in the corridor. "It's okay honey, just had to let it out is all." He covered his bloody hand with a paper towel and offered a reassuring smile. "Just can't believe she'd do that, not Marion. She brought that damned thing into our house!"

Kathleen put her arms around him. "My God Joe, what should we do?"

"We're gonna do nothing honey. She's got herself into this and she can get herself out. She's a cop for God's sake. She knows how the system works."

"But Joe—"

"No Kathleen, listen to me. What we do is sit here and wait, then when they come and ask us, we tell 'em everything we know. It's the only way to protect ourselves and our boys."

"Protect ourselves?"

"She stayed with us Kathleen. While all of that was going on she was in our house and doing God knows what behind our backs. She even took that damned disease out of her precious town on purpose. For Christ's sake! The same disease they used to kill a Senator!

"They're gonna tear our place apart and we're gonna let them. If it looks like we're trying to hide *anything* then we'll end up in a jail cell right next to her. So no Kathleen, we won't do anything except our duty as decent honest citizens."

There was a long pause before Kathleen let out a long sigh. "You're right Joe." They stood holding each other for another minute before she spoke again. "Come on, we need to get back to our boys."

Back in the room the TV was still on and the twins were standing in front of it watching as the newsreader spoke in breathless tones. "We now cross live to an undisclosed location where Washington Record journalist Mike Fanning is believed to be with one of the terrorists."

The image switched to Mike. His face was pale and over-exposed in the glare of a single bright light but around him was only indistinct darkness. Even with the poor image quality it was easy to see he was anxious.

"I have been brought here alone this evening to interview two men who purport to be the last un-captured members of the terrorist cell responsible for Senator Hanson's death. I was allowed to bring a TV news camera but it is being operated by one of the terrorists so I must apologize for any technical problems."

A voice answered from the darkness. "I know how to run a fucking camera dammit. Just get on with it."

Kathleen grabbed her boys and dragged them from the room to howls of protest. Joe hardly noticed as the interview continued.

"You can't use that word, they'll cut you off."

"For fuck's sake! Every kid in America uses that word every fucking day."

Mike shrugged. "I don't make the rules, OK? If you keep swearing they'll cut you off no matter what you have to say." He stared into the light until the voice replied.

"They won't cut me off. They got delays and stuff so they can just bleep me out. Now stop being a damned pussy and interview me."

"Uh, alright then, perhaps we can start with you telling me which terrorist group you are part of?"

"That's easy Mike; it's the US fuckin' army."

52

Building twenty three was at the far side of the Chan Yen Institute; at least fifteen minutes' walk from the residential building and the gardens where Du had been spending his time. He wasn't sure if he was even allowed back here, but no-one tried to stop him as he climbed the plain concrete steps and opened the door.

There were no guards inside and Du followed the signs up to the fourth floor. He passed a few men in lab coats on the way but they paid no attention except perhaps for noticing that he was dressed in a suit and tie.

The sign outside room four hundred and seven said "Laboratory Administrator – Please Enter." Du knocked and opened the door to see a plain office with only a desk and a couple of simple wooden chairs. The walls were bare except for a faded anatomical chart on the far wall.

Dr. Fen was at the desk reading. He looked up and smiled as his visitor walked in. "Du! I am glad you could see me."

Du moved one of the chairs in front of the desk and sat down. "I was told to come. I didn't think I had a choice."

Fen nodded. "True, you didn't. But I am glad to see you anyway."

"Why am I here Fen? Do you have news of my family?"

"No Du. I have asked many times but they tell me only what I need to know. Still, there is good news. I am to travel to Beijing."

"That is good news for you indeed Fen. But I doubt I am here just for that."

Fen smiled again. "Please hear me out Du. There is some difficulty between our government and the Americans around this fungus. We have new information so I am being taken to address our diplomats in person.

"When I am gone someone must take over as administrator. There is no one at Chan Yen more qualified to run a laboratory than you. I put your name forward and the request was approved."

Du bowed slightly as he replied. "I am in your debt Fen, but surely I am still blamed for what happened at Jouchou?"

"I have explained in my reports Du, that you were not the cause of events at Jouchou. You were infected in America and could not have known what you carried."

"So I am trusted again?"

"You are trusted with this job Du, beyond that I do not know. But to run this laboratory you must know its secrets, so it is no small trust."

"Yes, it is a good beginning." Du felt hope for the first time since arriving at Chan Yen. "So tell me Fen, when do I learn these secrets?"

The scientist laughed. "They have been in front of you since you sat down." He pointed to a pile of papers on the desk.

Du leaned forward but saw only inscrutable charts covered with columns of smudged lines. "I have seen these before Fen, but I cannot read them. You must explain."

The scientist searched about on the desk, speaking as he did so. "Those are electrophoresis gels, but I have something much better here." He lifted up a sheaf of papers and held them out to Du. They were covered in an endless series of closely printed letters.

"These are DNA sequences. We have been working on them since I arrived here and they prove the infection at Jouchou is not from your laboratory. The fungus that infected you was modified."

"A mutant?"

"No. A mutation can only change one or two sequences at a time. This fungus has *thousands* of extra sequences. It couldn't possibly have happened naturally."

"Then how?"

"There is only one way that I know of. Someone has *deliberately* added those extra DNA sequences to this fungus."

Du stared at the scientist. "Deliberate! Who did this Fen? Who made this thing that has ruined my life?" Du grabbed the papers from Fen's hand and pored over them looking for his answer. But they were as meaningless to him as the charts had been.

Fen waited for him to calm before replying. "Ten years ago it could not have been done, except by the most advanced laboratories. But the technology is moving fast. Today almost any graduate student could do it if they had the right equipment."

A deadly fungus; deliberately modified and connected with army research. There was only one conclusion and Du exclaimed "It's a weapon! Someone has made this fungus into a weapon and they were testing it on me."

Fen reached over the desk and retrieved the sequences from Du's shaking hand. "I don't think it is a weapon. The understanding of DNA is just not that far ahead. Sequences can be read, they can even be cut and joined back together, but no one knows enough to actually *design* something like this. We really can't know in advance how it will behave.

"No, I think the behavior of this fungus is accidental. Whoever made it was hoping it would remain harmless, but they didn't *know* that, and it turned out to be deadly."

Each of the doctor's explanations left Du more confused than before. "If they couldn't predict the outcome, why add the sequences? Were they just stumbling around in the dark?"

"Have you heard of junk DNA?"

"*Junk* DNA? No." Du assumed an explanation was coming and said no more.

"DNA is a sequence of chemical codes. The sequence tells the cells how to produce proteins, enzymes etc. When you put all the codes together you have enough information to build an entire organism. What most people don't know is that usually there are far more codes than are necessary. Some of the codes are for useful proteins, but most of them have *no function at all*.

"Now, some of it we simply don't understand, but for most organisms well over half the DNA is useless. The codes don't produce *anything*. That's what we call 'junk' DNA and we really don't know why it's there. Maybe it's old sequences that evolution has left behind. Maybe the coding process is just inefficient. Maybe it's something else.

"I think the artificial sequences added to this fungus are junk DNA. I think they were meant to be inert, not intended to change the behavior of the fungus at all."

Du opened his mouth to speak but Fen moved on to the next part of the explanation.

"About five years ago in America some academics put a document on the internet. The army asked me to review it and I said it was wild speculation. After a few months the document was removed. The rumor was that it had been classified, but I've never been able to confirm that.

"The academics suggested using mild infections to penetrate terrorist organizations."

Du laughed. "America gets its revenge by giving al-Qaeda the sniffles?"

Fen ignored the interruption. "Imagine you could infect just a single member of a terrorist organization or maybe even just an ordinary criminal. They infect their associates, who in turn pass it on to their associates. It's a mild infection remember, so these people might not even know they were sick.

"Eventually of course the infection will spread to the whole population. But before that happens there is a period where only the original vector and his close associates have it. By tracing the infection a government could find the associates."

Du grasped the concept, but it had obvious flaws, even to someone with as little knowledge of biology as him. "But this is impractical. The government would have to administer medical tests to everyone they suspected! That would give the game away. Even if they could do it, a certain portion of the population would be infected already and resources would be wasted chasing around after innocent people."

Fen nodded. "That's true, and there's a third problem too. It only works if the associates are in close physical contact. I don't think there's any way around that, but this fungus does answer your two objections.

"Firstly, junk DNA may not have any biological function but it still has a unique sequence. You could pick any junk DNA, add it to the fungus and that makes it instantly identifiable. No one would be infected with that specific strain because it has only just been created. So now it stands out clearly in the general population. You could prepare hundreds of different strains, each one unique, all just sitting in the lab ready to go.

"Secondly, this fungus infects the skin and it lives in sweat. Even if you think you're not sweating there is always moisture on your skin, so there is always somewhere for this fungus to live. Once you're infected then *everything* you touch gets some of it left behind. If you touch another person of course, you pass it on. But if you touch a doorknob or a handrail or sit in a car, there will be a trace of the fungus left behind.

Fen was speaking quickly now, barely pausing for breath. "So this residual fungus is what we're after! The government can send agents into an area to take samples from surfaces in public places. Anywhere the junk DNA turns up, their vector or his friends have been.

"That kind of mass testing used to be impossible. But now it's cheap, easy and efficient."

Du was not convinced. "But your fungus *kills* people Fen. It has done it everywhere I have been since I left America. It is a weapon."

Fen replied patiently. "It makes less sense as a weapon than as a tracking device. Despite what we have seen it's just not harmful enough to be a weapon. It kills some people horribly, but most it doesn't affect at all. Even if it was sprayed directly onto an enemy they could counter it too easily.

"I am convinced Du, the deaths are accidental. Maybe the junk DNA was cut in the wrong place and some ancient protein was activated. Maybe they just messed up and it's not junk after all. Whatever the reason, I think this thing was never meant to be noticed by anyone and the people who made it got a nasty surprise."

53

Mike Fanning was speechless, sure of the words he had heard, but not at all sure he believed them. Aware that he was live on air but unable to think of anything to say, he could manage only a barely articulate "What?"

The voice from the darkness replied with an impassive tone. "The US army Mike, you've probably heard of us."

"But—"

"What's wrong Mike? You think only the damned ragtops can be terrorists? Well wake the fuck up! We were all born in America and we're all damned proud of it. We all fought in Iraq and we're damned proud of that too. We are not affiliated with any other organization and we represent the interests of no one but ourselves."

The shock was still visible on Mike's face but he'd managed to regain control of his faculties. He was starting to get angry too. The thought that US soldiers were responsible was too much even for his indifferent journalist's view of the world.

"If you're such proud Americans then why do you support the terrorist agenda? Why are you killing Americans? Did you go native over there in Iraq?"

"Jesus Christ Mike! You think we give a fuck about the hajis? You think we're doing this for their sake?"

"Well then, why did you launch a biological attack on your own country? The one you swore to protect. The one you're so proud of."

"Alright cut."

"Cut? You wanted to be interviewed. You can't chicken out just because you don't like the questions."

"Yes I wanted to be interviewed but now I've changed my mind. It's just gonna take too damned long if I have to listen to your idiot bullshit. So new game plan. You shut up, I talk. We all get out of here a lot sooner."

Mike nodded agreement. The camera stayed on him as he waited for the soldier to talk.

"Okay then, listen up America. I was sent to Iraq along with a whole lot of your other sons and daughters to save the world from WMD's and rescue the oppressed Iraqi people from tyranny and injustice. 'Course when we get there it turns out there *are* no WMD's and hey guess what, the Iraqi people don't *want* to be rescued. Well not by us anyway. They just want us to fuck off back home.

"So I'm in Fallujah and I sent my men off on patrol. They come back shakin' with some story about a house full of dead hajis who'd puked themselves to death. Now these are tough guys. They've seen a lot of bodies by now and nothin' gets 'em scared like this.

"I watch the patrol video and sure enough. These hajis have just bled to death through their mouths and noses. Now we're operational right? We don't really care how they died so long as they're dead. We just move on and don't think nothin' more of it.

"Then some of the guys get sick. Within days man, just days, they're dyin' like those hajis. I sat and watched my men die like they were no better than those scum and there was nothin' I could do.

"I sent reports to everyone. Medical alerts, bio-war notices, you name it. I was raisin' hell but then I get the word. Official notification from the fuckin' US Army. It's a local disease and it's been handled. No further action required but hey it's fuckin' classified, you know for morale, so don't mention it or else.

"A few weeks later I get transferred back home. They said it was compassionate grounds but we were stretched so fuckin' thin back then that *no one* got to go home early.

"When I get back they give me a pay rise and a nice safe job in security. Nothin's said right, but they make it clear they're lookin' after me and I better do right by them too. Only they must've been idiots because they fucked it up.

"I moved around a lot, just couldn't get to feelin' settled anywhere. So one day I'm working security for some research lab and I'm just curious right? I'm checking in the labs and one of the beaker jockeys has left some papers out. This guy has photos there of *my* men. Some of 'em covered in blood, some of 'em all clean and cut open.

"It was some project called Longarm but these papers were from another place, one I hadn't even heard of before. So I applied for a transfer and they must've been asleep at the wheel 'cos they let me go. Took me two years 'til I was head of security at that lab and I could find out what happened to my men. That's when I got really pissed-off.

"Those fuckin' assholes had built the damned thing! They took a fungus and put some extra shit on it so they could track people then they turned it loose in Iraq, trying to find al-Qaeda.

"Now that was their first damned field test right? It's the war on terror after all so anything goes and hey, it's only hajis right? Only *my* men got to die along with them.

"I read their fuckin' report right there in the lab. My men would've been OK except they'd been exposed to DU and that made 'em vulnerable. The fungus just came along and finished 'em off. Same for the hajis."

Mike interrupted. "A lot of people won't know what DU is."

"Yeah right. They don't tell the nice folks back home what kind of evil shit we're doin' over there. Well DU is Depleted Uranium. They make shells out of it and we shoot it at the hajis 'cos it makes 'em die. But that shit is fuckin' toxic man and it gets *vaporized*. Everyone breathes it in. You think this fungus is bad? You wait 'til all those soldiers and hajis start havin' deformed kids. I tell you—."

Mike interrupted again. "Okay you've made your point. We're here to talk about your recent activities."

"Whatever. So anyway, I don't know how much shit you'll take from anyone but that fungus was it for me. I found a few more guys to help me out. It's not that hard you know, to find ex-soldiers fucked off with the way they were treated in Iraq. We put together a plan to get the public's attention. They were all running around with 'support our troops' stickers on their trucks and we thank 'em for that, but no one ever told 'em just how bad their troops got fucked-over.

"We picked on Hanson 'cos that slimy asshole was voting to send us guys to Iraq at the same time as he was gettin' kickbacks from the all the corporations makin' money from the war. Someone had to make the sacrifice and he was perfect.

"We wanted to make him sick with DU but we couldn't get our hands on any so we had to use drugs. Then we gave him the fungus. Got him good too. Asshole died by coughin' out his fuckin' lungs, just like my men. It was my most successful operation."

The soldier stopped talking long enough for Mike to ask a question. "What about the others? The people who died in Virginia and China and Australia. What about the quarantine and all the chaos you have inflicted on innocent Americans. The one's you expect to support you now?"

"Collateral damage. That Chinese guy was just a plain old fashioned accident; turned up at my lab right when I was stealing the damned fungus. He wasn't supposed to be there until the next day but some idiot screwed his schedule.

"As head of security I had to be there while they showed him around. They introduced me, I shook his hand. Must've got some fungus on him. I knew how to clean it off but I guess no one bothered to tell him. He went away and spread it around the world.

"Goddamn was I surprised when I saw it in the paper, about those hicks dying in Virginia. We all dressed up in our black suits to do damage control. Went out there and pretended to be DHS, told 'em all to shut up or we'd arrest 'em. Nearly worked too."

Mike repeated his question. "And the people who died. What about them?"

The soldier was mocking. "Exactly Mike, what about them?"

"So you're happy to tell the people of America you put their lives at risk, you actually killed some of them, and that is no big deal?"

"Christ man, I was bein' sarcastic. Who cared when my men died? Not the people who should have. Not the army or the politicians. Now at least we've got their attention."

"But what about the spores? They put us all at risk surely."

"Damn you're stupid. Those spores are bullshit! Some back-woods doctor looks down a microscope and before you know it the whole damned country's too fuckin' scared to breathe. Let me be real clear Mike. *You can't breathe this thing in.* You have to *touch* it. Even then it won't do you much harm 'til something *else* makes you sick. That Chinese stuff in this morning's paper is all true."

The interview continued for another five minutes. Mike tried to get the soldier to explain his motivation in more detail or to admit that what he had done was wrong but he was not about to be swayed. He had set his mind on revenge and that revenge had been achieved. The consequences for anyone else just didn't matter to him.

Mike interviewed the second soldier. He said that he was dying from injuries received in Iraq and this was a suicide mission for him. He was sorry for the unnecessary deaths but the Senator had deserved it.

He started to read a list of names; it was the men who died from the fungus in Iraq. He had only read the first two when a flash overwhelmed the camera's circuits and turned the image pure white for a moment, then black.

The audio kept working and shots could be heard above a cacophony of shouting. It lasted only twenty seconds before there was silence then the sound of heavy boots and a new voice shouted. "Get that fuckin' camera out of here; and what's left of that damned journalist too." There was a crunching sound of metal and glass breaking, and then even that was lost.

54

Marion muted the sound on the TV in her motel room. She assumed the soldier and his companion were dead before that TV camera hit the ground. The public announcement would be that they had opened fire on security forces and had died in the ensuing gunfight. For all Marion knew, that might even be the truth. If Mike was lucky he might even have survived to tell about it.

As the ad break started she carefully sorted through the few clothes she had with her and changed into the most comfortable ones. Then she collected her keys and wallet and put them in her pockets along with her badge.

She took the bullets out of her gun and put them in the drawer on the left-hand side of the bed. The gun itself went into the drawer on the right-hand side. With that done she put her shoes on and made sure she was wearing her glasses. Then she lay back down on the bed, put her hands behind her head and returned to watching the TV. She was ready now and there would be no excuse for violence when the time came.

The news had moved on to discussion of the day's events. The Record article was mentioned of course, but there was little attempt to understand any of the details. The focus of the analysts and commentators was entirely on the following day's election. They were only interested in how the candidates had responded to the news and what it might do to their chances.

Marion had done her utmost to get the truth about the fungus out to the public. Not to influence the election but to save her town. She had risked everything for Fulton and she had succeeded, but she had also failed. The truth was in front of the public, and so far no one seemed to care.

She lay on the hotel bed and told herself it would be different after the election. It didn't matter who gained power, there would be a need to restore order and the fastest way to do that would be to remove the quarantines and emergency measures that were causing such great disturbance. The terrorists were no longer an issue. It simply had to happen.

It was another fifteen minutes before the hotel door came flying into the room in a shower of splintered wood. Marion stayed on the bed and kept herself perfectly still as the room filled with shouting men and guns. She turned over when she was ordered and moved her hands down behind her back. Her last thought as she was dragged from the room was that at least she had done all she could for Fulton.

55

"And so the die was cast for the Fulton Four and this funny little band of conspirators found themselves sucked into a maelstrom. Only partly of their own making, it would become far more powerful than any of them could have imagined possible."

Marion Quirke sat in the darkened cinema, amused by the narration. She had never liked the name 'Fulton Four', but it was almost inevitable. It had been invented by the media after the Washington Record published their story. The four were Marion, Alison, Shona, and Sanjay, even though two of them had never even been to Fulton and Sanjay was never named in the Record article.

"All they wanted was to tell the world a simple truth. That the Fulton outbreak was not airborne, that its spores were harmless. It is impossible to tell through the long lens of history whether they were immensely brave, immensely naïve, or simply swept along by historical forces over which they had no control."

Marion decided that 'immensely naïve' was probably the best description for her 'little band' although each of the three descriptions had applied to them at some time. It would be good for the assembled audience to know that. She must remember to mention it when she spoke to them later.

As a guest of honor at the two thousand and thirty Vancouver Film Festival she was a hero to many in the audience, a freedom fighter, someone who had stood up to corruption and fought for democracy. The cinema was full of hip young people wearing retro t-shirts declaiming 'Free the Fulton Four.' Some of them hadn't even been born when Fulton had its brief turn in the headlines.

Marion's speech was scheduled to happen immediately after the documentary ended. She had agreed to speak because at seventy-nine years old it seemed like the last chance she would get to explain herself and her actions. Besides, the researchers had been so considerate when they interviewed her. They really had listened. She hoped the film would put an end to the 'freedom fighter' myth, at least in her case. She had fought for Fulton and for nothing else.

The documentary was named 'Something in the Air' and it told the story of the Fulton Four from the death of Bernadette Sutton through to the public release of the President's investigation. So far it had been reasonably accurate and its tone was carefully objective although somewhat self-important.

Marion had allowed herself to drift along with the story but she roused herself when it reached the point of her detention. She was always fascinated by what had followed.

From the moment Homeland Security broke down the door of her motel room she had ceased to be an actor in the drama and had become... what? Less than a pawn, less even than an observer; she became a non-entity. Someone to be remembered perhaps, but that was all.

Marion's detention unfolded in much the same way as those of Alison, Shona and Sanjay. She was treated more kindly than Alison because she did not challenge the authority of her captors. She answered the questions promptly, honestly and fully. As a cop she knew the best response was to cooperate. She would not avoid jail but she would likely get a better deal and they'd figure out the truth sooner or later regardless.

The questions did not last long. It must have quickly become clear to the DHS that the four were not involved in any terrorist activity. After what seemed like less than a day Marion was transferred to a regular jail cell, although she was still kept completely alone. She was never told where she was, how long she was likely to be held or what might happen to her.

Each of the four remained in this limbo for over two months.

To the political right they were traitors and they should be treated as such. To the left they were heroes, misguided perhaps, but heroes nonetheless. Brave citizens forced into drastic action by incompetence and outright corruption within the machinery of government.

The balance of power shifted significantly against the Fulton Four on Election Day, when many voters went to the polls scared and with no idea what was going on. They were afraid and confused and they blamed the President.

In public the President took the loss with good grace. The people had spoken and he was obliged to obey them. In private he was angrier about the loss than he had ever been about anything. To have his four long years of hard work end in such disaster was unthinkable and yet it had happened.

The President had promised an investigation. He had promised a thorough and complete public reckoning. In the two and a half months between the election and the end of his term he made damned sure that it happened.

The report was released on January eighteenth, only two days before he would leave the White House. It concluded that the United States undoubtedly faced a real threat from the Fulton fungus. It also concluded that the true nature of the threat had been exaggerated; mistakenly at first by Shona Price, then deliberately by those with vested interests.

The report did not mention MS. As the most powerful vested interest involved he had succeeded in covering his tracks. There was no evidence, physical or documentary to link him to the fungus. It was accepted that the director of his laboratory had acted without the proper authority in creating the fungus. There was even security footage of him destroying the labs last remaining samples just days after the fungus was released.

The Department of Homeland Security was also squarely blamed by the President's report. It had allowed a cadre of rogue agents to run operations with no oversight or constraint.

They had carried out unauthorized research with genetically engineered and biohazardous materials. They had engaged in field trials that took the lives of US military personnel.

They had concealed the existence of the terrorist threat to Senator Hanson and delayed effective action against the terrorist group. They had undermined the integrity of the intergovernmental panel.

In the final days of the President's term there was a purge of those agents and many of them were arrested and charged. The trials took place under the new administration however and due to political support for the agents many charges were dropped or reduced. Most of the sentences imposed were light and few of the agents faced any serious punishment.

As for the Fulton Four, the report stated they had broken any number of laws but their actions did not support the terrorists in any way. More importantly, their actions were never *intended* to support the terrorists. They had been foolhardy but this arose from a desire to reveal the truth about the disease in Fulton and to resolve the situation.

The President could have pardoned the Four, but he did not. He declared that although he had some sympathy for them, U.S. citizens should not be allowed to break laws just because they disagreed with the actions of the government or its agencies.

Balancing his choice to see them punished was an equal distaste for what the new administration would do to them once they took power. Consequently one of his last acts as President was to issue an executive order declaring that the Four should be tried as individuals for any specific crimes they had committed and that anti-terror legislation should not be applied in their cases.

The documentary ended by describing the fate of each of the Fulton Four.

"Sanjay Ramalingam was charged with participating in a criminal conspiracy. He was convicted and served two years in a Federal prison. On his release he returned to India where his wife and children had gone ahead of him. They had been subject to repeated death threats and other acts of intimidation that started shortly after his arrest.

"Shona Price also served two years on conspiracy charges. She lost her medical certification as a consequence of her illegal autopsy on the young boy, Tommy Sherman. Little is known about her subsequent life and she could not be contacted for the making of this documentary. It is rumored that she traveled to Africa as a humanitarian volunteer, but this rumor has never been confirmed.

"Alison Grove received the harshest sentence of all. As a Federal employee and a member of the inter-governmental panel she was bound by law to keep confidential all information provided to her in those roles. By communicating with the reporter Mike Fanning and the others in the Fulton Four she had abandoned her duty knowingly and deliberately.

"She served ten years of a twelve year sentence and was barred from ever working for the Federal government again. Her book 'Terror and Deceit' was published while she was still in prison but was withdrawn shortly after by the publishers when a legal challenge established that much of the content was still subject to national security restrictions.

"The brutal nature of Alison's detention along with her later experiences in prison changed her forever. She still lives in Atlanta but now devotes all her time to prisoner advocacy and organizations dedicated to preserving civil liberties.

"Marion Quirke served five years for criminal conspiracy and for failing to cooperate with Federal emergency personnel. This last charge referred to her breaching of the quarantine cordon around Fulton."

Marion knew the rest of the story. The time in jail had been particularly tough on her. Many of the prison guards and her fellow prisoners considered her a traitor and to make it worse, she was an ex-cop. She survived by doing exactly what was required of her and keeping to herself as much as possible.

There was no point going back to Fulton. Marion had received many hateful letters in prison. They made it clear she would suffer swift retribution if she should ever return to the town. Only a year into her sentence Dale Reynolds had visited to say her house had burned to the ground. It looked like arson but despite Dale's best efforts there was never an arrest. Folks in the town just wouldn't say anything.

On her release Marion took a bus across the border into Canada. It was the saddest day of her life, sitting high above the road and knowing that with every second she was getting further away from the only place she had ever truly wanted to be.

THE END

ABOUT THE AUTHOR

 Born in Wellington, New Zealand; Douglas studied at Victoria University, graduating with a Masters Degree in Physics. Since then he has been a professional software developer, which he loves.

Douglas was also co-director of an IT company in Wellington for a few years. This, he didn't love, but it taught him many important lessons and he's grateful for the experience.

Now working for a company in Melbourne, Australia he chooses to continue to live in Wellington because of its cultural life, its natural beauty and the fact he can mountain bike right out his front door.

Douglas decided to try writing after friends complemented the emails he sent home while travelling. When he discovered National Novel Writing Month, and its promise that a first draft could be written in thirty days, there was no holding him back.

To find out more about Douglas and his writing please sign up for his occasional newsletter at:

www.sporesdontevenbreathe.com

www.ingramcontent.com/pod-product-compliance
Lightning Source LLC
Chambersburg PA
CBHW070740180626
46818CB00007B/2929